All Shapes and Disguises

Lee-Anne Stack

ISBN 978-0-9939130-1-3

Cover Design and Photography by Lee-Anne Stack
https://leeannestack.wixsite.com/lee-anne-stack

Dedication

To my parents, Carmen and Ervin Stack,

whose vision, unique talents and herculean efforts
created The Camp and its magic for
generations of family and friends.

Love and miss you every day.

Table of Contents

Prologue

She relaxed into the layers of pillows piled against the rough log wall of the cabin. She didn't think much about pleasantries and comforts anymore; they were commodities that had long been forsaken and mostly forgotten, but her feather pillows felt bottomless, as though they might wrap around and swallow her up. And she would let them.

Listening to the scraping of the birch branches abrading her roof, she mentally added tree trimming to her already overburdened to-do list. She never wrote anything down, believing that once she started relying on written lists she would start to forget and that just wouldn't do.

She looked over at the seedlings sitting in pots covering the worn brown plaid of her couch. With the May long weekend still a week away it was too early to plant her garden.

Her arms felt heavy and cumbersome. She stared at them resting on top of her woolen blanket. At forty-eight the skin on her hands was already dried and wrinkled with age spots dotting the crevices. They were adaptable hands; capable of filleting a fish with meticulous precision and strong enough to build her cabin.

The white sucker fish were running early this year. Using her favourite recipe of bacon and brown sugar she had spent the day smoking and canning the start of next winter's supplies. It wasn't heavy work, certainly nothing out of the ordinary, so she couldn't understand why her arms were as heavy as fallen trees.

Her thoughts were softening, losing focus, while her body felt like it was dissolving into the bed. The sound of twigs snapping underfoot brought her back as her eyes sought out her rifle. She wanted to put an end to the bear that had been trying to break into her cabin but somehow, it didn't seem that important right now. There was a pressure on her chest and she wondered why the blankets were so heavy. She tried to move them off but her arms were not connected anymore. Looking at them she wondered whose arms they were and why they were on her bed.

With the pillows cradling her in their embrace the woman struggled to pull air into her lungs. Her eyes, frantic to find the source of the problem, desperately searched the room. Light from the evening sun glinted off a silver picture frame capturing her gaze. As her peripheral vision collapsed, she found comfort in the eyes of the man in the frame. They stared at each other momentarily until her lids closed, one last time.

Chapter 1 - The Trail

The trail spoke of beavers, moose, fires and rebirth, all in one breath. Hints of roots rippled centuries of debris while fallen trees created perfect hide-and-seek playgrounds for small and agile creatures. Through the variegated green of the trees the laughter of sunshine danced on the creek.

A recent fire had ravaged fifty miles of forest with only water bombers and luck halting its decimation of The Camp by a few hundred feet. The trunks of the scorched trees were already being cloaked by fast growing tag alders and poplars.

Returning my attention to the path, I watched the bobbing of the woven wood pack that my father had strapped to his back. It was a staple of the trip, always packed with essentials and the essential extras.

"Remember the old Findlay Oval?" Dad asked as we hit a spot that had usually been slippery with mud. "She finally developed one too many cracks, so we buried parts of her here to raise this section and help dry it out." Half turning back he looked over his shoulder.

My mind squealed, Noooo! It just wouldn't be The Camp without the old wood burning stove. It was the hub where we cooked, baked crusty Italian bread and toasted our tootsies on those winter days when we had snowshoed across the bay. It liked to be fussed over, having its drafts adjusted, feeding it with the fallen wood of the forest, nurturing its life.

"But…" I stopped dead in my tracks.

As Dad kept walking his voice found more accommodation in the surrounding woods than my ears. "…Honeymoon Suite … smaller… fit…"

Since I was a kid I had never handled changes at The Camp very well. None of us had. It was *The Camp*. Perfect just as it was. Changes need not apply. Apparently I had not outgrown that.

I hustled to catch up. "Did you say that you moved the stove from The Honeymoon Suite into the main cabin?"

"It's an even better fit."

"But what's in the Honeymoon Suite?"

"Remember the little old pot-bellied stove that was in the basement at Grandma's house? When she put the new furnace in, she decided to renovate, so out it came." Shrugging his shoulders he adjusted the straps from the pack. "No one cooks in the 'Suite' so there wasn't a reason to have a cook stove in there - just one for heat." It might have made logistical sense, but I was still struggling to adapt to the change.

My grandparents had built The Camp around the time when my parents were newlyweds, so it has been in the family for decades. After Mom and Dad moved from Timmins to the west coast we had made the trip back every year to northern Ontario to spend our holidays fishing, swimming, calling loons from the end of the dock and learning that it takes very little to make the best memories. Surrounded by Crown land, we had no neighbours in our bay and originally, the deadheads in the channel kept most boaters out. Over the years boaters removed them but we still don't get much traffic which suits us fine.

For me, walking the 500 or so metres of the trail is part of the magic. Recent visitors might be announced by the tracks they've left and decades of hearts have revved into the danger zone when a bear, wolf or moose print was discovered.

The trail has evolved over the years and can now accommodate a small truck or 4 x 4, but I still prefer the intimacy of walking.

Breaking through the clearing with the blueberry patch on both sides, The Camp greets me. I'm sure I can hear it say, "I've missed you. Please come in. You can relax now." And I do.

Two small steps up to the deck and I stop to take in the scene that is the wallpaper on my mind's desktop. Moose creek, which the trail follows, flows into the bay in front of the cabin. It's still sporting the same stumps, clumps, beaver lodge and reflections that I had seen on my last visit, three years ago. Looking straight east I check out the Point to see what has come and gone, but its profile seems unchanged - gnarly stumps, long grass and tall snags - all clinging to their boggy bottom. On the other side of the Point is another creek bringing water from the north, which merges with the first and drifts out past the old logging camp into the main lake.

I'm home.

Going through the opening rituals, Dad and I get the place ready for the rest of the company who will join us later: curtains opened, wood brought in, mousetraps checked, food put in the fridge and a quick peek inside the candy dish to see if fresh licorice allsorts are in residence.

The 'new' woodstove sits in the corner and I decide to make my peace with it. No water tank on the side, but we never really used the old one anyway.

Unlocking the outhouse, I put extra toilet paper in the mouse-proof tin and grab the water bucket to refill it. It may be an outhouse, but we have all the amenities, including a sink and gingham curtains.

"Hey, where did the boat come from?"

Perched upside down on two logs was an old fibreglass rowboat, its history described in the patches.

Coming out of the tool shed, Dad walked over to me. "Remember Sadie Ramier? She had a trap ground just north of here – along the Whitefish."

"I know her name - there were some pretty amazing stories about her." I realize that I'm drumming my fingers on the hull as I try to conjure up what I've heard. "Didn't they call her Cougar Sadie?"

Nodding, Dad chuckled. "Do you know how she got that name?"

"I don't imagine it's because she likes young men."

"You know the saying that when you see a cougar, it's only because it's let you? Well, Sadie was legendary for her stalking abilities. The old timers said she could blend into the forest and you'd never see her." Dad is not easily impressed, but I detected a note of reverence. "When she was just starting out about twenty years ago, a poacher made the foolish mistake of moving in on her trap line." Dad was smiling.

5

"Sadie's stealth was cougar-like; the guy didn't have a clue. He leads her right back to his trailer. She waits until he put his gun away and then she pounces." Dad leaned in closer. "Now this fellow is well over six feet tall and no lightweight. Sadie pins him in no time flat; hog ties him then recovers all of her stolen pelts and animals. Anyone else would have beaten him to a pulp, but not Sadie. She takes this guy's traps, weapons, stretchers, everything, and lectures him on the evils of stealing. Hauling him into the back of her truck, she brings him into town and before dropping him off in front of one of the bars, she writes "Poacher" in indelible ink on his forehead." By this point Dad was laughing. "Sadie walks into the bar, gives the story to some of the other trappers, then asks if any of them want some free gear. She figures this guy has been poaching from everyone, so they all have a stake in it. Well, you can imagine that once they hear the poacher is outside, they want to get in on the action, but by that time the guy was long gone."

Dad laid a hand on the boat. "Trapping is hard going. It's a rough, solitary life but Sadie loved it."

"Hey, I just realized that you've been speaking of Sadie in the past tense."

Pursing his lips Dad nodded. "They found her in the spring. She died of cyanide poisoning."

"Seriously?"

"Yeah. They couldn't confirm whether it was suicide, murder or an accident. They had no suspects or motive and there was no note, so they decided it was accidental."

A soft yet deep whooshing sound caught our attention and we turned just in time to see a great blue heron disappear over the treeline, the raucous *roohk, roohk roohk,* alerting its mate of his arrival, echoing across the bay.

"Ah, I see that Mintrude and Stanley are back." Ever since my grandparents built The Camp, there have been a resident nesting pair of great blue herons. There is speculation that this is the third or fourth generation, but they've all been called Mintrude and Stanley.

Staring over the bay, I wondered what Sadie's final moments were like.

Chapter 2 - Plus Two

"Ahoy, Captain Kate, permission to come aboard?"

"Colin, you twit, it's a cottage, not a boat."

Standing at the steps; the noonday sun ablaze on his red curly head, he nodded towards the deck. "Is this not a deck? Does a ship not have decks? Are they both not made of boards? Hence, I believe that 'coming aboard' is an appropriate term."

Pearl, my long-time friend and construction partner, put down her bags of food and placed a hand on her boyfriend's shoulder. "The man has a point. And I'm not talking about the one on top of his darling little head."

"Well, then, permission granted."

When first encountering The Camp and its environs, it looks like a log cabin with log out-buildings sitting on top of a little hill with wooded shorelines across the water. Quiet and peaceful. For anyone with a history here, there's a built-in release mechanism that activates as you walk the trail. You renew an intimate acquaintance with the magic and connectedness; not just the land but with yourself. You aren't even aware of the transition until you take a moment to notice your shoulders are more relaxed, your breathing quieter and deeper and the muscles around your eyes have softened. For the uninitiated, they look around, give a whistle and a head nod then comment on how beautiful it is. It's only a matter of time - time and acquaintance, until they too, are wrapped in the folds of the enchanted. Looking around, Colin's head was bobbing. "This is amazing. I can't believe you've managed to keep this place a secret."

Dad came alongside the new arrivals with an armload of kindling for the stove. "Did you have any trouble finding the trail?"

Pearl gave Dad a hug. "Not a bit. Mind you, we would have been snookered if you hadn't left the orange tape on the road sign." Digging into her pocket she pulled out the tape. "Removed, as per your instructions."

"How many years has it been since you've come for a visit?"

"Far too many. I was trying to figure it out - about four, I think." Looking around she smiled. "You've put in a new dock."

"That was one of last year's projects. The ice is murder on them."

Dad turned to Colin. "I'll just get rid of this load of wood and give you a tour."

Pearl and I smiled at each other. One of my Dad's tours could mean anything from a friendly beer out back to a "Here, can you hold this burlap bag?" At which point he'd start walking away saying, "I'm just going to put my boots on. Now make sure you hold it tight, that snake in there is not too happy." And off he'd go.

Grabbing the suitcases and groceries, we sent the guys off while we unpacked. As we were putting the last of the food in the cupboard, Dad came in and washed his hands.

"What did you do with Colin?"

With a low chuckle he nodded towards the east side of the Honeymoon Suite. Colin was shovelling dirt into a large wood-sided square with screening on the bottom. He'd search through the soil breaking apart the clumps and bits of debris, shake it about, then search some more before finally dumping it to the side to start the whole process again.

"You pulled the old, I-found-a-small-nugget-of-gold-just-over-here-and-haven't-had-a-chance-to-dig-around.- Do-you-want-to-give-it-a-go? on him! You get more projects done with that one, Dad. What's it this time - a new garden?"

"No, too late in the season. I thought I'd put in a horseshoe pit."

Colin had taken his shirt off by this point and was stopping every few seconds to swat a mosquito. "That's a bad spot down there for bugs. I guess I should bring him some spray."

We watched a s Dad wandered back down to the excavation site. Colin barely looked up as he was sprayed with repellent and kept to his task with a frenzied focus.

Pearl sat in the red rocking chair in front of the window. "He doesn't get a lot of exercise being a doctor. He'll sleep well tonight." She gave the chair some encouragement and settled in, rocking contentedly. "He really does have nicely defined muscles. Not too hard to watch."

"Speaking of sleep, I thought you two would like the Honeymoon Suite."

When Pearl didn't answer, I walked over to the window to see what was happening at the open-pit mine. Colin was absorbed in his sifting task and just behind him Dad was grinding something into the dirt at the edge of the hole. Pearl pointed a finger at my father and looked at me, her eyes open wide in admiration. "Your Dad always goes the extra mile, doesn't he?"

"It gets him the best results. He's got a stash of iron pyrite in the tool shed. That's how he got the boys and me to dig the hole for a new outhouse years ago." I watched my father saunter over to the Honeymoon Suite and unlock the door.

Pearl turned back to watch the men. "You know, everyone loves to pitch in, all he'd have to do is ask."

"Yes, but who has more of an adventure - those digging a new outhouse or those looking for gold?"

Chapter 3 - Lucius

T he soulful sax of Stanley Turrentine accompanied the afternoon sun's journey across the cloudless sky. Pearl and I put the suitcases away while Dad worked on the little outboard motor and Colin continued his quest for gold. Finding my Dad's chunk of fool's gold fueled his enthusiasm and he was focused on his task.

Rooting through the fridge, I came up with a container, its separated compartments filled with cheese, kielbasa, olives, pickles, cucumber spears and tiny tomatoes. Dad had just come in to refill his glass. Pointing to the repast I asked, "Mom?"

"You know how she wants to make sure no one goes hungry." He opened the cupboard, grabbed the box of crackers and shook some onto a plate.

We set out the food on the long wooden table on the deck and switched the playlist to some livelier music.

I called down to Colin. "The gold will still be there tomorrow, come and take a break."

Picking up yet another shovel of soil, Colin yelled back, "Just two more loads and I'll come up."

"He can't dig much deeper - he'll hit water soon."

Pearl piled some sausage and cheese on a cracker. "Have I mentioned that he can be a little obsessive?"

"Nah." I said. "More focused than obsessed."

"Really? Do you remember when he decided to build a drone? He didn't sleep for two days."

"Yes, but he got it up and flying. I'd say that was determined."

10

"Whatever you want to call it, he's like a terrier - he doesn't give up."

Without saying anything to us, my father walked into the cabin, grabbed a bar of soap and a towel from the sink then wandered down and stopped a foot away from the good doctor. Straightening up from his task, Colin turned and listened intently then nodded. Sticking the shovel into the ground, he took the soap and towel and walked out on the little dock.

When Dad returned, we looked at him with eyebrows raised.

"I told him that I wasn't sure that I had properly staked that part of the property and needed to check with the Ministry to ensure it was our claim and not someone else's."

"Devious."

Dad shrugged his shoulders and smiled. "The horseshoes are in the toolshed."

*****

By four o'clock Dad was getting ready to go.

"Won't you stay for supper?"

"Thanks, but you kids get settled in. Your uncles have invited your Mom and me over to play euchre. I hate to pass up a chance to win some money." He shrugged his backpack into position and gave us a few last-minute instructions. "The fishing rod is all set. I put a smelt on the hook – the pike really like them. See you in a few days."

He didn't get more than a few steps before he turned back around. "Kate, do you remember where the ammunition for the .22 is?"

"In the night table?"

"Yup. If you're going to do any target practice, don't shoot into the woods. A bullet from that rifle can travel over a kilometre."

"Right, pop can in the water, it is."

I was lost in thought as I watched my father disappear into the forest wondering how many feet had trod that trail, when a shout from Colin brought me back.

"Thar she blows!"

Turning, I watched him scamper down the hill and onto the dock. You could hear the zing of the fishing line as it pulled against the lock. "Man, this is a big one. Look at him go."

The red and white bobber had disappeared below the surface and when it popped up again it was about half way to The Point.

Grabbing the rod he pulled it out of the holder just as the bobber vanished once again. "Oh, man, this is going to be an epic struggle for survival. It's brains and brawn against basic instincts. Homme contre poisons. Hombre contra los peces, Skin. . ."

Watching from the deck I wondered if I should go down and get the landing net.

"Pearl, has Colin ever been fishing before?"

"Probably at a fun-fair when he was a kid."

"So he's never pulled in a Northern Pike?"

"That would be my guess, especially the way he's jerking that rod around. Colin! Honey! Smooth motions, don't jerk the line or it'll snap."

"Should we go down and help?"

"With him doing the herky-jerky? I don't fancy the odds of us coming away unscathed." Pearl grabbed her phone. "But I will record it for future entertainment."

We could hear Colin furiously reeling in, not having taken off the lock. Before Pearl could start the video recording, Colin was yelling, "Woah, buddy! Woah, woah! Holy freaking fins, he's coming right for me!"

The buzz of the reel had stopped and Colin stood statue-still. I couldn't figure out what was happening until I noticed the bobber creating a wake as it skimmed along the water heading straight for the dock. Noticing the absence of sound, Pearl looked up from the screen on her phone. "What the heck . . ."

Scrambling up from our chairs we stood at the side of the deck, mesmerized by the progress of the bobber. About two yards out, the float disappeared into the depths.

"Shit, it's like freakin' Jaws! What the hell is down there?" Pearl's eyes were wide as she pointed to the bobber returning to the surface about ten metres out into the main channel of the creek, just sitting there.

Without warning it jerked and was once again speeding towards the dock, plowing up the water in front of it. Still holding the rod and reel in both hands Colin turned slightly. I wasn't sure if he was going to bolt for the safety of the shore or wait to see what the creature had in mind.

One more depth dive and then nothing. No bobber, no fish, no sound. It was like the air got sucked out of the world. The water was still and dark. Colin stood there with his jaw slack. He started to turn towards us to confirm that he wasn't the only one who had just seen the action, when an eruption of water, gaping mouth and a pike of glimmering goliath proportions hurtled into the air, contorting its body with flips of its tail. Razor sharp teeth glistened in the sun and with one last twist, the hook flew free of its mouth. Splashing down, it rolled on its side and with a mighty flip of its tail, returned to his aquatic realm.

At times like this there's usually one of two responses. Either everyone is talking at once, or else there is absolute silence as brains scramble to make sense of what the eyes just took in. This was one of those quiet times where we all just stood, cemented into place, kind of working our jaws like three demented fish out of water, struggling for air.

Slowly and gently, Colin, placed the fishing rod on the dock, turned and walked the short distance up the hill. He looked over at us with eyebrows raised and mouth slightly open as if frozen in mid-sentence. His right hand came up with his index finger pointed up to the sky then aiming it down to the lake, he kind of gargled a noise, turned and walked into the cabin. We could hear the seal release on the fridge door, the clink of glass, then the whoosh of a bottle cap being popped off a beer.

"Did you happen to record any of that?"

"Nope, not one second."

"I've never seen a pike leap out of the water before."

"Nope, me either."

"Want a beer?"

"You bet."

"Want to go swimming?"
"Never again."

Chapter 4 - Outhouse At Night (or, Do I really have to go?)

The hauntingly beautiful wail of the loon enticed me from a deep sleep. I laid there, listening to the silence between the calls, letting my mind drift. When the loon's pleas were answered by its mate, I threw back the covers and grabbed my camera.

Beams from the three-quarter moon slipped through the slits between the curtains casting moon shadows on the painted wooden floor. Unlatching the doors, I stepped slowly and silently onto the deck.

Mist drifted above the water in a landscape of mystical magic with the moon spotlighting a path on the stage. My breath caught in my throat as the loon slipped into the light, lifted its head and infused the night with another eloquently beautiful call for its mate. Its silhouette, soft in the haze, made a striking picture, but an odd sense of voyeurism stopped me from raising the camera. There was an intimacy in this moment that felt wrong to capture. I watched as the bird glided away towards its mate until the mist obscured any trace of him. And then I watched some more, not wanting to break the spell.

*****

I was unaware of the passing of time. Then, like a hypnotist's snapping fingers, my own call-of-nature pulled me back into the night. Right - the outhouse. Out back. In the dark. On the edge of the forest. Do I really have to go? Can it wait a few more hours?

Nope, apparently not.

I can do this!

Yup, I'm a chicken. A chicken with a very vivid imagination and a healthy fear of what creatures are waiting just beyond the reach of the light.

I *know* a wolf pack is not lying in wait for me, nor is it likely that a deranged escapee from the local jail has set up a blind, sitting patiently, waiting for me to walk out in the middle of the night. But knowing and fearing do not always communicate well. There are gaps in the transmission and it's in those gaps that imagination feeds. Maybe, in my case, gorges.

In my defence, there are bears. Big bears. Big, black bears that one can surprise. And a surprised bear is not a creature you want to encounter. At night. In the dark. All alone.

Come on, what are the odds? Well, the odds of winning a lottery are infinitesimally small, yet every week, in every province and state, people win lotteries.

This line of un-reasoning was not helping so I just grabbed my camera and marched along the cabin then into the four-metre danger zone to the outhouse. I'm not sure why the camera was important - maybe to capture my last moments in mortal garb or possibly to swing and smack the snout of an attacking beast, but whatever it is, it gave me confidence and I slowed my pace and felt empowered. Striding assertively, I opened the outhouse door and let out a blood curdling scream as a monster moth dive bombed me.

Freakin' moths!

Chapter 5

The moon taunts him with dancing shadows. He's too exhausted to make sense of the shapes and movement of the dark-and-darker, and the pain in his right hip distracts rationalization.

The wind and dropping temperatures are keeping the mosquitoes at bay but the occasional hardy individual rises from the forest floor driven to seek its fortune.

An ominous shape, larger and more threatening than the surrounding ones catch the man's peripheral vision. He's not sure if it has moved or the branches of the neighbouring trees are creating the illusion. His first encounter with a bear that day hadn't gone well and he's not looking to test his luck again.

Caught in mid-stride with his weight bearing down on the damaged hip he stands stock-still. The pain is screaming obscenities in his head as he slowly eases back onto his good leg. The wind is in his favour and he tries to catch a hint of an odour, but the only smell is that of the damp forest detritus.

Still not convinced the black mass doesn't pose a threat, he remains motionless. Gradually, he becomes aware of sounds outside of his own pounding heart. Crinkling leaves, sighing evergreens, then the scampering of tiny unseen feet. Risking movement he slowly turns his head towards the sound, trying to track its owner with his eyes. Before he can zero in, an enormous winged creature silently navigates the branches and swoops down to capture a meal in its viciously proficient talons. When the owl lands on top of the mysterious shape in question, tension escapes the man's muscles and he draws in a large breath.

As he watches the bird reposition its catch, the moonlight stipples the white feathers of the snowy owl. Once finished its meal, the huge ghostly creature lifts its head and intense, intimidating yellow eyes bore straight into him. A spine-shivering screech pierces the night and with this last reproach the bird fans the air with its huge wings, lifting itself above the trees and away.

Chapter 6 - "Ah"

The bacon sizzling in the electric frying pan created incomparably superb aromas. Through the large open window, I heard the scrape of the door in the other cabin, the thudding of racing feet, a squeal and triumphant shout, then a maniacal laugh as the outhouse door slammed shut.

Initially, I had discouraged Pearl and Colin's relationship - for the good of the group. We were such good friends and I worried that if they ended up in an ugly place, it would put me in the middle, with my best friend and construction partner on one side of the firing range and my landlord and buddy on the other.

I don't think I've ever been so happy to be wrong. Now, I can't imagine our lives in any other format.

Setting the round oak table for breakfast, I noticed Pearl scampering down to the dock where she dropped a towel from her shoulders revealing her athletically muscled body, sleek in its one piece bathing suit. "Geronimo" infused the warm morning air as she ran the length of the dock and executed a perfect shallow dive.

"I could watch her for hours on end." Turning, I saw Colin standing on the deck, hands casually resting on his hips.

Flipping the bacon onto a plate lined with paper towels, I grabbed two mugs of coffee and carried it all on a tray out onto the deck. By this time Pearl was a third of the way out to The Point.

The admiring smile on Colin's boyish face morphed into a full grin as he picked up his mug and a slice of bacon.

The silence between us was comfortable with only the faint, soft rhythm of Pearls strokes and the occasional cawing of a crow to keep us company.

"Do you miss him?"

I had expected the question, but I hadn't yet decided on my answer. I hoped my sigh would help me clear out the clutter of thoughts eddying in my mind.

Colin waited patiently.

Chewing on some bacon to buy a little more time, I mentally pulled up a mini slide show of Andrew. As I viewed the images, I watched to see how I felt with each memory that passed.

It's not like I hadn't spent countless hours thinking about him, about us, about not-us. I had existed during painfully tumultuous weeks trying to sort out how I felt, what I wanted my future to look like, and acknowledging what my future wasn't going to look like. But it wasn't that easy. I discovered my heart is like a kaleidoscope where a simple little change in perspective presents a whole new world to contemplate. I had pretty much settled on a point of view - but every once in a while, that darned kaleidoscope moved.

"Yes."

Colin nods. "Me, too."

"And, no."

"Yup."

"The condensed answer is that I miss what I thought we could have had. I miss the original Andrew. My battle has been to look past that into the truth. He was, and still is, a good man with a kind view of people and the world. He is fun and easy going, but once he moved from Tofino to Victoria and realized how much of the world he was missing, his restlessness was too overwhelming - for both of us."

I picked up my mug only to discover that I'd already finished my coffee. Colin nudged the plate of bacon towards me.

Pearl had reached The Point and was heading back.

"Would you consider getting involved again when he comes back?"

"That's easy to answer." Smiling at my friend, I shrugged. "It all depends on who he is when he comes back."

"Ah."

"And the addendum to that is; I'm not going to drift around, waiting."

Colin's freckled hand patted my arm. "That's our Kate!"

A gargled scream shattered our focus.

Running down to the dock we watched Pearl hydroplaning the last ten metres to the shore with a string of obscenities curdling the air.

"Son of a bitching, Lucius! That bastard brushed my leg and scared the freaking shit right out of me!"

"Lucius?"

Colin wrapped the towel around Pearl and by his shaking shoulders I could see him working hard to supress a laugh. "Esox Lucius is the Latin name for the Northern Pike. I thought it was most fitting given the nature of that beast."

"Well, Lucius has met his match! He may have won this round but I'll be damned if he wins the battle!" Pearl leapt onto the dock and shook a fist at the water. "I will win! You will die! Kate, get the gun! Mama's going fishing."

"Honey!" Colin snuggled up to Pearl's back and wrapped his arms around her. Kissing her shoulder, he pulled her tighter. "Shooting fish is illegal, unless it's in a barrel. And then it's just plain foolish." He spared a hand to stroke her hair. "We'll get him, the proper way. Remember they have teeny-tiny brains. How hard can it be?"

A distant cawing was heard – bearing a striking resemblance to a laugh.

*****

The sun twinkled through the large birch at the front of the deck, so I slipped my sunglasses on. "I thought you weren't ever going swimming again."

"I totally forgot about the devil's spawn." Pearl stopped towelling her short blonde hair and dropped her arms. Spikes and swirls poked in all directions giving her a mad-scientist appearance. Damn, she can absolutely rock that look with her pixie-shaped face and large blue eyes.

"When I stepped out on the porch this morning and saw the water, it called to me. Smooth as glass; just begging me to dive right in. An invitation I've never been able to resist."

Placing a plate loaded with a staple Camp breakfast of eggs, bacon and toast on the deck table, Colin lightly touched Pearl's back. "How's your heart?"

"I may have cleared out a few arteries - but it's pretty much back to normal now."

"So what's on the agenda today, ladies?"

Pearl's eyes were mere slits as she leaned forward. "Fish fry."

I stretched and gave my head a tilt towards the back of the cottage. "Well, if you two want to take the boat out, I've got some things I want to do around here. The little Merc is in the tool shed."

A piece of jam-slathered toast halfway to Colin's mouth stopped in midair. "Aren't you coming with us? This is the opportunity of a lifetime. The ultimate catch. The world's largest pike just waiting to be landed. Lucius on a lead. . . Come on!"

I really hate missing a boat or fishing trip, but I also want to give them some alone time. Let Colin and Pearl make their own memories of this place. And, honestly, I was looking for a little quiet time to just sit in the red rocking chair in front of the huge open window and remember.

Chapter 7

The ominous shape, upon closer inspection, had morphed into the root system of an up-ended fir tree. What initially had been a terrifying threat was now a shelter for the night. Gathering branches from the downed tree for cover requires more strength than the man possesses, so with the dirt and roots at his back, he cocoons into the forest debris to escape the cool night and passing voracious insects.

Sleep immediately overcomes him but the pain in his hip is an insistent alarm clock that keeps resetting itself during the course of the night.

Shivering, the man transitions from a restless sleep to an awareness of his surroundings. He slowly pushes himself to a sitting position, shaking his arm to retrieve it from its numbed state.

Noticing a fat earthworm emerging from under a leaf, overlapping thoughts of, 'Gross', 'protein', and 'don't think about it' stop his hand from grabbing it - for a brief second. Hunger is a master that demands commitment, so he reaches out, snatches the worm and tries to slip it past his taste buds and straight down his throat. As slimy as worms appear, they don't slide down a dry throat very well, and this one stuck half way down. He had been saving the last of his water until he was absolutely desperate but as he starts to gag and heave he decides that time has come. He tries to flush the worm down with one swig but a second one is necessary to complete his breakfast. Hooking the empty water bottle to the back of his belt he works at distracting himself from the imagined wriggling in his stomach.

The early morning light presents a different world - one filled with information and possible options. Rolling onto his hands and knees, he tests his leg by stretching it out behind him. A shooting pain insists that he drop it back down. Discovering that crawling works, he moves around the edge of his shelter until he can pull himself up holding on to the fallen tree. Keeping his weight off his leg he shifts and turns to sit on the trunk. As he surveys the deadfall around him for a possible cane or walking stick he smacks the back of his neck killing two mosquitoes.

A long stout branch is within reach. He strips away the rough bark near the top then places it between his knees. Taking a deep breath, he leans into it for support and finds it holds up under his weight. After a few tentative steps, the man is relieved to discover he's able to move with considerably less pain.

Closing his eyes, he hopes if he listens hard enough he might hear the sound of water but after a moment he purses his lips and decides his next move is to look for open space where the mosquitoes might not be as abundant and where he can hopefully find some higher ground. The little blood suckers are starting to come out in full force and it becomes obvious his repellent from the day before has long ago worn off so he sits back down on the log and pulls his red plaid shirt up over his head. Next he takes off his t-shirt and working quickly, slips his long sleeved shirt back on, tucking it in his pants. Draping his t-shirt on the top of his head he twists it around so he can look through the arm hole. His ball cap goes over top of this and pulling his sunglasses out of their case he works them through the arm hole and rolls the short sleeves around the frame. His pants had come untucked from his socks during the night so he stuffs them back to ensure his ankles don't get molested.

The woods of Northern Ontario can present hundreds of kilometres of the same dense forest with underbrush that impedes travel and his movement is ponderously slow. His stomach is becoming more and more vocal while his tongue tries to suck moisture from his parched mouth.

Noticing a stand of birch he moves towards it where the underbrush isn't as thick. He finds a grouping of ferns which hold droplets of morning dew. Lifting his homemade mosquito headgear, he gets down on his knees and begins licking the drops from the plants.

Chapter 8 - The Creature at the Point

From my vantage point on the small dock, I took inventory of the stock in the boat. "Got everything? Rods, tackle box, net and bait?"

"Check."

"Sunscreen, hats, towels?"

"Check."

"Water? Libations?"

Colin tapped the small blue cooler behind his seat. "Plus some pepperoni sticks, chips and apples."

Pearl raised one eyebrow but said nothing.

"Paddles?"

"Rats, forgot the paddles."

Turning, I ran up the slope to the Honeymoon Suite and grabbed both paddles from the small deck.

As I passed them to Colin, Pearl pulled her baseball cap down as far as it would go and saluted me. Colin had decided to go Mexican, covering as much of his fair skin as possible with a large sombrero.

Pearl gave the pull cord on the Merc a couple of quick jerks and it brrrmmmed to life. Giving the dock a shove, Colin touched the brim of his sombrero, nodded and called out, "Mañana, Senorita."

Before putting the motor into reverse, Pearl shook her head. "Honey, that would be 'luego'."

"Si Señorita. Mis apololgies. Mañana, luego."

"Goof."

"Can I drive?"

"No."

"Please, please, p-u-h-l-e-a-s-e?"

"Sit down before I dump you out of the boat." Pearl pointed to the red bench seat. "If you behave, you can drive once we get onto the main lake. There aren't any deadheads there."

As Pearl swung Cougar Sadie's old boat around, I noticed it had a name written in script on the starboard side; *The Elgin*. I made a mental note to look that up to see what it meant.

Heading off towards the main lake, Colin grabbed both sides of his sombrero and held them down. If it were any bigger he could use it to paraglide.

*****

Being the only cottage in the bay allows you a fair amount of freedom without ticking off the neighbours so after a second cup of coffee, I cranked up the music to an unusually loud volume as I wandered around doing odd cleaning and maintenance jobs. Taking the broom into the outhouse, I noticed the orange gingham curtains looking a little less orange and decided they could use a wash so I unhooked them, grabbed the wash bucket and went back into the cabin to retrieve my eco-friendly soap.

Looking out over the lake as I head to the dock, I became aware of something bobbing on the surface, just off The Point. I wondered if it was Colin's sombrero, but then it appeared to be waving at me. I tentatively waved back but couldn't quite make out what or who it was so I ran back to turn off the music and grab the binoculars.

It took a few seconds to figure out the strange apparition. Initially, it looked like some huge-eyed bug wearing a baseball cap until I realized that the eyes were actually sunglasses. "I could . . . some help. . ."

Holy shit.

Kicking off my sandals I hustled down to the dock. As my feet hit the planks I remembered the canoe so I turned and ran over to the small dock. Bugger, it was chained to the tree. I started to head back to the cabin for the key when it occurred to me that there were no paddles left. Bugger, bugger, bugger.

Ah, pool noodle. But that will just slow me down. . . Looking out again, the person didn't seem to have made any progress but at least he/she was still afloat.

Right, lifejacket.

"I'll be right back," I yelled across the water as I opened the door to the Honeymoon suite. Ducking inside I grabbed a lifejacket, scrambled down to the water while putting it on and jumped in.

Strokes are awkward with the safety device on and it seemed to be taking forever to swim the distance. As I got closer I could hear a deep baritone saying, "Thank you!"

I noticed he wasn't struggling, in fact he was hardly moving and his shoulders were out of the water. It didn't make sense. He wasn't making movements like he's treading water. My brain was flashing little warning signals that said, "This does not compute." That and the fact that I couldn't see his face under the weird headdress were making me slow down.

From about five metres away I stopped and let the lifejacket keep me afloat. I really wasn't sure what to say to this fellow but decided to not get any closer until I could figure things out.

Raising a hand he waved and said, "Hi." The movement caused him to tilt sideways and a "Whoah!" rushed out as he slipped sideways into the water and then grunted.

"Sorry, lost my footing."

Footing? It took me a second to realize that he'd been standing on a stump or deadhead well below the surface.

"Are you able to swim?"

"It's rather painful. I've injured my hip so I'm down to one leg."

Unsnapping the life vest I removed it then swam closer to pass it over. "Here, put this on. I can hold the strap and drag you back." Now that I had a moment to get a better look, I realized he'd pulled a t-shirt over his head, which would make sense given the voracity of the bugs, but I still couldn't see his eyes or his face, which left me at a distinct disadvantage.

As I held the vest open for him, he leaned in to slip his arm through the hole, lost his balance and toppled forward, catching my shoulder and dragging me down underneath him. I started to panic. Struggling and kicking wildly my foot met with resistance as I connected with some part of him, which helped propel me away and to the surface.

I could hear, "Sorry, so sorry." as I coughed and tried to clear the burning from my lungs. "Lost my balance. . ."

People and water can be scary things. Drowning people are known to cling - with understandable desperation - to their rescuers, pulling them down to a watery end. I had no idea who or what this guy was and I was not going down to any depth with him so I swam a few feet further away.

"Are you okay? Really, I'm so sorry." Having put the life jacket on backwards, was breast-stroking towards me.

Floating on my back, I kicked to propel myself away.

My face must have displayed my concern for Mr. Baritone stopped and let the jacket suspend him. "Sorry, my name is Ben. I've been lost since a bear and I had a turf disagreement yesterday." He started to extend a hand in an offer to shake mine, but caught himself. "Hey, you know, if you want to swim ahead, I'll stay behind a bit, give you a chance to get out of the water, call someone. . . whatever."

He doesn't *sound* like a deranged killer. But then again, my experience with ones of that ilk was limited to a sociopathic woman who presented rather polished. Okay, maybe as polished as a bench in a whore house on payday - but I digress, that's another story. Besides, what are the odds that I would encounter more than one in my life?

"Are you okay to swim?"

"As long as we're not racing I should be okay."

Feeling a little guilty I swam ahead but when I stopped to look behind, Ben was lagging, but not too far.

"How bad is your hip?"

"I don't think it's broken, but it's certainly not right. I had two walking sticks that helped in bearing weight, but I wouldn't want to run any marathons."

Floating on my back I continued to scissor kick. "So you've been lost since yesterday?"

"Yesterday morning. I was out picking blueberries in a patch about a kilometre this side of the Whitefish. Apparently it was already spoken for."

The dock was only a few feet away so I turned, took a couple of strokes and planted my feet on the sandy bottom. Ben seemed to have found a cache of energy and was only a few metres behind.

As he came abreast of the dock, a huge sigh escaped from somewhere behind his t-shirt. Placing his hands on the dock, he heaved himself up, twisted and sat down with a solid thump and another sigh. "I think I'll just stay here for a while." His shoulders were slumped as he leaned his forearms on his thighs.

"I'll be right back." Sprinting up to the cabin I grabbed a couple of towels, a can of juice and the leftover tray of cheese and crackers.

Ben didn't look up as I sat down beside him on the dock. "Can I help you take off your t-shirt?"

"Ah, yeah, that would be great. I'm feeling a little wobbly." Reaching up he worked his sunglasses out through the armhole and placed them on the wood planks.

I lifted the t-shirt off his shoulders and over his head, creating a striking black mohawk with his wet hair. No need to suppress a grin - the look on his face told me his hair was not the front runner of his thoughts at that moment. In fact, I don't ever recall seeing anyone with an avocado hue to their skin. I hesitated in passing him the juice but figured it would give him an immediate boost or the heaves. Either way – it'd be an improvement over his current situation.

He wasn't moving and his eyes were focused on a little water bug skating on the surface just in front of his legs.

"You did say your name was Ben, didn't you?" Nothing. "Ben?"

Shaking his head he turned to me and I noticed his eyes were espresso brown, set in a soft downward slope - rather like Paul McCartney's. The line of his nose had a small deviation with a scar just to the side. I watched his eyes focus on my face, blink a few times, then open wide. "I'm sorry, I must have zoned out." Looking down he spied the juice then looked back at me questioningly.

Picking up the can I popped the little lever and passed it to him. As he started chugging it I watched his stomach and chest spasm.

"You might want to start by sipping."

Quickly putting the can on the dock, Ben slid into the waist-high water and turned his back to me.

"Are you. . ." is all I got out before the retching started. Apparently he hadn't eaten a lot because the contents of his stomach spewed into the water didn't amount to much, and I immediately wondered if minnows would find this smorgasbord appealing. Fortunately, I'm not a sympathy-retcher.

"Sorry."

"It's okay, Ben, don't worry. This doesn't bother me in the least." I did decide, however, not to get back in the water and instead put my hand on his back and gently squeezed his shoulder. He seemed to be rallying a bit as whatever was in his stomach was now gone.

"I may have eaten a bad worm or two."

My arched eyebrows were my only comment.

Picking up the juice he swished a bit around in his mouth, spit it into the water then drank the rest of the can. He appeared to be taking the weight off his hip by leaning sideways on the dock.

"Is it better when you sit or is that still painful?"

"Sitting's good." Pulling himself back up on the dock he turned and smiled at me.

His colouring was decidedly better so I passed him the container of food. "This might be an improvement over your recent diet. Have at 'er."

The struggle between epic hunger and politeness lasted a mere three seconds. He appeared to inhale the food. While he was appeasing his hunger, I grabbed his t-shirt, popped it in the bucket with the curtains and walking to the end of the dock I scooped up some water and gave them a quick wash. Turning back to Ben I noticed him staring with some intensity at my legs. Oh, so not on, buddy. I was about to make a comment when he nodded and pointed to my left calf. Looking down, I saw two huge bloodsuckers gorging.

"Ahhhhh. Shit!" Running up to the cabin I was sure I could feel the blood being sucked through the punctures. Gross! I grabbed the salt shaker and ran out on the deck where I knelt my left leg on the bench and vigorously shook the salt until the black creatures were writhing in a blanket of crusty white crystals. There was a momentary pang of guilt as I watched them drop off my leg, but I was willing to let it go in this case.

Chapter 9 - In the Beginning

The thick plastic disc nailed to the top of the stump made a perfect seat while I waited outside the outhouse.

The door opened and Ben placed his left leg on the ground. Holding the door frame while taking the weight on his injured leg, he brought his right one down beside it.

"Let's get you off that leg." I slipped under his left arm and even while protesting that he was okay, I felt his weight transfer and the burden of pain shifted to rest on my shoulders.

"We should get the weight off that hip so there are two choices – the lounge chair on the deck or you can lie down in the cabin."

"Deck chair would be perfect." I noticed that his voice sounded a bit constricted, like he was holding it in to control the pain.

"You're in luck, you know. When Colin returns from his fishing expedition, you'll have the services of a first-rate doctor."

"So far you've been doing a pretty good job of taking care of me." He hobbled up the steps onto the deck. "And I can't thank you enough."

After settling Ben into the wooden lounge chair, I realized that his lips were blue and what flesh was exposed was ruffled with goose bumps.

"How about a pot of tea and some dry clothes?"

He started to shake his head in protest, paused and smiled. "That would be great."

With the kettle plugged in, I rummaged in the armoire for some clothes.

Walking out onto the deck my breath caught as I was treated to an expanse of well-muscled chest and arms. Oh! Oh, sweet mama!

There was a towel draped over the arms of the chair and underneath it Ben was struggling to peel off his wet jeans, which were not going down without a fight.

"Tell you what. You hold the towel and the arms of the chair and I'll pull the jeans from the bottom."

There was a momentary pause as we sized each other up.

"Well, I don't seem to be making much progress this way. If you're okay with that I'm good to go." He sounded sure but I thought I detected a faint pink hue migrating up his neck and face.

Grabbing the bottom of his jeans I gave a yank that produced nothing but a grunt from me. A few more tugs and still no progress.

"I'll go get the tea, you slide the jeans as low as you can and I'll be back."

Balancing the tray with the tea accoutrements and cookies, I backed my way onto the deck and placed it on the table.

"There, got it."

I turned and Ben was smiling up at me pointing at his pants resting around his knees. "Sorry, I don't seem to be able to rotate my leg out to get the pants all the way off." He was visibly shaking with cold, and most likely fatigue, so I grabbed the bottom of his jeans, yanked them off and draped the heavy wet denim over the deck railing.

"Here, wrap your hands around this." Passing him the mug of tea I dragged the little side table with the cookies, milk and sugar closer. "Do you want some ibuprofen for the pain?"

"That would be great."

As Ben doctored his tea and his body, I held up a large blue hoodie. "This should be big enough." Wrestling it on, it looked more like a second skin as his shoulders and chest stretched the fabric. "Sorry, I don't have anything larger." I was a little taken aback as he smiled up at me. There was something about his face...not quite familiar but maybe endearing?

His feet and legs, protruding below the draped towel, were tinged with blue. Holding up an index finger I smiled. "I've saved the best for last." His face displayed a quizzical motif as I held up a pair of pyjama bottoms. "I couldn't find any pants that would fit you, but even better – I found these. Now, just so that you know, they aren't just *any* pyjama bottoms. These belonged to a Cardinal. Cardinal Legault."

Ben's laughter echoed across the water. "Well, I never thought I would see the day where I was excited about getting into another man's pants."

Chapter 10 - A Shove and a Pop

W arm clothes, a blanket, tea and the potent summer sun worked their magic and Ben finally stopped shivering but the drooping eye lids and dark circles that surrounded them still spoke of exhaustion. I found excuses to leave him alone in the hopes that he might fall asleep but he stubbornly clung to social mores by trying to maintain the conversation with a stream of questions. Whether or not he was actually taking in the answers remained to be seen.

"I'm just going to pop into the cabin to do some prepping for supper. Can I get you anything?"

"Can I help?" He motioned to his lap. "If you have a cutting board I can do vegetables, or peel potatoes or whatever..."

He responded to my smile with a shrug. "You've been a life-saver and I feel like a burden."

"You've been no trouble. A bit of excitement makes for an interesting day." Lifting up the pot of tea I nodded to his cup.

"No thanks, but some water would be great. I'm probably a few pints short."

Rummaging through the cupboards I couldn't find a water bottle, so instead grabbed a large glass stein and filled it with spring water we had collected the day before. As I reached for the door handle I stopped and looked outside through the screen. Ben's head listed to one side at an awkward angle. I decided to give him ten or so minutes to get into a deeper sleep before I would try tucking a small pillow between his shoulder and neck.

Instead of starting the salad, I stayed inside and settled into the red wooden rocking chair that has resided in front of the large windows since The Camp was built. Many dreams have been conceived in this chair, many hours of contemplation and incalculable time spent in perfect bliss looking out over the bay, watching the unfolding of nature, time and people. All to the rhythm of the rocking chair.

The sun had shifted slightly, about an hour's worth, towards the west, when I noticed a small boat emerging around the edge of the tree line, off in the distance. Looking through the ever-present binoculars I could easily pick out the ridiculous sombrero dancing in the wind. I looked though the screen door and saw that Ben was still asleep but his blanket had been tossed aside. I slipped out the door and sat on the chair beside him.

When Ben first arrived I had asked about his night spent outdoors. He had summed up his ordeal with a shrug of his shoulders and a vague comment about not being the most pleasant night of his life and something about being visited by an owl which, according to native legend, might be a good or bad omen. With this in mind I thought a gentle awakening might be in order so I softly called his name. His breath deepened and his eyebrows lifted as if asking a question, then his eyelids slowly opened like he was hesitant to leave the dream he was immersed in.

Ben's eyes caught mine and after a millisecond lag, he face glided into a smile. "Oh. Hi. Sorry, I guess I drifted off. Have I been out for long?" He noticed the pillow and nodded his thanks.

"Just an hour or so. I imagine you have a bit more catching up to do than that, but it looks like Colin and Pearl are coming back and I thought you might want to have a few moments to wake up before Colin gets his hands on you."

"That sounds rather ominous."

"Nah, he's one of the best. Pretty amazing, actually. But don't tell him I said that."

Turning to look at the approaching boat, Ben's only comment was a low-throated "Hmm" as he spied Colin holding down the sides of his sombrero which made it look like a ridiculous oversized bonnet.

I nodded towards the boat. "Be right back."

Standing on the little dock, I caught the gunwale of the Elgin and snugged it up to the dock. "So, how was the expedition?"

Grinning like a toddler with fists full of frogs, Colin held up a brace of sizeable pickerel. "And here, my dear, is our supper!"

"Excellent! I did a little fishing of my own – look up on the deck and see what I caught."

Pearl turned and looked. "Oh, yes, I see Kate did go a-fishing? Hmm, he looks like a keeper, but is he housebroken?"

Colin climbed out of the boat and elbowed my arm in a gentle jab. "Looks like you win the trophy for the largest catch. Did he put up much of a struggle?" Shrugging his shoulders, his head bobbed forward as if looking closer would give him some answers. "Well? What's the story? I'll bet it'll be a good one."

"He was standing on a stump out by the point." Pearl's head turned as she looked at me out of the corner of her eyes, then up at Ben who was now holding his hands out in an I-know-it's-a-crazy-story sort of way. "He was chased by a bear, injured, got lost and spent the night in the woods. He's in a lot of pain when he tries to walk so when he came out of the bush near the point and saw The Camp he thought it would be easier to swim than walk."

"Injured, you say." the doctor questioned.

"Yeah, his hip."

"Well, I haven't made a house call in a while – let's not keep the lad waiting." And off Colin marched, handing his fish to Pearl and tossing his straw hat to me.

I hustled up the incline after him and left Pearl to secure the boat.

Colin was already introducing himself as I caught up. "I hear you have an interesting story to tell."

"It's a bit different – not one you'd hear at most cocktail parties, but probably not all that unusual around these parts."

"Right, first off, what's the damage and how did it happen?"

Ben described how he was out at his favourite blueberry patch when three little bear cubs came running out of the forest. Knowing that mama wouldn't be far behind he started backing up slowly but not soon enough. The sow stood on her hind legs, snapped her jaws a few times then charged. "I knew not to run, but I just couldn't help it. A protective mother bear coming straight at you is one terrifying sight and she just kept getting more and more massive with each step, so I turned and ran. There was a steep slope just behind me that I failed to negotiate and ended up tumbling down and hitting a tree at the bottom." Ben looked around and shrugged. "I put my hands over the back of my neck and head and laid there for the longest time hoping she wouldn't follow me down. Fortunately, the cubs started bawling and she went back. I discovered that I was having trouble walking and needed to find a different and easier way back and that's when I got lost."

Colin nodded as if that explained things. "So, where's the pain?"

Pearl and I settled right in, shamelessly horning in on the medical assessment.

"My hip. That's what hit the tree." Ben pointed. "On the right."

"Does it give out when you walk?"

"Yeah. A crutch kind of helped but it was better when I could support myself on both sides."

"Right, let me wash up and then I'll to do a few little tests to see if it's what I think." As Colin disappeared into the cabin, Pearl laid the pickerel on the grass and climbed onto the deck.

With hands freshly washed, Colin nodded to Ben. "We'll need to get you up and onto the picnic table."

"Kate, your assistance, please." Lifting Ben to standing, it was easy to see that he had stiffened up and was having some trouble moving. "Has Kate given you ibuprofen?"

"Yes, she's been an excellent nurse." Through his grimace, Ben smiled and put his arms over our shoulders. We manoeuvred him onto the table.

"This test, should you be interested, is called the FABER test, and will tell me if your pelvis is misaligned." Taking Ben's right leg he flexed it. "Okay, now let's put your right ankle on top of your left thigh, now let your knee fall to the side. I'm going to put pressure on this leg and on the opposite hip. You tell me if this causes you pain."

Ben's quickly exhaled breath gave us his answer, but he followed through with a quick, "Yup."

"Excellent."

Pearl shook her head. "He's such a sadist."

"And you love me for it you little degenerate." Colin gently placed Ben's leg back on top of the other one. "It's excellent because it's suggesting that this is a nice, easy fix. I'm going to try two other tests, just to make sure, and if they indicate the same results, I should be able to pop that joint back into place."

Ben sighed deeply. "You mean it's not broken?"

"Doesn't appear to be - looks more like your sacroiliac joint has shifted out of position. The soft tissues are swollen and will be a little tender for a few days but you'll be able to walk and pick blueberries in just a few minutes."

Colin continued torquing and prodding his patient until he was satisfied with his diagnosis. Walking around the table he asked Ben to shift onto his uninjured side with his opposite hip and knee fully flexed. Standing in front, he supported Ben's right knee as he hung it off the table. "Try to relax and let everything go." Tapping Ben's hip he smiled. "I'm going to apply pressure to your shoulder, and a little opposing force to the ischial tuberosity which, literally translated means, I'm going to twist you like a pretzel." Placing his right hand on the front of Ben's shoulder, Colin leaned over the patient, applied pressure to the back of his pelvis, waited for a second or two then gave a sharp shove. An audible pop snapped the air. "And now you can walk again!"

Ben eyed the doctor as he sat up. "Okay, let's give this a go." He stood up wearing a questioning look which quickly transitioned into a full out grin as he tested his ability to move.

"I'd recommend a little walking to get everything moving in the area, but take it easy. The area is traumatised and needs some TLC."

Pearl gave Colin's shoulders a squeeze. "My little wizard."

"All part of your full package deal, Ma'am."

Chapter 11 – The Invitation

T he sun still had a bit of a journey before it put itself to bed but a cool wind off the bay was picking up momentum. I zipped up my sweatshirt. Colin waited until Ben closed the outhouse door behind him before speaking. "Even though he hasn't said as much, Ben's been through some trauma and a lot of pain. I wouldn't mind keeping an eye on him for a day or two. He should be taking it easy for a bit, and I'm concerned about him walking through the trail; both the length of it and especially with it being uneven in so many spots."

"Okay. I don't have a problem with that."

"I thought for sleeping arrangements, you and Pearl could sleep together in the Honeymoon Suite, Kate, I'll take your bed and Ben can use the bunk bed."

Pearl and I eyed each other up. She had the good grace to blush and I shook my head.

"Is there a problem, ladies?"

I just smiled while Pearl stuttered. "The last time Kate and I shared a bed, I was dreaming and thought it was you. Let's just leave it at that."

Colin obliged the story with a leer.

"Hey, there's no problem here. You guys stay where you are, I'm sure I'll be fine in the bedroom with Ben out in the main cabin. I don't see him as the Night-Stalker type, and besides, there's that big hook latch on the bedroom door."

Pearl shook her head. "Yeah, like you've got a good track record in assessing men."

"Hey, I did all right with Andrew!" My indignation was unfounded. Andrew had been the exception rather than the rule so my friends had good reason to be concerned about my out-of-commission creep-meter. "Well, what do you two think about him?"

Pearl shrugged. "I have to say he seems okay."

"Colin?"

"Okay, our bed is within hollering distance, and, as you say and there is a lock on the door. Besides, he'll probably crash and burn when he hits the pillow tonight."

I walked over to the railing and grabbed Ben's clothes which were still wet and now cold. "Let's move this party indoors. That wind is getting the best of me – which is a perfect excuse to make a fire."

Ben stepped up onto the deck with a smile and an armload of wood. "How's that for timing? I wanted to do something before I left..."

"That's very thoughtful of you, but Colin was just saying how he wanted to keep an eye on you for a bit and we could always use a fourth hand for Euchre, so if you're able, and no one is waiting for you, you're welcome to stay for a day or two."

Colin nodded. "Besides, you need to eat, and navigating that trail right now is not something I'd recommend."

With pursed lips and brows hunkered down hooding his eyes, Ben resembled a caricature. He shook his head. "No, no one is expecting me, but you've already really put yourselves out and I'm not comfortable imposing further."

Colin shrugged with a smile. "That's cool. However, I've just put in a long day fishing and I'm more than ready to pour everyone a lovely glass or two of Pinot Grigio before I fillet the pickerel. And, after we partake of said beverages, no one will be in any condition to drive you back to wherever you are staying."

Our guest looked around at the three of us. "Okay, but only if you let me help with dinner."

Colin picked up the fish. "We never refuse help. Besides, we're always up for a good story and I'm getting the feeling that you've got one for the telling."

Chapter 12 – No Suckers Here

C olin laid the sheets of newspaper on the edge of the deck, placed one of the pickerel on top with the filleting knife pointed at the fish's belly. He stopped and looked up at me. "I imagine it starts out something like an autopsy, but after that I'm a little unclear."

"Yeah, that was always my mother's domain. I'm not too good at that."

Ben waved a hand. "Hey, more than happy to help. I can show you with the first one and you can try the second one if you're game.

"I'm always game – and according to Pearl, at times, gamey. But that's another story."

Ben pulled a chair down onto the grass so he didn't have to stoop to get the job done. "Ninety percent of the work is in how sharp the knife is, and of course the angle. Thumbing the blade he nodded. "This'll do nicely." Placing the knife behind the fish's head he made his first cut. "Okay, to start, you slide the knife behind the gill plate, right down to the backbone. Don't cut through, but instead, turn your blade in the opposite direction and, only going in a little bit, slide it all the way down the backbone to just in front of the tail."

Tapping Pearl on the arm I inclined my head towards the cabin. "Pearl, can you help me with the salad, please?"

"And miss the demonstration?"

"Yeah, just for a minute."

Once we were at the counter at the back of the main room, I leaned into my friend, speaking quietly. "Just a heads-up, girl, I'm quite capable of cleaning a fish – but the trick is to never let *them* know. That

42

way, you don't get suckered into cleaning every bloody fish that gets caught. They catch 'em - they can clean 'em, and I'll cook 'em."

"You're wise beyond your years."

"I have my moments."

Chapter 13 - And Now You Know... Some of the Story

"So you're a teacher?" Colin passed the wooden salad bowl to our guest. "What grade?"

"I teach at a high school near Toronto." Ben pinched the salad between the serving tongs and dropped it into his bowl. "I've got grades nine through twelve, in the tech stream."

"Tech, as in computers?"

Nodding, Ben smiled. "Construction; design and environmental."

Eyebrows raised, Pearl and I gave each other a look.

Ben had seen the look pass between us and sat back in his chair.

I jumped in. "Well that's cool. Pearl and I do renovations."

"In Timmins?"

"No, we live in B.C.- in Victoria."

"You've come quite a distance for a holiday."

We gave Ben a brief version of my family history and found he was a focused listener, looking directly at us as we spoke, taking in our stories and responding with nods and smiles.

Pearl had used a generous, though some might have described it as sadistic hand with the spices for the fish coating and we found ourselves opening a second bottle of wine to anesthetize the blazing tissues in our mouths. As she apologized repeatedly, Colin shook his head and patted her arm. "It's all good, my little clam shell. Cells in the mouth reproduce quickly. We'll have brand spanking new taste buds in no time at all."

Ben was busy wiping the perspiration from his forehead. "Are you kidding, this is exactly what I needed. Who knows what parasites I consumed eating worms and drinking lake water. I'm sure those little devils have now been taken care of." He raised his glass. "And we've given them a proper send-off."

"To proper send-offs." said Colin as we clinked our glasses.

We sank back into the wooden captain's chairs and collectively sighed. The heavy round oak table with the red and white checkered table cloth was littered with the remains of our empty dinner dishes. Ben looked around at us, nodding. "And this is where I come in handy. I need to move a bit before I stiffen up permanently, so I'll get the dishes."

Pearl started stacking the plates. "In restitution for my scorching fish coating, I'll help."

The large metal dishpan had been heating up on the wood stove and was ready for business. Adding some dish detergent, Ben pulled it to the edge and dipped our wine glasses in.

It's the simple little things that can catch our interest. Things like knowing how to wash dishes, offering to help prepare, jumping in to contribute; these are little check-marks on the "Hmm, interesting" list. Okay, those and a wonderfully broad back, well-muscled legs, an engaging smile that includes the eyes, and, oh yes, hands. Solid, strong, clean hands. But I digress.

I felt Colin's eyes and turned to see him smiling at me. He whispered, "You're staring, dearest."

"Just admiring a well-raised gentleman."

"I think the phrase 'well-raised' has a different meaning for you right now."

I'm pretty sure he caught my blush before he caught the hand towel that I whipped at his head.

*****

As Pearl passed around the large tin of assorted cookies I realized that we still didn't know any more about why Ben was in Timmins.

According to Pearl, beating around the bush was not how you mined information.

"So Ben, what brings you to this neck of the woods?"

A slow smile extended across his stubbled face. "My uncle." He seemed to be gathering his thoughts as he stared at the table cloth. "My uncle, Carl. Carl Gabrielsen." When he looked up I realized he wasn't seeing our faces but instead seemed to be observing a familiar and maybe comforting inner video. "I used to come and spend a lot of time with Carl while I was growing up. He was twelve years older than me, but he was like a big brother. He would take me fishing, hiking and teach me about life in the forest. Carl was a very passionate and committed man and it came through in everything he did." Ben leaned back tipping his chair onto the two back legs. "He had a cabin that he stayed in, over on the Whitefish. Belonged to ...," Ben paused and brought the chair forward and leaned onto the arms. His voice became soft "... belonged to a very special lady Carl wanted to marry. But, she kept putting him off thinking that he should commit to his passion - which was biology and the environment. She didn't want him to be stuck working a dead-end job. I guess she was worried that she was holding him back. She kept telling him to go back to school and get a degree."

There must have been a wet log in the wood stove as a loud bang cracked the air which pulled Ben from his story. Looking up at the ceiling he sighed. "I'm sorry, I got lost in the telling. I still miss my uncle, even though he's been gone for sixteen years."

I put my uneaten cookie down on a napkin. "So, you still come up to the cabin when you can?"

"Yeah, but I'm not sure for how much longer. The lady died and ... well ... it's complicated."

Clapping his hands then rubbing them together, Ben looked around and raised an eyebrow. "Someone mentioned Euchre, earlier. It's been a while but I'm up for a game if you are."

Pearl nodded. "You're on!" Turning in her chair she reached behind and pulled the little glass knob on the drawer in the green table. "Oh yeah, still where they've always been!" and she lifted out a deck of cards.

*****

Two hours and uncountable laughs later, it was noted that eyelids were drooping and the card-playing was getting sloppier – time to call it a night.

The interplay between Colin and Ben was very subtle, but from my viewpoint in the dark recesses of the bedroom, I caught Colin looking intently at Ben then slightly incline his head in the direction of my room. I couldn't see the look on Colin's face, but our guest had no doubts about the meaning. He spread his fingers wide, held up his hands and shook his head. Colin gave a little nod, clapped him on the shoulder and said he'd see him in the morning.

Chapter 14

T he creaking of wood on wood yanked the man out of a
dreamless sleep. The curtains made a backdrop upon which the
silent leaves and limbs of the birch trees were backlit by the bright
moonlight. Through slitted-eyes, he watched as Kate tip-toed through
the cabin. He kept his breathing full, wondering if that was how he
sounded when he slept. He was curious as to why she stopped to pick
up her camera with its large, long lens and was tempted to follow her
outside. After a brief internal debate he rolled over onto his right side
and stared at the log wall. Knots and textures captured his vision and he
drifted back to sleep.

Chapter 15 – Hips & Squats

T he sound of the cast iron frying pan connecting with the cast iron of the wood stove caught my attention. I had been drifting in and out of sleep for a while, enjoying the fluidity of the transitions. And just as engaging was the opportunity to relax into the comfort of the bed; stretching, repositioning, and allowing the whispering of the trees to lull me back to sleep.

Now I was curious as to who was getting the breakfast started.

The plush texture of the sheepskin mat greeted my feet as I sat on the side of the bed listening to the sounds on the other side of the door. There seemed to be a lot of poking around in cupboards so I assumed it was one of the guys because Pearl knew where pretty much everything resided whereas neither of the guys would. Damn, but I'd make a good detective! I smiled at my delusion.

There are smells that touch your heart: the ocean, the forest, or maybe that of your Grandfather's pipe, and ones that connect directly to your stomach. I find the airborne molecules of fresh brewed coffee, with a companion odour of bacon frying, score a direct hit to both. Standing in the bedroom doorway I allowed the delicious aromas to carry me into the day. The orchestrator of said delights was nowhere to be seen. Through the large west window I watched as Ben struggled with an armload of wood on one side while putting his weight into a long pole on the other. I hurried to open the door for him. His smile through his stubbly beard was bright, but the squint of his eyes told the real story.

"Hip out again?"

"It appears to be, though not as bad as before."

"And yet you still got the fire going and breakfast started?"

"Hey, where would I be without all of you? Probably... I don't even want to think about it." He dropped the wood into the box behind the stove, turned and leaned over the counter, sweat dappling his forehead.

"I got this. Stretch out on the couch and we'll get Colin up here to work his magic again." As Ben started to argue, I just shook my head and pointed to the green plaid couch. "You're doing more damage by weight bearing." After sighing, he tried to walk as if it didn't hurt, but I could see he was white-knuckling his walking stick.

Pride? Stubborn? Or a combination of both – it doesn't really matter. It's a blessing and a curse of some particular members of our species.

A loud, triumphant, "Hah," sounded from the vicinity of the other cabin. Pulling open and lifting up the huge mullion window that looked easterly out over the bay, I latched it to the hook hanging from the ceiling.

On the small deck on the front of the Honeymoon Suite, Pearl was performing squats while carrying Colin on her back. He was holding on with one arm while making lassoing motions with his other. "... four, five!"

I looked over at Ben who was watching with wide eyes and mouth slightly agape. He nodded in appreciation and simply said, "Impressive." Then, as an afterthought, "You'd never know it – she's so... so... delicate."

"Yup. And Colin keeps getting sucked into bets with her that he continually loses." I turned back to the cupboard and grabbed some plates. "But really, I think he doesn't mind losing because he loves watching her, and probably does it just to see what her limits are."

Ben shook his head and smiled then looked up at me. "So, do you have anyone who checks out your limits?"

An innocent enough question, and said in a casual, off-hand manner, so I replied in kind. "No, not really."

"'Not really' allows for some interpretation."

I reached into the bedroom and grabbed the broom just beside the door. There's always sweeping to be done around a wood burning stove. And, it gave me some time to question why I had added 'not really.'

"Nah, Pearl and Colin make sure I don't become complacent."

Colin appeared on the deck, grinning, "Did you see her? Amazing."

Through the screen door I asked, "What did this bet cost you?"

Colin grinned. "Dishes for two days. Totally worth it!" He opened the door and took in the tableau. "Ah, not quite the tap dancer you were last night?"

Ben shook his head. "But I can still play the violin."

"Good lad. Let's move into my office-slash-torture chamber... sorry, adjustment room and get you back to dancing form." Leaning down, Colin hoisted Ben's arm over his shoulder helping him up and they hobbled out onto the deck. Through the door he called, "Carry on, Kate, breakfast smells delicious."

Pearl danced into the cabin then promptly dropped into the red rocking chair. "Yes! No dishes for two days."

"Right, but how are your legs."

"I can barely walk, legs are pure rubber." Jerking her thumb towards her boyfriend, "But I'm not letting him know that."

"Can you get the toast going?"

"Only if I can do it from a chair." She grabbed the yellow stool and pulled it up beside the counter. Popping in the bread she pushed down the lever and asked, "So, are you up for a little exploring today? We thought we'd take the snorkels and masks out to the sandbars."

"Sounds like a plan." Through the window I checked out the guys on the deck. "Looks like Ben will be keeping us company for at least another day. We can't send him back to his cabin if his hip is still going out."

Pearl just looked at me and smiled.

"Whaaat?"

"Nothing. Just noting how happy you sound."

"Hey, can you not tell the difference between happy and concerned?" I asked.

"Why yes. Yes I can."

"Twit."

*****

Passing around the plate of bacon, Ben exclaimed, "Man, it's like magic! One minute I can barely move and then next, poof ... I'm looking for a swing partner."

Movement and conversation stopped as we all looked at Ben. "Excuse me?" I think my mouth may have had a slackness to it. "Swing?"

Ben managed a conspiratorial smile even while a blush bloomed upwards from his neck. "Uh, yeah." He looked at Colin, then Pearl and shrugged as he turned back to me. "Swing dance. That was something that my uncle's girlfriend taught me when I was a teenager. She was amazing." A smile of memories lit Ben's face. "You never would have expected it from her. She was a basic kind of person. You know, not simple, but just not frilly. She lived a tough life, but man, when you put the music on, that woman was possessed. She transformed into whatever culture or creature the music called for." His head swivelled slightly then tilted. "She was quite amazing."

"So, tonight, if we were to find some souped-up jazz music," Colin waved a piece of bacon and nodded towards the deck, "we could clear the dance floor and you could give us some lessons?"

Chuckling, Ben nodded. "Because I can't even begin to repay you for all your help and kindness, the humiliation I would suffer in trying to pretend that I knew what I was doing, would be a small price to pay." The wiggling of his eyebrows gave promise to an entertaining evening.

"Right! Then, it's Swing Night on Moose Creek." Colin stood and started collecting dishes. "But for now, it's time to do a little aquatic archeological dig over on the sandbars."

Pearl's legs had apparently recovered from her squat challenge as she stood up and declared that she would get the snorkels and masks from the cupboard in the other cabin.

Ben helped Colin clear and clean while I gathered towels and snacks and found an old pair of swim trunks for Ben.

Within twenty minutes we were ready to go. Walking down the hill and crossing over to the small dock, we carried the supplies for our outing. Colin had put the motor on the back of the boat and was grinning like a little boy about to slip a bug down someone's shirt. "I get to drive today, huh?"

Pearl and I just looked at each other. After sighing, I relented. "You can drive on the way back."

Colin gave the trucker's air-horn-pump and scuttled to the middle bench while I climbed into the back by the motor.

As we settled in I looked up to see Ben standing statue-still. He didn't appear to be breathing.

"Ben? Ben, are you okay?"

He pointed at the boat and whispered, "What's the name of the boat?" And before we could answer, he turned, walked off the dock and around the shore so he could see the other side of the craft. Within seconds, a cast of sad and confused played across his face which then became ashen.

Not being sure what was going on, we stayed silent and waited for Ben to collect himself. A minute or so passed before he looked at us.

Chapter 16 – The Elgin

Ben regarded me with brows stitched close together in either concentration or confusion, or most likely, both. Pointing at the lettering on the side of the boat his mouth worked to form words that couldn't seem to find their way out into the warm morning air.

We waited.

"The Elgin." He shook his head. "Um, Kate, could you please look on the transom, in that corner?"

I turned and looked. Written in faded black marker was 'BB – 38'.

Ben closed his eyes. "BB - 38, right?"

"How'd you know?"

Pearl and Colin looked like they were watching a tennis match with their heads swivelling in unison back and forth as they and looked at Ben then me.

"Where did you get this boat?"

"My dad said he got it from a trapper he knew. Cougar Sadie."

"Yeah. Sadie Ramier."

"Wow. You knew Sadie! What does BB – 38 mean?"

"She put that there." A half smile appeared on Ben's face. "Those are my initials. I caught a thirty-eight inch pike – biggest catch of the summer. She said it had to be memorialized. I was fourteen. Oh, man, she was something." He cast his eyes back down to the name on the boat.

"So you were a friend?"

Ben looked skywards and rolled his shoulders back like he was releasing something that had been pent up. "She was my uncle's girlfriend. She's the one who taught me to dance." His sigh was long and belly deep. "She's the one ... she was everything to Uncle Carl." Ben's arms hung loosely by his side - he seemed to have slipped into a fog of memories.

A little breeze had started rippling the water creating a gentle rocking motion in the boat. Pearl and I looked at each other. She lifted her eyebrows and I nodded.

Pearl placed her hand on Colin's shoulder and stepped onto the dock. "What's say we stay here right now, put on the kettle and, if it's okay with Ben, hear a few stories about Cougar Sadie. She sounds pretty special."

Colin passed the cooler to Pearl. "I'd like that. We can always go to the sandbars this afternoon."

Chapter 17 – And the Plot Thickens

We sat at the table on the deck with the warm breeze whisking away the steam from our coffees. Instead of telling us about Sadie, Ben looked at each one of us in turn, and asked what we had heard. Being the only other one at the gathering who knew of her, I retold my father's story of the poacher and Cougar Sadie's solution to his thievery and how she got her name. Pearl smiled as she nodded her head in admiration. "Awesome. She sounds like a most unusual woman."

"Yeah, she sure was." Ben's large hand wrapped around his mug but he didn't lift it up, just slowly slid it back and forth.

Colin placed his arm over Pearl's shoulder and gave her a little squeeze. "So how did she die?"

"Cyanide poisoning." Ben pursed his lips.

The doctor's head tilted down while his eyebrows arched up. "Cyanide poisoning? Now that's not something you hear every day. Accidental?"

"That's what the final report said." Ben's head shook slightly. "An old trapper friend, Marcel Dubois, found her. You know, these guys are tough old birds. They spend their lives living as much off the land as they can; a lot of them are pretty reclusive and they might not make friends easily, but they all loved Sadie. It really hit everyone hard."

Leaning into the table, I used my elbow for leverage and turned further towards Ben to study his expression. "It doesn't sound like you're convinced it was accidental."

Ben looked at me, then across the table at my friends and finally over at the water to his right.

There are people who can easily read others' tells, like a good poker player can pick out the tells or unconscious signals of the other players and figure out whether they are bluffing or if they're excited about the hand they're holding. Usually I'm not great at it, but Ben wasn't so hard to read. I had noticed that one of his tells was the rubbing of the back of his fingers along his chin. This appeared to be his thinking-tell. Then again, it could also be a biding-time or uncomfortable-situation movement. As I watched the action of his hand, I believed it to be all three. There was an internal debate raging inside.

Colin waded in. "Cyanide? Why would a trapper have cyanide?" He pulled Pearl in a little closer. "She didn't poison the animals, did she?"

Ben's eyes widened. "Oh, hell no! Not Sadie!" His chest expanded before he blew out a long breath.

Again he studied the three of us and nodded as if giving himself permission to tell us more. "Timmins is a mining town – it was one of the largest gold mining centres in Canada." Taking a gulp of his coffee he continued. "Mining is tough and it's dangerous. It's mostly open pit now, but before, the miners would get into cages and descend anywhere up to 5,000 feet – about one and a half kilometres, for their eight-hour shifts. My uncle took me down when they used to have tours. It's not a life for just anyone." Ben pursed his lips. "Of course the security was really tight but some guys found a way to... liberate gold dust and nuggets."

I jumped in. "You mean high grade?"

Ben's eyebrows lifted. "That's right. I forgot your parents grew up here."

"Only my Dad. Mom had just come for a summer job working at the provincial park when she met Dad."

Ben smiled as he scratched his fledgling beard. "Well, let's just say that Sadie inherited some gold. She held onto it for years because even though there's a black market for high grade, it's pretty dangerous. If the police don't get you, there are plenty of fellows who'd be more than happy to put you in the hospital, or worse, stealing it from you. Trapping isn't a very profitable business and Sadie's needs were simple. She grew and hunted the basics, but vehicles, insurance and taxes have to be paid so she figured out a way to sell the gold without raising too much suspicion."

Ben had our complete attention.

"Sadie would go around to garage sales and second hand stores buying up old cutlery, small metal serving plates, decorative items - inexpensive stuff. She would smelt down the gold, then dip the items to coat them. She could sell them on the internet or to buyers down south without raising warning flags. She even made some medallions and other bits of jewellery. But, in order to process the gold from its raw state, you need to use cyanide."

Pearl's eyes were slitted in concentration. "So how did they find her? I mean, was she found with a pot of gold bubbling in front of her?"

Ben's lower lip pressed up into the top one as a soft snort blew across them. "No. The police never knew about her gold smelting. She died in bed."

Colin and Pearl looked at each other. Pearl turned back to Ben. "So, if she was in bed, how do they figure it was cyanide and accidental?"

"That's just it. They haven't come up with anything that makes sense." Ben stared into his coffee mug, his eyes hard with a steely determination. "When the toxicology report came back saying that her death had been caused by inhaling hydrogen cyanide they searched everywhere and found a container of it in her work shed, but because it was covered in dust and was at the back of a shelf, they assumed it hadn't been used in a very long time and therefore couldn't have been the direct cause. Finally, they looked in her wood stove and ascertained that she had been burning plastics and must have inhaled enough to kill her."

"That sounds reasonable." said Pearl.

Ben looked directly at her. "Yes, it would be a reasonable assumption if she was foolish enough to do that. People think trappers and folks like Sadie are simple and have no education... and some are.

But not Sadie. She was always reading and taking courses in subjects like languages, chemistry, botany... she was a diverse and well-informed woman. She would never burn plastics indoors. In fact, she would never burn plastics, period. Because she lived off the land, she had a great respect for it. But with no suicide note and no foul play evident, they concluded it was accidental."

Slowly shaking his head from side to side Ben pursed his lips again. "But it gets better. Part of the investigation included me."

I had two sets of warning bells going off simultaneously in my head. The first set warned me to be very careful about my instinct to defend and protect someone whom I considered to be a good guy and a new friend. I tend to accept people into my life at face value. Historically, this has been a double-edged sword. The second and more resonant set of chimes were telling me to defend and protect this man whom I considered to be a good-guy and a new friend.

And, like most people, I am inclined to listen to the loudest noises. "As in you were called to give information about Sadie or..." I shrugged, "...or?"

Ben smiled and nodded. "...or – I was a suspect." His hands splayed out on the table as if showing they were empty. Leaning back, he again looked at each one of us in turn trying to assess our responses.

"Why you?" asked Pearl.

"Because I'm the sole beneficiary." Ben smiled at the looks on our faces. "You wouldn't think there would be much of an estate… and why me?" Lifting his left leg over the bench, he straddled it so he could look directly at us. "As I mentioned, Uncle Carl was the love of her life. I think, in a way she felt responsible for his death because she had insisted he go back to school. It was on a return trip from the university in southern Ontario that a drunk driver in an SUV crossed the line and killed him." Ben's brows drew closer together as he looked down and stared at his hands for a moment. When he tilted his head up he was grinning. "Anyway, Sadie had a brother, Raymond, but they'd gone their separate ways years ago after a falling-out so she mentioned him in the will – specifically, her words were, '...and for my brother Raymond, I leave nothing but my best wishes that he smarten up, learn to behave himself and finally get a job and act responsibly.'"

"Ouch." Colin smiled. "And how did brother Raymond take that bit of advice?"

"Like a hound on the hunt - a lot of baying, sniffing around and chasing scents. But then he backed right off, which leaves me suspicious and, to be honest, a little nervous."

We waited.

"Raymond's income is questionable. He does odd short term jobs, but has a decent truck, lives girlfriend to girlfriend and disappears for periods of time. When the will was read, he accused me of taking advantage of his sister and coercing her to leave everything to me. Then it escalated to him accusing me of murdering her. But, of course there were no grounds for that – five classes of students vouching for my presence eight hours away, as well as parent-teacher interviews in the evening kind of cleared me pretty quickly."

"So why do you think he backed off?"

"No idea. It doesn't make sense. But it doesn't end there." Ben was shaking his head. "The will is being held up, not by Raymond, but by a real estate agent by the name of Sterling Harper."

Pearl snorted. "Sterling?"

"Yup, that's his name."

"Why's he contesting the will? Was he a friend?"

"Now here's where it gets really interesting." And, on cue, a cloud slipped underneath the sun bringing a quick cool breeze that raised the hair on my neck. Ben hadn't noticed the weather drama. "Sterling has a signed agreement to purchase Sadie's properties, for about one-tenth of their value. That's impossible on many levels. First of all, Sadie would never, ever sell her properties. They were her life. She wouldn't move into town, or anywhere else for any amount of money, let alone the paltry sum that this crook was offering her. Her land was how she lived, made money, grew her food. She was not a person who could ever work in an office or a store, so this made no sense. Sadie couldn't live off of what he was offering."

Pearl was shaking her head. "But he had a signed agreement. Where did that come from?"

"That's just it – it seems to have appeared out of nowhere. Sadie and I talked at least every couple of weeks and she never mentioned anything about selling."

"Wait a minute." I cut in. "You said properties, plural. She had more than one?"

"Yeah. She had the three acres on Adikameg River where she lived, and she also had the cabin further down the same river – closer to the highway. It's where I always stay when I visit. Sadie wanted me to have some privacy and it made the place looked lived in. You know, so it was less likely to get broken into."

"Adikameg? You mean the Whitefish River?" It took me a moment to put the pieces together. There had been a lot of information coming at us over the last two days. "That's right, that's where you said you had met up with the bear."

Ben was nodding. "Yup."

"So, what do you think is going on?" My mind immediately jumped to the obvious. "Do you think he forged her signature?"

Ben leaned in closer to me, the brown of his irises almost eclipsed by his pupils. "That's exactly what I think."

Chapter 18 – Now What

"So what are you going to do?"
    "I'm contesting the sale but it's not looking good."
"How so?"

"He's got a signed document and..." We waited while Ben shrugged and sighed. "...and he's a local. With connections. Seems like there's either a few backroom deals happening or relationships, or whatever. I'm being stonewalled."

I think best while doing things and my mind was slogging through the information so I got up and went into the cabin to grab more coffee and some fruit. I picked up some paper and a pencil and added it to the tray. Ben was waiting to open the door for me, his brows pulled together and his eyes trying to read my face. "Hey, I'm sorry. I didn't mean to bring everybody down and ruin your day with my problems."

Colin jumped in. "What are you talking about? You didn't ruin anything. We were going out to do some digging – well we're still digging, but now we're mining in the muck of human depravity. This kind of digging..." and in a theatrical voice added, "...is far more captivating." He looked around to see if anyone else was as pleased with his analogy as he was. I granted him points with a small groan.

Ben topped up everyone's coffee and passed the bowl of fruit around while I wrote Sadie's name in the middle of the paper. In separate circles orbiting her I added Ben's name, Raymond's, then Sterling's. To the side, I listed gold and property. Ben tapped the sheet. "Don't forget to add 'trapline'. The rights for that are up for grabs as well."

Pearl asked, "How does that work?"

"Unless the property is owned by the individual, the trapline reverts to the Crown. There is a consideration, however, that if a trapper has a helper, then the helper stands a good chance of being able to acquire the rights. And yes, Sadie had taken on a helper two years ago – a fellow by the name of Jasper Lebeau."

"So we have another possible 'person of interest.' How is this playing out?" Pearl bit into an apple.

"Needless to say, Harper is trying to push this thing through as fast as he can and I'm running out of resources." Ben turned to me. "I'm open to any suggestions. Kate? Anything?"

"Of course you've questioned the signature."

"Yeah, but he had a guy all lined up who is supposed to be an expert, so I brought in my own and he said it was 'inconclusive' as to whether or not it was her signature. Apparently, if it's a forgery, it's a good one."

Ben stood up and walked to the railing on the deck. I watched as his head lowered slightly and his shoulders rounded. My first response was to comfort him but I held back and before my indecision could be conquered, Ben straightened up, pulled his shoulders back and spoke to the water in front of him. "I don't care about the money." He turned back to us and with his eyes narrowed and lips pinched into a firm line his face had taken on a determined countenance. "No, it's not the money. It's everything and it's all wrong."

A lot had happened in the twenty four or so hours since we'd met, but morphing right in front of us was a man capable of an intensity I had not imagined. In the four steps he took back to the table, you could feel the power of his leg muscles driving down into the planks. Leaning over he grabbed the edges of the table. There was a faint creaking of wood. "It's about what happened to Sadie. Whoever did this has to be accountable. They have to pay for what they did. She was the most decent person you could ever meet. She didn't deserve to be murdered! She didn't deserve to die!" His fist came down more softly than I expected and the muscles in his face transformed back into more familiar lines. "I'm sorry. I'm so frustrated and..." he sighed and sat down "... and I'm out of ideas. And, I just hate to see some slime bag get away with this."

I didn't realize that I had leaned back and as Ben's intensity subsided into more of a sad resolve I brought my posture back to neutral and blew out a long breath. This didn't escape Ben's notice and his hand made it halfway towards mine before he twitched and drew it back. "Sorry."

Forks in the road-of-life force decisions upon us. Do we go this way or that? Do we take the easy path through the flowered meadow or the one with boulders and rushing rivers? Do we trust or don't we? I was looking down two distinct paths and neither one had more pull on my judgement than the other. And in the middle, I could just make out a narrow footpath wandering right between the other two. As far as I could see down it, there appeared to be side paths that led to the other two main ones - the ones with the signposts that said, "Help a Friend - Right the Wrongs." and, "That Was A Little Too Intense – How Safe Am I?"

I was good with the path labelled "Indecisive."

For now.

We'd see.

Chapter 19 – Just A Thump

Looking intently at Ben, Colin shook his head. "No worries, man. I can totally understand why you would be so upset. It's never easy losing a loved one, especially in such a heinous manner."

Pearl patted Ben's hand. Smiling in appreciation at her gesture, he turned to me. "But I think I scared the hell out of Kate." Before I could say anything, he reached out and this time took my hand in both of his. "Kate, I really am sorry. I'm not a hothead. I'm not an aggressive guy. I guess I'm just protective of those I care for."

Concern and contrition fleshed out Ben's face. Damn those eyes. I didn't stand a chance. "No worries. That's not a bad thing." He continued to watch my face looking for signs that it matched my words. I felt my muscles relaxing into a smile.

"Hey, enough about my problems." Ben stood up. "How about we get back in the boat and go out to the sandbars. Maybe we can even do a little trolling along the way." He pointed to the Elgin. "It would be great to drop a line over her side again. Man, we spent a lot of time over the years in that boat – and all of them good."

"Oh yeah. There's a monster pike out there that's just begging to be hooked on my lure again." While Colin relived his encounter with Lucius, Pearl and I put more food and ice in the cooler, grabbed the sunscreen and hats and joined the guys on the little dock.

Ben was checking out the tackle box, crooning. "This baby will bring him in for sure." He held up a three-inch red devil spoon. "But you want to keep it moving with all those deadheads on the bottom."

Colin had settled himself on the wooden bench seat in the middle of the boat and was sporting an old hat that must have been unearthed from some dark corner of the Honeymoon Suite. The straw brim hung down in defeat while the yellow plastic flower stapled to the red band bloomed out perkily even though the colour was dulled by years of dust. Pearl handed him the sun screen that he artfully applied to his face, temporarily muting the bridge of freckles that had assumed a position of dominance across his nose.

Pearl joined Colin while I set myself up at the stern; checking the gas can and confirming the motor was secured tightly to the transom. Ben continued to root around in the tackle box then turned his attention to the rod and reel. "I learned to cast on a bait caster just like this. It's perfect for trolling." Giving the line a test pull he added, "I like the weight of this one. Sturdy."

We sat and waited.

After a few moments Ben took a deep breath, turned and reviewed the seating arrangements. "Yeah, this was my favourite spot when I was young." Untying the bow line, he stepped down and sat on the little seat in the front, leveling out the boat. His teeth were framed in a full smile that contrasted with the sadness softening his eyes.

Pearl reached out and grabbed the fishing gear and life jackets before pushing us away from the dock.

I held the primer bulb and gave it a couple of squeezes then made sure the motor was in neutral before giving the throttle a small little twist. As we lazily drifted towards the main dock Ben dipped a paddle into the water and pushing against the sandy bottom, shoved us away from the shore. The motor fired up on the first crank. I was glad that everyone was sitting when I flipped it into reverse as I wasn't too smooth on the throttle and we jerked backwards. Colin started moaning, something about whiplash, so I switched it to forward and gunned it. Guess it would have been more effective if there had been a decent sized engine and we weren't loaded down, but the noise did drown out Colin for the short time it took us to get to the Point.

Pearl had already passed the rods to the guys so when I slowed the boat to trolling speed they were ready to cast their lures. With a gentle flick of his wrist, Ben's spoon landed outside the small wake and quickly slipped into the waves as it was pulled along. He let out a little more line then pressed his thumb to the reel to stop the unravelling. Colin, sitting on the left side let the barbs of his lure dip into the water and held it at the surface, watching the mini wake it created.

Pearl nudged him. "Honey, you usually tend to catch fish by letting the lure sink into the water."

"And that's what has me concerned." Lifting his hook up so that it hovered above the surface, Colin looked around the boat. "There's not a whole lot of extra room in this boat right now and I was trying to figure out just where we'd put Lucius should we catch him."

Ben nudged the tackle box. "There's a stringer in there. We could attach him to that and drag him in the water."

"No, no, you don't understand," insisted Pearl, understanding the situation. "He would be dragging us."

"Riiight." Ben stuck out his leg. "Now pull the other one."

Colin and Pearl looked at each other and shrugged. "Okay, man, you catch it; you put it on the strin..." Colin's warning was cut short as a soft thump was felt through the boat. I grabbed the motor, flipped the release and tilted it up so the prop was out of the water. Scanning behind I expected to see a submerged deadhead, but there was nothing but the soft movement of water as the boat slowed down.

With mouths pursed, in unison, Colin and Pearl whispered one word. "Lucius."

Ben still didn't look convinced but I noticed that he was reeling in his lure.

Chapter 20 – Sandbars and Superman

Ben kept a lookout for deadheads as we cruised through the tight spots and once out on the main lake the trip to the sandbars took only ten minutes. The water was low and clear allowing us to spot the aquatic sand dunes easily. I cut the motor and dropped anchor. There wasn't much current so the boat drifted lazily, casting a shadow on the shallow edge of the underwater plateau.

Decades ago, after the dam was built at the end of the main lake, the water rose substantially and with a substrate of sand, over time the small islands began to wash away. These particular islands were of special interest, as there had been an old Hudson's Bay trading post nearby. They had used this area as their dumping grounds so scouring around might produce wonderful artifacts left behind over a century ago. As a kid I used to row out and tether my boat to the small bushes clinging tenaciously to the ever-shrinking land to unearth bottles, axe heads and other exciting finds. Now, with the islands submerged, no greenery remained but the sand was willing to disgorge treasures at its leisure.

A quick shiver traversed my body as I jumped into the cooler water of the main lake. We had only two masks and snorkels and one set of fins so we took turns cruising the perimeter with the plastic shovels while the other two shuffled around moving the sand with their feet. No treasures were immediately apparent however the entertainment value of water play and friendship put smiles on everyone's face.

"Oh no you don't!" Pearl bent over peering into the water. Her hand hovered over the surface, then with a slight hesitation she reached in and plucked a black tubular object between her fingers. Plopping it into her bucket she shook her head. "Not today, you don't."

"Is that what I think it is?"

"Yup. A big juicy one, to boot."

"How the heck did it get way out here?"

"Swam, would be my guess."

"They're not supposed to be out here. This is a no-bloodsucker zone!"

"Yeah, well you can post all the signs you want, I don't think they can read."

"Maybe he's just lost."

Pearl pointed to the space between us. "Okay, but it looks like he was leading a parade of lost friends."

A breeze had temporarily ruffled the surface of the lake, reducing our ability to see clearly into its depths. However, as I bent over to get a closer look I had a flashingly brief moment of fascination as multiple undulating black torpedoes honed in on my legs.

"Shit! Shit! Shit! Holy freaking shit! They're all around." I was in water well up my thighs, and my efforts at high stepping away acted more like a dinner bell than an escape method. They were between me and the boat and their numbers were multiplying. Exponentially.

I looked over at Pearl who was calmly plucking them out of the water and adding them to her bucket.

"Are you crazy? There're enough of them to suck out all of your blood," I screamed as I swirled the water in front of me in an effort to dissuade the little buggers. I'm sure the whites of my eyes were predominant. When I panic, I do it wholeheartedly. And with great alacrity, I might add.

Without warning, my legs were knocked out from under me and as I began to fall backwards, a solid set of arms lifted me high out of the water. Trying his best to refrain from laughing, Ben pursed his lips. "It seems that bloodsuckers are rather fond of you. Extra sweet blood, perhaps?"

My heart was hammering away and I knew I should be embarrassed but adrenaline had completely devoured that emotion. Wading through the hordes of evil creatures, Ben made his way to the Elgin and gently placed me on the rear seat. I was dumbstruck as he winked and without even glancing in the water around his legs, he leaned over and pulled out a little minnow net from under the middle seat. He nodded towards the bailing scoop, smiled and encouraged me to reduce their numbers from the safety of the boat.

Everyone has a built-in alarm setting. An evolutionary necessity that helped us identify possible threats to our existence. Throughout time, this inherent feature has served us well. Mostly. In some cases, and yes, I will stand and put up my hand, there are those who take it to the next level and beyond. I'm not proud of it, but in my defense, I would like to say that there are very few situations in which I will have a full-on blowout. Standing in the middle of a swarm of threatening and repulsive blood-sucking creatures is right at the top of that list.

I looked up at Ben who nodded and tapped the corner of his forehead as if touching the brim of a hat. I hadn't even noticed the mask and snorkel that he'd placed on his head and with two hands he brought them back into position, turned, and like a half-naked Superman, dove out towards deeper water.

Just call me Lois.

Chapter 21 – Mechanics 'R Us

As we had been preparing to return from the sandbar, the wind became substantially more vigorous along with a swing in its direction. After everyone piled into the boat and removed any offending uninvited hitchhikers I pulled the cord on the motor with no success. In fact, we all gave it a go, and – nothing. Various ideas were floated as to the reason, but the situation didn't change. We were sitting in a full boat in the middle of a large body of water with a strong headwind and only two paddles. Oars would have been nice.

Even with rotating paddle duties it had still taken close to an hour to make the trip just to the Point. The wind was steadily increasing and we decided to tie up to one of the deadheads for a bit, hoping for a reprieve. As none seemed to be forthcoming we struck out on the final push to The Camp. There was no fighting the wind, so we tried to stay in the lee of the trees around the edge of the bay in front of the cabin. Hugging the shoreline, we pulled ourselves along on the logs and long grass. There was a break in available handholds and the wind used this opportunity to send us sailing over to the opposite side of the bay. With only sixty metres between us and the dock, the ending was merely a tantalising promise. Ben looked at Colin, pointed to the bow rope and smiled. Colin shrugged his shoulders and offered the fins to our new friend. "No, I'm good. You take them 'cause, trust me, you don't want to touch the bottom!" The briefest shadow of revulsion flickered across Colin's face before he jammed his feet into the fins, clumsily stood on the middle seat and executed a shallow dive towards the deeper channel in the creek.

I should take a moment to explain that the creek is not really a creek. It used to be before the dams were built, but now it's more like a creek flowing through a small body of water that opens up into the bay in front of our place. So there's movement and it's a little deeper in the middle, but the south shore opposite The Camp is still full of fallen logs and detritus which created a perfect spawning ground for imagined creatures and quagmires.

Ben followed Colin into the water and we threw them the rope. The last leg of our adventure had been completed within minutes.

As Ben pulled the boat onto the landing spot beside the little dock, Colin held the stern fast from his position in the water. Pearl unloaded the rods and reels then stepped onto the wooden planks before Ben secured the boat to the large spruce tree.

"Food! I need food! And a beer!" Colin, wading onto shore, grabbed the rods and tackle box then headed directly for the cabin. We were right behind him.

Hummus, crackers, cheese, chips, gummy worms, cookies – a veritable smorgasbord upon which to refuel our depleted stocks was quickly laid out on the table along with four frosty beers. The assault was intense and shameless.

"Man that was a workout!" Pearl flexed her biceps.

Taking a pitcher of water out of the fridge, Colin asked, "So what do you think is wrong with the motor?"

The quickly consumed beer and treats had sated the hunger and we could now focus on the problem of the motor. "Spark plug fouled?" was my only suggestion.

"Dirty gas?" supplied Pearl.

"I've worked on a few motors in my time," offered Ben. "Happy to have a go at it."

"I'll start supper, if you want to give him a hand, Kate." Pearl's eyes were innocently wide. "My darling assistant can help, even if he is on wash-up duty." She batted her lashes at her partner and blew him a kiss.

"Tacos? Cervezas?"

"Si, perfecto."

Tilting my head towards the Elgin, Ben smiled in return. "Let's get to it."

"Go ahead, I'll get the key to the tool shed."

By the time I returned to the boat, Ben had finished loosening the clamps and was lifting the sixty pound motor with ease. Gently placing it on the dock he stepped up beside it.

I grabbed the gas can so we could check it for dirt or water.

Ben one-handed the motor up the little slope to the tool shed and stood patiently while I opened the lock.

The shed also doubles as wood storage with room for a season's requirement lining the back wall. It's big enough to work at the bench and move around, but with the two of us in there, the space became charged with intimacy, made more so by the fact that we were both bumping into each other as we looked for the various tools needed to accomplish our repair.

A delicious tingling accompanied Ben's touch on the back of my waist as he propelled me towards the workbench. "Seeing as you know your way around here, and you're no stranger to small motors, what would you like to try first?"

"Shall we go with water in the tank to start?"

"Sounds good. Do you have a cup or tin to drain the carburetor into?"

I grabbed a glass jar off one of the shelves and removed the cover. Ben picked up a screwdriver to loosen the screw at the bottom of the carburetor. As the gas drained into the jar we could see the offending water bubble sitting in the bottom.

We knuckle bumped as Ben smiled. "Well done - mystery solved. Do you have a spare gas can?"

Looking under the bench I pulled out a five-gallon can. Empty.

"No worries, we can run into town, dispose of the old gas and pick up two cans of fresh." Ben stopped. "Sorry, I'm jumping in here." He sighed. "If I can get a ride to my cabin, I'll take the gas cans in for you. I'd be grateful to help out – you know, try and repay you for all of the help you guys have given me." His hand reached out to rest softly on my forearm and soulful brown eyes held mine with such intensity that I felt myself leaning forward.

"Hey, how's it going in there?" And what felt like a frigid bucket of ice water assaulting me, pushed me back on my heels. From the bedroom window Colin hollered. "I don't hear any motor sounds coming from your vicinity. Come to think of it, no swearing, either. What's up with that?"

Ben exhaled deeply and smiled. The world swirled back into focus and I became aware of the smell of gas and realized I was clenching the jar lid in my hand. My voice felt disconnected as I replied. "Mostly fixed, just need some fresh gas."

"Cervezas are being served."

Was I saved by cervezas or thwarted? It was a toss-up. But apparently I was starting to lean to one side.

Chapter 22 – The Challenge

The après dinner game of Aggravation was ramping up with alliances being struck and un-struck as favours, promises and full-on bribes were anted up. I called foul to anything of a very personal nature given that Pearl and Colin would have us at a disadvantage. I did think of a few that would have given me a great deal of pleasure, but I censored my inner beast and refrained from voicing them.

"Shall we make this a little more interesting?" Colin's face displayed a simple grin but his denim blue eyes sparked with challenge. As my mother would say, you could see the horns growing out the top of his head.

"The loser has to jump in the water and swim for two minutes, by themselves."

Pearl pointed to the ominously dark water lit only by the rising moon. "But Lucius is out there. Just waiting. And he's probably insatiably hungry." She shook her head. "I've already had one personal and up-close encounter with him yesterday – that's quite enough."

Yesterday? Was that really just thirty-six hours ago? That was P.B. - pre-Ben. How did so much get packed into such a short time? Part of me felt like I had morphed into a different life or straddled two different planes of existence, all a little surreal yet here we were. Ben was grinning at Colin, however there was something else there, something almost tangible. As their focus on each other intensified no words were spoken but they were obviously communicating, giving me an opportunity to study Ben a little closer. Given the intimate and detailed nature of all that we had learned about him today, the comfort I felt was one born of a much longer friendship.

"I'm in," was Ben's response.

I was not liking this at all. Ben and Pearl were closest to bringing the last of their players home with Colin not far behind while I was at least three or four throws behind them. Bugger it all. "I'm in!" I mean, it's just a fish! And he has to sleep at some point.

Pearl quickly assessed the board then nodded her consent. "But first, a little Mexican courage." She went to the cupboard and pulled out a bottle of Tanteo Cocoa tequila along with four shot glasses.

"Salud!" The peppery chocolate flavour enchanted my taste buds. Man, I could predict trouble on the horizon with this stuff!

Picking up one of the dice, Ben rolled it briskly between his hands as he looked at each of us and smiled. I wasn't sure but I thought I detected the slightest of winks when he turned to me. He threw a five, which, with the way his last player was positioned, would allow him to jump into the centre and take the short cut. Instead, he moved his orange marble along the perimeter of the board taking the long way Home.

Pearl looked at him and smiled. "You've just earned a complimentary shot," as she poured Ben a second glass of tequila.

Colin and Pearl made it Home within the next three rounds, while it was obvious that Ben was doing everything he could to ensure that I didn't lose.

*****

As we stood at the deck's edge, a light thudding of feet on the dock broke the silence of the lake followed by a splash then a whoop of exhilaration. Ben's head of dark hair and expansive shoulders were highlighted by the portable spotlight I held, which augmented the moon's reflection on the water's surface. I played the light around him looking for the ominous fin to surface.

I turned to Colin. "What the hell was that all about?" I whispered.

Colin replied just as quietly, "Just seeing what he is made of."

"Look, I appreciate you wanting to play the big brother here, but, come on, he doesn't have to pass your tests to get to me."

Colin put his hand on my shoulder and paused. "Point taken." He shrugged. "But every time your heart gets broken," tilting his head at Pearl, "we both feel it."

I kissed Colin's cheek then slipped my fingers under the waistband of my shorts pulling out the top of my underwear. "It's okay, I've put on my big-girl-panties today."

A gargled yelp echoed as Ben began thrashing. "What the hell was that?"

Long arms stretched out, pounding the water, pulling their owner towards shore. There was a sense of urgency mixed with a modicum of style which appeared to give the facade of nonchalance. As Ben planted his feet on the sandy bottom near the end of the dock he stood up and gave us a wave. Stepping forward, he broke into a grin that immediately turned into a full-on yell as he slammed his hands onto the dock and in one swift move, hoisted himself out of the water. In the play of the spotlight beam where Ben had just been standing, we could see the flick of a tail.

Ah, the return of Lucius.

We stayed up well into the night, plotting Lucius' demise, or at least schemes to relocate him as far away as possible. Tequila helps lubricate the imagination but can also send it spiraling into absurdity and by the end our ideas were infused with futuristic weaponry and fanciful creations.

The large jar of peanuts and bag of jelly beans were as empty as the bottle by the time we all fell into our respective beds.

Chapter 23 – There's Only One Marcel Dubois

The sun struggled through the clouds as we sat around the picnic table hoping the coffee would help revive our brains as well as our energy. There was little conversation for the first fifteen minutes as our bodies absorbed the caffeine.

Ben rubbed the back of his fingers against his chin. "If I could catch a ride to my cabin a little later, I'll grab my truck, go into town and pick up some gas for the boat. Is there anything else you need?"

My recovery time hadn't run its course so a head-shake was all I managed. And, if I am to be truly honest, my mind was scurrying around wondering what I should do or say to Ben. My conflict was creating a minor maelstrom in my already foggy brain and the swirling clouds gave me only fleeting glimpses of ideas. I'm definitely not a fly-by-night-one-hit wonder but more of a let's-see-how-well-we-fit-together-before-taking-this-to-the-'Holy-Wow' next step. Then, circling the periphery of this tableau was the lighthouse beacon of reality that illuminated the fact that this could only ever be a short summer fling.

It was appearing, though, that hormones are magic and can obscure, and even make common sense disappear into thin air.

And, really, if you take away all of that, this man who had pretty much just dropped into our laps, was a super decent guy who was great to have around. Okay, and to look at. But I digress.

I realized that Colin had been responding to Ben's question and my focus zipped back to the present. Colin had said that he wanted to pick up some supplies and offered to drive in with Ben in the afternoon.

I volunteered for brunch duty and pulled together a basic repast that was consumed with more enthusiasm than I expected. I love an easy crowd to please.

After cleaning up, Pearl asked Ben's opinion on how he would approach correcting a settling issue with the Honeymoon Suite that was causing a window and door to stick. The three of us spent the rest of the morning reviewing the situation while the good doctor caught up on some reading.

As it turned out, my struggle over whether or not to have Ben continue his stay with us was easily settled.

"I have a jack and some concrete slabs at my cabin and would be more than happy to help you level the Suite."

Well that would be worth an extra day or two.

"And, I noticed that there are a few gaps between the logs. I'm pretty sure there's a bucket of chinking there as well." His smile was broad. "Besides, I owe you a few meals and I can pick up some peameal bacon at the butcher's for a start."

"Peameal, creamed corn and mashed potatoes?"

"Is there any other way to eat it?"

Pearl was not to be left out. "Yes, how about for breakfast? Sandwiches? Snacks?"

Apparently hormones are not the only driving factor in decision making.

As Colin was getting ready to drive Ben to his cabin, I lingered over a last cup of coffee while staring out over the water. In the distance, what appeared to be a large box-like structure with glinty bits came floating into view. As it made its ponderous journey towards us, a soft grey plume of smoke flowed from a stovepipe creating an aerial legacy.

From the cabin Ben commented, "Well, I'll be." Grabbing the binoculars from the window sill he came out onto the deck and trained them on the approaching vessel.

"An acquaintance of yours?"

Ben was grinning. "Kate, we are in for a treat. This is quite an honour to be visited by none other than Marcel Dubois, legendary character of Kenogamisi. If you want to know something about anything – he's the fellow to ask. It'll cost you – but it's always worth it."

Ben passed the binoculars to me but kept his eyes on the floating vessel.

The structure was covered in green tar paper with black wooden strapping overlapping the joints. A Dutch door gave access to a walkway that ran the length of the houseboat. The glinty bits were not only windows but a variety of buckets, shovels and implements of questionable usage.

"So what kind of 'payment' are you suggesting?"

"Nothing expensive, just useful. Some produce, meat, you know, food items, or things that he could use like a shirt or rubber boots. He won't ask for anything, he'll just kind of stare at something, or hint that he has to go into town to buy an item. It's how he survives."

Pearl and Colin rounded the corner. Pearl pointed to the approaching vessel, raised her eyebrows and looked over at us. Ben gave her a brief synopsis of the soon-to-be-met character.

Colin rubbed his hands together and as he walked across the deck chuckled, "Sounds like my kind of guy."

Ben's grin got bigger. "Oh, I think, Colin, you will have met your match."

Watching the houseboat grow larger as it approached, my eyes didn't know where to look. The front deck had a table with one chair and an assortment of boxes of varying shapes, sizes and colours. Centred on the table, was a bucket with all manner of wildflowers exploding from it. Perched above the front windows was a large red plaque with white routed letters proudly proclaiming this to be the Florence. Beside the scripted letters, there was a painting of a small bird – which I thought might be a nightingale.

There was no sign of the captain but the honeyed voice of Pat Boone coming from hidden speakers crooned the arrival of Florence.

When it was obvious she was making her way to our dock, I put the binoculars on the table and looked at Ben. "Care to make the introductions?"

"My pleasure."

Pearl and Colin, so as not to crowd the dock, stayed up on the deck to watch.

As eclectic as the vessel was, there was a grace and stateliness about her. The engines throttled down, then off. With perfect precision, its momentum tenderly carried 'Flo' towards the edge of the dock.

Ben's foot met the bumper inches out just as Pat Boone's song drifted into the final bars to create a perfectly choreographed arrival.

I could see a silhouette of someone moving to the dutch door but was unprepared for the manifested version.

Topping the measuring stick at maybe five and a half feet, a gnome-like character stood in the doorway. Two coal black eyes were set in a face that looked to be constructed of weathered pine tree bark etched with deep crevices. Grey hair projected out of his chin and from under the edges of a black knitted toque. Belying his smaller stature, there was a solidness about him that suggested he could wrestle with a full grown black bear then sit down for a pint of beer with him. He squinted at the two of us and quickly nodded to Ben. I wasn't prepared for the tight little rheumy voice that crackled with a smoker's congestion. "You're Carl's nephew." His eyes shifted to me, lingering. "And you've got the look of an O'Malley. You must be Shamus' daughter. Come from out west." The comments were statements, not questions.

"Why yes, yes I'm Kate. And you must be Mr. Dubois." My extended hand was firmly grasped. "And, you're correct again, this is Ben Brodan."

Ben stepped forward to shake hands. "It's been a few years, Mr. Dubois. I'm surprised you remember me."

Marcel nodded and smiled. "No trick there, lad. Sadie used to talk about you all the time. She had your picture in a locket and didn't hesitate to show it off every time she could." He shook his head. "Bad business that. I'm sorry for your loss, son. They didn't make two like Sadie. She's greatly missed."

"Mr. Dubois, can I invite you up for a coffee or a beer," I asked, pointing to the cabin.

He looked up at the sky. Satisfied that the sun was over the yardarm he nodded. "Heck, yup, a cold one would go down good right now."

Our guest scrambled up the little incline with a nimbleness belying his age. Coming on to the deck, I introduced Pearl. As they shook hands he nodded and pursed his lips. "Good strong hands for a girl. You're no office worker."

"Kate and I have a renovation business back in Victoria."

"Do ya now?"

"Yes, and this is my boyfriend, Colin."

"Mr. Dubois, it's a pleasure to meet you."

Our guest eyed Colin as they shook hands. "And what do you do?"

Colin smiled. "I like to poke and prod people and ask a lot of questions."

"Sounds like that nosy Etienne Bisette. But no, your eyes are kind so you can't be like that troublemaker." He took this opportunity to cough up some phlegm and spit it over the side of the deck. I got the impression he was making a derisive statement about this Etienne character rather than just clearing his lungs.

Still holding Colin's hand, his eyes continued to search as he pulled him in a little closer. He took a few sniffs and scrunched his face up. "There's a book sense about you." Dropping my friend's hand he took half a step back. "Nope, you're not a lawyer 'cause you don't smell, and you're not a dentist 'cause there isn't a mean streak in you. I can't picture you sitting behind a drafting table losing your head to a bunch of drawings, so you must be a man of science."

Colin threw back his head and laughed. "Well, sir, you nailed it. I'm a family physician."

Marcel's head turned slightly as he eyed Colin. "Heh, heh, heh. A doctor, eh?" And without hesitation, Mr. Dubois started untucking his shirt. Before any of us could react, he had it whipped off over his head revealing a pair of long johns that may have started out being white but had, over the years or maybe even decades, transmuted into a grey-black-brown blend of shades. A strong, pungent odour found its way into our nostrils.

The old trapper didn't seem to notice as we in the non-medical profession, collectively stepped back.

"It's this patch on my back, Doc. I can't get a right-good look at it. Feels scaly. I tried bear grease, goose grease, even made my special secret paste but it won't go away. I just want to make sure it isn't that nasty 'C' word. What 'cha think?"

The three of us slipped away as quickly and quietly as the smoke from his houseboat chimney. The Honeymoon suite seemed like the best reconnoitering spot to give them privacy. Pearl was peeking around the curtains while Ben and I smiled at each other. "Oh yes, you did call that one! We meet some pretty unusual characters in our line of work but he's totally unique. Does he wear those long johns all year round?"

"I think he only takes them off to change – and at what intervals, I'm not going to hazard a guess."

Pearl shuddered.

Ben shoved his hands in his jean's pockets and rocked back on his heels. "Laundry day at Marcel's is quite the production. Sadie described it to me. He puts everything in a mesh bag and drops it overboard for an hour or so to 'presoak'. He boils up buckets of water for a big metal tub, adds some of that detergent for babies..."

"Ivory Snow?" offered Pearl.

"Yeah, Ivory Snow. He says he uses it because it's soft on his skin and smells nice." Ben mimed the next steps. "He dumps everything in, stirs it around with a paddle and lets the water cool off. When that's done, he puts it all back into the mesh bag and drops it into the lake again to rinse it off. He usually tries to time it so that he can drag it behind if he's going somewhere – but he's got to watch out for deadheads." Ben was smiling now. "Once, while Uncle Carl and I were out fishing, we turned into a small cove to do some casting. Mr. Dubois' houseboat was moored and he had hung his laundry to dry on the trees. Normally, you would think that it would have been a colourful sight, but with him, it was pretty much all the same shade of muddy grey; shirts, sheets, underwear... everything."

At this point Pearl and I were at a loss for words. I mean, what can you say?

*****

Pearl, being our reconnaissance person, noted that Marcel had his clothes back on and he and Colin were sitting at the table on the deck.

"DeKuyper gin. That's the ticket for the broncheckles." Marcel slapped the table. "Cures them every time."

Colin nodded. "Just DeKuyper? No other gin will work for the..." he lowered his head slightly looking just underneath his eyebrows at Marcel, "... for the broncheckles. I'll have to try that remedy."

"Yup, only DeKuyper. And beaver castors. Steep them in a bit of boiling water for twenty minutes, add the gin, and Bob's-your-uncle. You'll sleep like a baby and when you wake up you'll be fit as a fiddle."

Colin looked over at us. "Mr. Dubois has been giving me some really interesting remedies." Turning back to our guest he asked, "But, you know, beaver castors are pretty hard to come by. Where could a fellow get his hands on some?"

Marcel eyed him up. "Well, I'll tell ya. Some could be traded for a bottle of DeKuypers."

"Excellent. We're going into town later. I'll pick some up. Where can we find you?"

"Well," Marcel scratched his head through his toque. "I've a mind to go up the lake. As long as you keep this under your hat, there's a blueberry patch up about six or seven bays north of here there that only I know about. The berries are extra big and as long as I can get to them before the bears do, I can pick baskets of 'em. Takes me a while to dehydrate them," he leaned back and squinted his eyes slightly, "but I've got a system. They're mighty tasty dehydrated. A good batch will do me for the winter." Marcel looked towards the trail. "And I see you've got yourself a good patch here."

Colin confirmed that we wouldn't be poaching Marcel's produce. "Yup, there're more than enough blueberries to satisfy our needs right here. In fact, if you would like to help yourself..."

"No thanks, that's right kind of you but quite all right." Marcel said.

Pearl came out of the cabin with bottles of beer, a bag of pepperoni sticks, pretzels and cheese.

We tilted our bottles towards each other, gave various toasts and took our first sips.

Ben slid the bowl of pretzels towards Marcel. "So I take it that Etienne Bisette is still around?"

The muscles on the back of Marcel's creviced, brown hand popped as he clenched the bottle tightly. "That good-for-nothing, nosy, know-it-all, son of a b... bee with an itch. I always told Sadie to watch out for him." Marcel hunkered in. "Him and his smarmy ways. HA! I wouldn't trust that slickered cockroach..." He paused, taking a short break in his rant and leaned in further towards Ben. "You know he was always snooping around Sadie. Asked a lot of questions. Not direct ones, mind you, oh no, he thinks he's too clever. Always indirect about her truck, or equipment." Placing a finger aside his nose, Marcel's eyes became slits. "But I know what he was really after. He was always snooping around because of the rumours of Sadie's gold." Marcel's wizened face contorted into a sneer. "He'd show up all Pomaded, dressed in his best bib and tucker, with some cheap flowers – HA! Sadie saw right through that crusty codger."

Well, here was a new piece to the puzzle. I looked at Pearl and Colin, who were staring at our guest, riveted with his story.

Ben's face looked conflicted and it took me a second to realize that he was working hard to suppress a grin. His mouth managed the task but his eyes were crinkled with delight.

"You know, Mr. Dubois, Sadie thought the world of you. She often told me about how you two would listen to music for hours on end. You've got quite a collection, don't you?"

Marcel's face had morphed into a beatific smile – his eyes softened, he smiled and gave us a rumbly chuckle. "Oh, lad, we had such great times. And your uncle Carl – he was a good man. Sadie was madly in love with him; and him with her." Patting his chest, he said, "Yup, we had a lot of good times together."

I noticed that his eyes were glistening and didn't want him to feel embarrassed but before I could distract him, he looked at each of us, let a tear slip into the crevices on his cheek and smiled. "Yup, it's a pity you never got to meet Sadie. A gem, she was. And I'm not embarrassed to say so!"

We let the moment sit quietly.

A splash retrieved us from our reverie. Marcel looked out over the water. "So how's the fishing been?"

Pearl became animated. "Well, let me tell you about that!" She pointed out to the bay. "Out there lives a monster. Not just big, but a monster that's evil. Colin had him on his hook, the beast leaped out of the water, spit the hook out and has been taunting us ever since. If we go swimming, he comes around and bumps into us to let us know who owns the place. I'm thinking he's just playing with his food."

"Heh, heh, heh. I see you've met Nellie. Kenogamisi's own Loch Ness monster."

"Nellie? We've dubbed him Lucius."

"The name suits. Yeah, Nellie, or Lucius has been around forever. Got quite the sense of humour!"

Pearl shook her head. "I don't think it's a sense of humour. It's a vicious, evil streak."

"Heh, heh. And she's wily. You don't get to be that size without learning a few tricks." Marcel waved his hand. "But not to worry, it's been warm and she'll want to move on to the deeper cooler water."

I wonder if anyone bothered to cc Lucius/Nellie on that decision.

Chapter 24 – Stocking Up

We gathered on the dock to say our goodbyes with promises to come and find him in the next few days. The afternoon was spent down to the last quarter and as Ben threw the mooring line onto the deck of the Florence, the speakers crackled to life with the sound of waves on a beach, then a guitar and finally good old Otis Redding singing about sittin' on the dock of the bay.

The departure was somewhat mesmerizing. We stood and watched until the vessel had passed the Point before smiles were shared with each other and the questions started.

"Who's this Etienne character?"

"What are broncheckles?"

But the most burning question in my mind was, "Okay, I want to know not only who the first person was to discover that boiled beaver castors made you feel better but *how* that discovery was made."

Ben smiled, still looking out, as if unwilling to let the encounter end, and watched Marcel navigate the deadheads around the corner towards the open water of Kenogamisi Lake.

My hand reflexively reached out to Ben's arm. "Visits with the past can be a mixed bag, can't they?"

Ben turned and stared deeply into my eyes for a brief second until a sad smile softened his face. He looked down at my hand on his forearm. By the time he had returned his gaze to meet mine, his face had assumed a happy expression and he nodded without saying a word.

Colin was addressing Pearl's question. "I'm pretty sure the 'broncheckles' are bronchitis. Gin is not necessarily a remedy that I would recommend – but maybe there's merit in adding beaver castors."

Pearl wrinkled her nose. "I'm assuming the castors are their testicles?"

Ben grinned. "No, they're the beaver's scent glands. Both the male and female have them."

Pearl's eyebrows made a quick leap towards her hairline.

"Poplar and willow bark contain ASA or aspirin and when the beavers eat the bark, apparently some of the ASA gets stored in their castors. It's an old trapper's remedy. Always a fun fact to trot out at parties." Ben started to laugh. "In fact, there is one trapper I know who has tacked a couple sets of castors to a board and when his daughter dates a new fellow, this guy brings him out to his skinning shed, nods towards the board and comments that those belonged to guys who hadn't treated his daughter with the utmost of respect. Culls the herd pretty quickly!"

Colin's head was bobbing. "Man, now I *have* to get some."

We decided to make an early supper then go into town for gas and supplies.

*****

While the guys chopped, diced and fried the various ingredients for tacos, Pearl and I battled it out in a supreme cribbage championship match. There's no need to recount who came out the victor as it's really not important. However, Pearl disagreed with that sentiment and did a victory lap around the deck, waving the cribbage board and pointing to her peg sitting in the winning hole.

We cleared the afternoon's dishes from the picnic table and got the napkins just as Colin called us in to come and build our own tacos.

Ben was recounting a Sadie story when I remembered the look on his face when Marcel was talking about the mysterious Etienne Bisette. "So what's the story with this Etienne character? Is he a possible suspect?"

Ben's laugh was low as he shook his head. "Etienne is the diametric opposite to Marcel and the two of them have been sworn enemies for as long as anyone can remember. Sadie once told me that it had to do with a woman – but no one is really sure."

"But could he have killed her? Sadie, I mean."

"Tell you what. We'll make a trip to Etienne's place after we get the Honeymoon Suite levelled and you can judge for yourself."

*****

It was seven o'clock before we finished cleaning up and we all decided to pile into the car and go to town. Pearl was driving and had chosen a CD with music from the 60s. With car windows down the music escaped into the warm evening air. There was almost two hours until sunset so the sun was still high enough to sit over the tallest of the trees on our left as we drove along Highway 144.

About ten minutes down the road we passed over the bridge at Adikameg.

"My place is just down that road." Ben indicated a hard packed path that seemed to be having a turf war with trees desperately trying to reclaim their native territory. "We can stop on the way back to pick up my truck and the stuff we need."

The liquor store was open until 9:30 so we hit the grocery store first and stocked up. With the butcher closed, Ben rooted through the peameal bacon until he found a slab big enough to feed a convention of carnivores. Perfect! There was a minor skirmish at the checkout that Ben won merely by not letting any of us close to the cashier. With eight grocery bags hanging off his fingers he shrugged. "This doesn't even begin to repay you for all you've done."

The liquor store still had a few customers besides us. When Colin grabbed two boxes with the cardboard inserts to hold our purchases I said a silent prayer for our livers.

"Don't forget we have to carry all of this through the trail."

"Good point. Bags it is. Except for the beer." He surveyed the selection, made his choice and added it to the cart. Again, at the checkout, Ben slipped in and handed the fellow his credit card while

Colin put the libations on the counter. When he realized what was happening the good doctor held on to the last two bottles. "No, man, this is my shout."

Ben reached for the two bottles still in Colin's hands and replied, "You can get the next round."

When Colin is doing some serious thinking, his top lip burrows into his bottom one which pushes his cheeks out and highlights his one dimple in his right cheek. This look can be held for seconds or, as in this case, just appear as the briefest of flashes. And in that split-second flash, I knew that he had done a full-scale assessment of the last two days: of Ben's situation and possible motivation, and what was fair for all concerned. Really, his RAM processing capabilities are lightning fast! He smiled and released the bottles to Ben's solid hands.

Pearl remotely popped the tailgate of the SUV and rearranged the contents to accommodate the newest purchases. Once on the road, I pulled out some trivia cards. Turns out, we are all pretty feeble at movies and entertainment but nailed it in the science and geography categories.

Ben pointed at the upcoming bridge. "Just up ahead on the left, after the bridge is the road to my cabin."

Pearl slowed and leaned forward peering through the windshield. "That's it, right... here."

Pearl negotiated the turn. The road was sloped, turned and almost immediately we were surrounded by the forest. While we travelled, Ben had removed his seatbelt to access his pocket. After a brief struggle, he laughed. "Right! Forgot that I was just going out for blueberries and didn't lock the door.

The headlights lit up a cabin.

"Welcome to Chez Ben's."

Chapter 25

Grabbing the corner of the double mattress the man's manicured fingernails disappeared into the thick foam. Flipping it over, he inspected the surfaces for any evidence of tampering. The box spring was lifted and given the same scrutiny.

He turned and surveyed the room yet again. It hadn't taken him long to disembowel the contents of the little cabin. Short of pulling apart the walls he couldn't think of where the gold could be hidden. No loose floorboards and an extensive inspection with the snake camera confirmed nothing was hidden in the space between the floor and ground. He couldn't bring himself to smash the dishes or destroy the furniture – he did, after all, have his ethics. However, he was thorough and all the furniture and crevices had been examined, cupboards and fridge emptied, even the outhouse had not escaped his search.

The last of the late evening light had mellowed into twilight and he flicked the flashlight at his watch. Putting his latex gloves back on, he once again checked the man's backpack for clues. He picked up the keys to the truck and quickly dropped them as his phone vibrated against his leg. Three long strides took him to the door where he scanned the road. Letting the screen door close with a snap behind him, he moved quickly along the far side of the cabin and slipped unseen into the woods as headlights fleshed out all that were caught in their gaze. Not waiting to see who or how many were in the vehicle he turned and crept down the bank to the waiting canoe.

Two paddles dipped in unison propelling them up the river.

Chapter 26 – Taking Stock

"Holy hell in a hand basket!" Pearl has such a colourful way of summarizing situations.

Ben walked around the cabin assessing the damage. Using the back of his hand he shoved the bedroom door open and stepped in, disappearing momentarily.

"Well, it wasn't kids."

The three of us just stared, not wanting to touch anything.

"Whoever did this was looking for something and either we interrupted them before they were finished or they were looking for something specific."

I moved over to the cupboard, which had been emptied. "You mean because they didn't break stuff?"

Ben motioned for us to follow him into the small bedroom. "Yeah, that and they checked out the mattress and box spring but didn't bother to slash them." The dresser had been pulled away from the wall and its contents were piled on the floor.

Colin apparently didn't have a mind for thievery or vandalism. "Maybe they didn't bring a knife?"

Pearl hugged her man. "Honey, don't give up your day job any time soon, okay?" She pointed back out to the other room. "There're likely some knives in the kitchen."

"Oh, right."

I wasn't sure whether or not to move anything but Ben had picked up some clothes off the floor and was stuffing them into drawers.

"Shouldn't we wait until the police come and, I don't know... maybe take fingerprints?"

Ben shook his head and expelled a little snort. "No, I don't think they'll worry too much about a bit of vandalism at a remote cabin."

"But what about theft? Don't you want to have something for insurance?"

He looked around. "I can't say for sure at this point – not until I do some cleaning, but it doesn't look like they've taken anything." Straightening up the mattress and box spring, he pulled the sheets off the floor and started remaking the bed.

Pearl stepped in and held out her hands for Ben to pass her the bedding. "Here, I can do this if you want to have a better look around for anything taken."

Ben handed over the sheets and put his hands on his hips. His eyes scanned the room and they seemed to stop briefly on the wardrobe standing in the corner, then move on.

Colin had returned to the living area and I could hear the click of his phone camera.

Ben moved to join him. "Good idea. I left my phone in the truck."

"No problem, I'll send these to you when I'm done." Colin bent over the table. "Hey, they didn't even take the keys to your truck. Man, they really were focused on something in particular."

"They were looking for Sadie's gold."

Having just helped Pearl clean up the last of the bedroom mess, we joined the guys. "Ah, of course, the gold!"

"Do you want us to spend the night here?" I asked. "You know, just in case they come back?"

Pearl nodded. "Yeah, we could take turns staying up."

Ben was gentlemanly enough to not laugh or mock our bravado, but instead, smiled and shook his head. "You guys are amazing. You're offering to put yourself in danger to help out someone you barely know." He raised his hands at our protest.

"They're not likely to come back tonight, or maybe ever. They gave the place a thorough going over and are probably going to go back to Sadie's to try again there."

"You mean someone broke into Sadie's cabin after she died?" asked Colin.

"Twice. And, I would imagine that if they're after the gold, they probably figure that I'll move it out of here after tonight."

We refrained from voicing the question that was plainly displayed on our faces. Ben laughed and shrugged. "I moved most of it already, what's left is what I figured Sadie would want to be given to her closest friends. Problem is I'm not quite sure how to do that. I can't straight-up give them the gold."

"Why not? I'm thinking it would be cool to have a bag of gold." Colin's eyes were wide with possibilities.

"Not around here it isn't. There's a lot of law enforcement dedicated to dealing with high-grade. Tough to sell and you can't trust that people will keep a secret." Ben's shoulders rose in a shrug. "And besides, there were always rumours about Sadie having gold, but if this got out – well... I don't want anyone saying anything bad about her. You know, questioning where she got it." This time only one shoulder rose up. "I just don't want anyone talking about her except to say what an amazing woman she was."

It's funny what a few simple words can say about a person, and in this instance the words spoke not only of Ben's kind and loyal nature, but also of how that resonated within me. As I studied his face, I felt a compression in my chest and a slight catch in my breath.

Chapter 27 – The Lyin', The Rich and The Wardrobe

"So now what?" I asked.

The corners of Ben's eyes branched out into creases of happy as his mouth turned up into a smile.

"Well," his head tilted towards the bedroom, "if I'm still welcome at your place, we can take the gold back there and figure out what to do with it."

"Ooh, ooh ooh!" Colin was shaking with excitement. "I have the perfect spot for it."

Ben's face read, 'Oh, this should be good.'

"Kate's dad got me digging a horseshoe pit by telling me there was gold there." Colin turned to Pearl, "Thanks, by the way for letting me in on that – I owe him one."

"Anyway – we could bury the gold in the pit under the stakes. That way, if anyone was using a metal detector they would assume it was the stakes and horseshoes."

Ben's hand clasped Colin by the shoulder. "That's really clever, however, it's just a little too risky out in the open. And besides, a metal detector can be set to differentiate between metals."

Colin's upper lip dipped into his lower one.

"How about we just take it back tonight and we'll look around for the best hiding place in the morning."

There were nods all around.

I raised my hand. "By the way, just how much gold are we talking about here?"

"Ah, right. You want to see the gold." He jiggled his eyebrows. "Follow me."

Into the bedroom we trooped trying not to crowd our host in the small room. He walked over to the wardrobe and muscled it out of the corner so that the wall side of the antique piece was revealed. Kneeling down, Ben pressed both ends of the trim board at the bottom of the wardrobe, releasing a pressure fit mount and off it popped. Reaching into the opening, he pulled out two small cloth sacks, each about the size of his hands.

Colin blew a low whistle while Pearl's stunning blue eyes were open wide and sparkled. It appeared that my response wasn't quite as dignified, as Pearl reached over and lifted my chin, closing my mouth.

As Ben stood up, he looked at us and laughed. "No, this is not solid gold, it's still in its raw form."

"That's okay, raw's good for me," Colin commented.

Ben passed one of the pouches to Colin whose hand immediately plummeted. "Holy quartz crystals, Batman, that's heavier than I expected."

Pearl reached out two hands and was better prepared for the weight of the second bag. She turned it over and inspected it from all sides. I'm not sure what she was looking for but to their credit, both she and Colin resisted opening the bags.

Replacing the trim board and returning the wardrobe back to its original spot, we decided to tidy up as much as we could so Ben didn't have to come back to a mess. It didn't take long with four of us working and within half an hour Pearl and I were back in the SUV with Ben and Colin following in the truck.

Chapter 28 – The Moose, The Man and The Moonlight

S leep was elusive after the drama of the evening. By 2:00 a.m. I was sitting on the side of the bed with the curtains opened, staring at the water but not really seeing it. The moon was close to being full and was playing light through the clouds as they journeyed on their celestial paths.

My father had always told me to look for what's not supposed to be there – and, sure enough, having known the silhouette of The Point for my entire life, there was a shape that didn't belong. It looked like an extra bush had manifested but then it started to rise out of the water. I watched in fascination as it grew and grew. Movement stopped and I tried blinking to see if that helped my vision. With slow, measured movements it changed direction and the outline of a huge bull moose, complete with an enormous set of antlers, presented itself.

The tapping on my door startled me. A whispered, "Kate. Kate, do you see it?" followed.

I jumped up and opened the bedroom door. Ben smiled and handed my camera to me. "Come on. We'll have to be seriously quiet because he'll hear the slightest noise."

"Okay, I'll shoot from inside, first."

I adjusted the camera settings to allow as much of the available light onto the sensor as possible. Because the lens was heavy and difficult to hand hold at a slower shutter speed, I leaned it against the large picture window.

The moon had found a patch of clear sky to shine through and highlighted the thousand pound bull's back and antlers, dramatizing the light and dark. Shooting and changing settings as fast as I could, I didn't take the time to check the results. Hopefully one of the images would work. After a few moments, the moose raised his head and sniffed the air. Ben and I actually held our breath.

I slowly lowered the camera and leaned back. Encountering the solid mass of Ben's chest I was caught in a maelstrom of conflicting responses, the most predominant one demanding that I lean in further and just accept the pleasures that awaited. However, as my thoughts and hormones coursed around bumping into each other, the door on the Honeymoon Suite opened and Pearl popped her head out.

Ben gave my shoulders a little squeeze and pointed to the moose whose head had swivelled in our direction. It felt like he was looking directly into my eyes. After a few seconds the beast lifted its huge head to check the information riding on currents of air then turned and walked with a stately gait back into the water.

We scrambled out onto the deck where Pearl and Colin joined us. Four sets of eyes watched the progress of the elongated head and heavy antlers glide across to the opposite shore. Climbing the bank with a grace that belied its size, he turned once again to briefly look our way. Then, with just a few strides, the forest swallowed its citizen.

As we sat, immersed in our personal thoughts, we watched the spot at which the moose had disappeared.

Scanning the shoreline, I tried to peer into the depths of the trees, wondering what stories were being played out in the darkness. Ben quietly stood up and moved to the edge of the deck where he stared out over the water. I wondered what story was playing out within him.

Chapter 29 – Hide and Seek

The two bags of gold sat on the picnic table along with four coffee cups, which had already been refilled a number of times that morning.

The white cloth sacks were quite unremarkable considering what they contained.

Ben's face took on a hard look as he picked one up. He stared at it through eyes pursed in disgust while his lips formed a tight line. Releasing it as though it was contaminated, he shook his head. "Is this the reason Sadie is dead?"

The noon sun played through the leaves of the birch, dancing light and shadow on the two pouches, making it difficult to imagine the evil the contents might inspire.

"How much is a person's life worth? Two sacks? Twenty? A mine-full?" Swirling the contents of his cup he brought it to his lips and chugged it down as if to rid himself of a bad taste in his mouth. His sigh was deep. "Who knows? Maybe the thieves were just taking advantage of a situation. Maybe it wasn't them who killed her." His hands splayed out on the table. "I guess it doesn't change the situation. I have to figure out how to convert this to cash and give it to Marcel and Etienne."

Woah, stop the smelting! "You mean *our* Marcel? And his arch enemy, Etienne?"

Ben's laugh was soft as he nodded. "But we won't tell them about the other one. It would crush them to learn that they shared the same level of friendship with Sadie."

Colin pointed to the gold. "It's complicated stuff, isn't it?" He rolled one of the bags over. "Amazing how this particular metal has changed the lives of millions, and really, changed the course of history." He paused. "You know, the more I think about it, it's changed how people established themselves, fought wars, enslaved, created empires, made and destroyed civilizations..." Tapping the sack with his finger with his head bobbing, he smiled up at us. "Wow! Complicated stuff."

Pearl leaned in and gave him a quick cheek kiss. "My dear, it's not half as complicated as you. And that's part of why I love you."

Colin's smile was full. "You mean you love me because of my mind and not this stunning physique?" He wrapped his arms around her shoulders and dipped her back. Her squeal of surprise was cut short by his kiss.

The interplay had lightened the mood and as I leaned back my peripheral vision caught Ben smiling at my two friends. He picked up one of the bags. "Okay, who wants to see what it looks like?"

Heads snapped forward as Ben released one set of strings. He tipped the sack and shook it until a thick plastic bag slid out. It wasn't immediately apparent what was inside as the plastic was coated in dust and dirt. "It's kept in plastic so any gold dust doesn't get lost. I knew a jeweller who had a rug from his workshop sent down to the States to have it processed. He said he made more money from the recovered gold dust than he made for the entire year in his business."

He unrolled the bag, reached in and picked through the contents. "Ah, that's what I'm looking for." He pulled his hand out, keeping its contents hidden in a fist. Holding it out to me he tipped his hand towards mine.

I held my hand out and he dropped nuggets into it. All three were quite different. The largest was a piece of quartz clad with chunks of gold. The second was a smoother piece of quartz with the gold running in veins. Colin reached over and picked up the third piece, which appeared to be a solid gold nugget. Turning it to view from all angles he whistled. "So that's what it's all about."

Ben sighed. "Yup. That's it."

"What do you think it's worth?"

Shrugging, Ben replied. "I'm no expert, but I would assume that little chunk would be around five hundred dollars. Maybe seven. I'm thinking its value is more than just its weight. People like to make these nuggets into jewellery or have them for display – so they tend to pay more."

Colin passed his piece on to Pearl. "What about these two bags together?"

"I really haven't a clue. If I had to guess, I would say maybe twenty to thirty thousand?"

This time all three of us whistled.

We all studied the pieces, holding them up in the sunlight. Colin reached into the pocket of his jeans and pulled out the piece of iron pyrite from my father, comparing the real with the fake.

After a few minutes of scrutinizing the gold, I was surprised to feel disappointment. I thought about that for a bit and realized that it wasn't sparkly or pretty, and in its raw form was pretty useless. There remained the fact that it was difficult to do something with unless you had nefarious connections or had obtained it legally. Colin was right, it was all very complex with possible horrific consequences should you become obsessed with it. However, it could be a positive game changer once it was processed and sold. Yup, complicated.

*****

Colin was briskly rubbing his hands together with his shoulders hunched up. Pearl shook her head. "You do love a challenge."

"Okay, ladies. Do your best." Colin pushed away from the dock. "You've got two hours to come up with a hiding place. And, once we come back, if we can find it in two hours, you're on the hook for cooking and cleaning for a week."

"Game on!"

Ben cranked the motor and the boys headed out.

"Where the hell do you hide two bags of gold?" Pearl looked at me and we both cracked up.

"Okay, in your wildest fantasy, did you ever imagine this being a scenario in your life?"

Pearl spread her hands out with the palms up. "And we can't even tell anyone. Bugger!"

We walked up to the deck, turned and watched the guys motor past The Point. "Do you have any ideas?"

"Plenty, but none that aren't obvious."

Pearl and I work well together. We systematically walked around each room and each building, eyeing-up possible hiding spots. Then we did it again, this time trying to imagine we were the ones looking for the gold. Upon review, each spot we had earmarked seemed obvious.

Our brains were tired after a full hour of searching so we stopped for a quick break. Sitting on the deck chairs we started to scope out some exterior possibilities.

"Hiding it outside just seems wrong. You know, with our luck, we find a hole in a tree and some squirrel comes along and decides to make a nest and tosses it out." Pearl drummed her fingers on the chair arm. "And underneath any of the buildings is just too obvious."

I felt my lip rise in a sneer. "The outhouse might work."

Pearl's sweet smile introduced a laugh. "I'm not volunteering for that particular duty." She shook her head. "And it's probably the first place they would look."

"Speaking of..." I stepped off the deck and turned to walk towards the outhouse. I looked up and caught a glimpse of Stanley, the great blue heron, soaring overhead. "Mwhahaha! Got it!"

*****

We had just enough time to hide the gold, return our tools, cover any tracks we had made and sit back down on the deck before the boat appeared around the corner. We watched its progress as we sipped beer from our frosty mugs.

The boys pulled up to the dock and Colin passed the rope to Pearl who snugged the Elgin up on shore. They unloaded the fishing gear and a cooler. As Ben stepped onto the dock he nodded towards Colin. "The lad has potential." Pointing at the cooler he continued, "Take a look."

Inside were three good sized pickerel.

"Well, that's dinner taken care of. Brilliant." I lifted my shoulders and hands and looked around. "What remains to be seen, however, is who is going to prepare it." Ben and Colin nodded to each other and we all checked our watches. "It's three o'clock, gentlemen. You have until five to find the gold."

It was obvious that they had been strategizing as Ben went straight for the main cabin while Colin headed for the Honeymoon Suite. Pearl and I had decided that we wouldn't follow them around in case we gave anything away so we pulled out the lounge chairs and reclined on the deck. We could watch Ben through the large window as he stood inside scanning the room. After a few minutes he stuck his head out the door. "Just to confirm – you didn't hide it anywhere personal, like in your suitcase, right?"

"Nope, nothing personal, so you don't need to go through my underwear."

A flash blush coloured his face.

By four-thirty they started to look a little panicked and stopped behind the cabin to discuss the situation. Pearl and I wandered over. Colin yelled, "Ah ha. We must be close as they haven't left the deck before this. They are getting worried that we're close."

We raised our hands in supplication. "Oh great and wise one, we were merely coming to offer you spirits to raise your spirits." Pearl held out two cans of beer while the boys looked at each other, back to us then down at the beer.

Ben shook his head. "I think you're right, Colin. This is just a clever ruse to distract us." He leaned on one of the metal bars of the stand holding up the water tank.

Pearl and I shrugged at each other. Passing one of the cans to me, her eyes opened wide as she pressed the now empty hand to her chest. "Try to do a nice thing for some people..." We turned and walked away. On the deck, as we popped the cans open, she leaned in and whispered, "Wow, they're good."

The beer frothed as we poured it into our mugs.

At one minute to five o'clock, Pearl stood on the deck holding an antique metal triangle and stick that had served, in decades past, to call the workers home for supper. "Gentlemen, the time is near."

Colin yelled from behind the cabin. "I've got it!"

I looked at Pearl and we both shook our heads. "No way, I didn't hear him get the ladder."

We walked to where the boys were standing out back. Colin was grinning. "It's up in the water tank, isn't it?"

Pearl shrugged. "I don't know. I don't see it in your hands, so I guess you haven't found it yet." She ran the metal wand around the inside of the triangle, setting off a raucous cackling from a couple of crows in the nearby pines.

"But I know where it is."

Pearl and I looked at each other.

"If you can produce it in five minutes we'll call it a draw." I had hidden the ladder not far into the woods, but the undergrowth was doing a nice job of keeping it from sight.

The boys were hunting behind the buildings when Ben noticed some broken twigs. He walked a little further and found the old, handmade wooden ladder nestled in the greenery. Moving quicker than one would think possible while carrying a ladder, he placed it against the water tank stand and started to shinny up. When he reached for the cap I yelled up that he needed to open it slowly. Colin was doing a little happy jig as Ben unscrewed the cap. He turned and looked down at us with his face establishing the fact that he was confused. Holding the metal cover out to us, he turned it over. "I was sure the sacks were going to be attached to this."

We let the moment linger in suspension.

The lines between Ben's dark brown eyes deepened and his head tilted slightly as if this movement would help clear the confusion. With slow, almost hesitant movements, he turned and slipped his hand into the hole. We could hear the faint tapping of his fingers on the metal as he explored inside. Determination had driven him to slide his entire forearm into the hole but the muscles above his elbow prevented deeper exploration. He withdrew his hand and looked down at Colin. "Looks like we're on kitchen duty, Mate."

Shaking his head, he placed the cap back on the tank but immediately pulled it off. This time he used his left hand to investigate, burying his arm once again up to his elbow. Pearl and I smiled at each other and shrugged as Ben pulled out one of the sacks. "Nicely played, ladies. You were banking on a right-handed person looking for this, weren't you?"

I wiggled my eyebrows. "Just another possible layer of security. It was Pearl's idea." We fist bumped.

Colin placed a hand on each of our shoulders. "Magnets in the bag?"

Pearl's smile was happy while still smug. "You just never know what you'll find in the woodshed. In this case – they are rare earth magnets. Heavy suckers, too."

Ben was still standing on the ladder with the gold in hand. "Kate, are you okay with me keeping these in here while I try to figure out what to do with them? I can't think of a better hiding place. Really, this is brilliant."

I shook my head and shrugged. "I can't see why not."

When Ben replaced the gold there was a dull thud as the magnet latched onto the inside of the metal tank. "Really brilliant!"

"And, ladies, even though it was a draw, supper and clean-up is on us tonight."

Pearl's arm snaked around Colin's waist. "So magnanimous, my little medical friend, considering we gave you an extension."

Colin leaned in and whispered something in Pearl's ear, to which she lowered her head slightly and looked at her boyfriend through her impossibly long lashes. The invitation in her smile spoke volumes.

"Hmmmph." I turned and walked away. "Have you two no shame?"

I gave a little jump as Ben's voice was just behind. "Apparently not." A little sigh escaped and his timbre lowered and softened. "I rather like it." I turned to look at him. "I haven't seen that kind of solid, loving relationship since Uncle Carl and Sadie." The softness in his smile and eyes held a depth of appreciation.

Chapter 30 - Images, Memories and Mellow

Colin stood and stretched before collecting the dinner plates. Bringing them over to the large metal tub on the wood stove he slipped them into the hot soapy water. "Ben, do you think we have time to visit Marcel before it gets dark?" There wasn't much to clean off the dishes as we had all but licked them at the end of a most scrumptious meal. Dipping one of the blue antique plates into the rinse water he passed it over to Ben to dry.

"If he's in the bay that I think he's in, it's only about twenty minutes up the lake, so, yeah, we should have enough time to make the trip and have a short visit."

I looked out at the early evening light. "Excellent. I would love to get some shots of him in this lighting. It's perfect." I added three packages of warm woolen socks that I had picked up on our trip into town, to my camera bag. "Ben, do you think he'll be offended if I give him these?"

"I don't think so, especially if you're wanting to take pictures of him. He'll see it as a fair trade."

*****

I cut the motor as Pearl reached out to grab the side of Marcel's houseboat. "Ahoy, Mr. Dubois."

"I'm over here." Waving to us from the shore on the far side of the bay was our gnarled gnome-like friend carrying a large white bucket. As Pearl lashed our boat to his, I watched as he made his way across the edge of the rocky shoreline, his step firm and sure. Marcel's home was tied strategically to two trees at a ninety degree angle and a ladder was straddling the distance to the shore along one of the lines. Without even touching the rope, he nimbly traversed the rungs and gracefully landed on his deck. "I wasn't expecting to see you so soon." Disappearing on the opposite side of the boat he yelled, "Come on aboard."

The deck was crowded with the four of us standing there waiting to be ushered further onto the vessel when Marcel's voice came from above. "Ah, I see you were all raised with manners." He pointed to the back of the houseboat. "There's a ladder – come on up."

I waited for the boys and Pearl to climb up then shrugged my camera bag onto my shoulders and followed. Hand hewn benches with storage boxes were set on either side of the upper deck. Marcel was in the process of removing a small folding table from one while Ben opened a couple of folding chairs. Our host pulled a piece of cloth from his back pocket and wiped the table down. "I don't get many visitors. Well, none that I worry about cleaning up for." Motioning to the chairs he instructed us to have a seat.

"I was out picking blueberries. There's nothing like the smell of the patch in the evening after the sun has baked it for the day." He turned and started pulling up a rope that was tied to the railing. We watched, mesmerized, waiting to see what was at the other end.

"Nope, I don't get a chance to break into this very often." Over the edge of the railing came a large wicker basket. Carrying it over to the table he pulled out a bottle filled with a deep ruby liquid. Next came five juice sized glasses, three of which were decorated with ducks and the other two with deer. He pulled out the same rag that he had wiped the table with and ran the cloth around the edges of each glass. I really hoped that the alcohol in the bottle was strong enough alcohol to kill whatever germs the glasses were now harbouring.

"This is from a batch I made two years ago. Raspberry liqueur. Picked them myself." Holding the bottle, he stared at it fondly. "This is mighty fitting seeing as I picked these from Sadie's patch." His head was doing a little bob. "Yes, sir-ee, that woman could make things grow from rocks."

Trying not to be obvious, I looked at Ben but needn't have worried as he was nodding in agreement. "My favourite was her garden medley. Did she ever make that for you?"

"Oh yeah. I used to bring a couple of rabbits to have with it." Marcel's eyes closed momentarily as he savoured the memory.

With a cough and a quick nod, he opened the bottle, poured some into each glass and passed them around. "To our very good friend, Sadie. May the good Lord see fit to make sure I end up in heaven so I can once again enjoy her company."

Marcel's eyes were intent on seeing our appreciation for his drink. We certainly didn't have to fake pleasure as the crimson liquid delighted taste buds all around.

Colin leaned forward. "Mr. Dubois, this is excellent. I've made blackberry liqueur before, but never was it this tasty."

The old trapper held his finger to the side of his nose. "It's all about when and where you pick them, lad, but most important is the full moon."

Hey, I'm not going to argue with success.

As he poured a little more in each of our glasses, he said, "You know, you never told me how you four got together."

Ben inclined his head toward Marcel and smiled. "Well now, there's a good story." Engaging his audience with direct eye contact, enhancing the story with just enough detail to easily visualize the drama while weaving in some self-deprecating humour, Ben's aptitude for story-telling was apparent. We were all mesmerized and I was surprised back into the present when I heard my name. I had been so caught up in his retelling of events that it was like being in a theatre watching an engrossing movie then all of a sudden pulling yourself back and becoming aware of your surroundings.

"And it was our Kate, here, who rescued me and saved my sorry behind from a most unpleasant ending."

Marcel's intense, coal black eyes shifted to mine. "Aye, I can see that she's a good lass, not without talents."

Ben's voice slipped in without hesitation. "You're right there, Mr. Dubois - many talents."

I'm sure it was the raspberry liqueur that brought the blood flooding into my face.

Pearl lifted her glass to catch the evening sun through its beautiful red hue and studied it for a moment. "Mr. Dubois, I'm trying to sort out how things work with traplines." Lowering her glass she tilted her head. "So Sadie's apprentice or assistant; he's now set to take over her trapline?"

Pursing his lips, Marcel nodded. "I haven't made up my mind about that lad. Knew his grandparents – they were good people. But, there's something not quite plumb about him." He looked off to the distant shore. "Sadie liked him well enough so maybe she saw something I don't. Then again, she was a generous soul – too trusting."

*****

Colin's grin bordered on maniacal as he held up his beaver castors. One man's treasure…,

With less than thirty minutes to sunset, we bid goodbye to our host and because our Maglight didn't really count as a running light on the boat, I opened up the throttle.

*****

Ben stood beside me as I downloaded the images from my camera. "Did you get any good ones?"

"Marcel is wonderfully photogenic. Just look at how his character is so perfectly expressed in his face. It tells a thousand stories." I pointed to one in which the evening sun highlighted his left side. You could almost feel the texture of the crags of weathered flesh etched in the darker, shadowed side. "To me, these speak of a lifetime of hard manual work with exposure to the elements, while the catchlight in his eyes proclaims a world of profound understanding."

Ben's hand rested gently on my shoulder and even though his eyes were focused on the computer screen, I could still feel them assessing me peripherally. When he turned to look at me, I felt my chest compress, leaving me short of breath. The warmth and delight expressed in his eyes gave me the feeling that I had accomplished something of great importance. I wasn't really sure what, but it pleased me, and I was quite willing to bask in the glow.

He turned his attention back to the images. "You've done a great job of capturing his story. I think he'd be pleased with these." We continued to review the pictures making various comments on cropping or processing possibilities and I was delighted to discover that he had a good eye for composition and technical aspects. He smiled when we came to the ones where I had focused on photographing the relationship between him and Marcel. "Hah. I didn't realize that I was in these."

"Do you mind?"

He studied them for a moment. "Not at all. In fact, if you don't mind, I'd love a copy of this one." He indicated one in which the two of them were intensely engaged in a conversation that was expressed by their animated faces and upper torsos leaning slightly towards each other. "I think this is where we were debating the merits of the Leafs versus the Canadiens."

I moved further down the page to an image of Ben staring intently into the glass of raspberry liqueur, his expression soft, thoughtful, and possibly in the past. Marcel was watching him with an expression equally as soft and thoughtful but his face communicated a tenderness that spoke volumes. "I think this is my favourite."

After a moment, Ben smiled and asked if he could have a copy of that one as well.

Giving my shoulder a light squeeze he turned and walked over to the fridge. "Care for a late night snack?"

I closed the laptop and stood up, stretching. "Sounds great."

Sitting in the captain's chairs at the old oak table, we consumed our repast and agreed that Colin and Pearl had missed delicious treats because they'd gone to bed early. I took out a bottle of Tennessee Honey liqueur and poured us each a generous measure over ice.

Ben softly sighed as he sat in the red rocking chair while I curled up on the couch.

I hadn't realized how long we had spent processing the pictures and found the softness of the sofa inviting me to rest my head. With so many nights of broken sleep, along with busy, entertaining and complex days, the golden liquid seeped into me and I relaxed into the realm of mellow. I briefly struggled to keep my eyes open but found there was no reward in doing so.

*****

It's a small little noise. Someone with no previous experience hearing it might think it inconsequential. Yet that tiny, insistent buzzing sound can draw a person out of a coma and set them to swatting. We've long known that heat and carbon dioxide are the main attractants for the insidious little creatures. There remained, however, the question of why they seem to focus on certain people with greater persistence. Once again, some unfortunate schmucks who subject themselves to experiments have allowed science to advance and uncover the answer to those poor people's plight. Apparently blood type and a higher concentration of lactic acid on the skin are now known to create a first-class dinner bell for mosquitoes. And, I would imagine that from the mosquito's perspective, it appears that I have been endowed with both of these gifts as the bloody little devils single-mindedly seek me out in a crowd. Maybe bloodsuckers have similar homing devices explaining why they like to attach themselves to me. But really, in either case, I have to work at keeping calm.

Having just been yanked from a most delightful dream I pulled the blanket over my head only to discover the buzzing was trapped inside my bedding cocoon. With probably a little more drama than was necessary, I threw the blanket back, sat up and commenced to swatting vigorously about my head. You'd think that having done these kind of moves all my life I would know that they don't work, but I guess I'm a slow learner...or maybe just optimistic...or maybe desperate.

The sharp little prick on my neck gave away its location and before she drew more than a litre of blood from me (they're really big and thirsty up in the North) I managed to give her a quick and efficient death. I'm considerate like that.

It was only after dispatching my mighty foe that I came to the realization that I was on the couch and someone, (my astute powers of deduction produced an immediate answer by the name of 'Ben'), had placed a pillow beneath my head and covered me with a blanket. Said benefactor was breathing softly in his bunk bed about a metre away. As quietly as I could stumble, I dragged my bedding to the bedroom, slipped between the cool sheets and let the night glide away from me once more.

Chapter 31 – And Now For Something Completely Different

Ben's laugh was low as he shook his head. "As I mentioned yesterday, Etienne and Marcel couldn't be more different."

"But could Etienne have killed her?"

"Tell you what. We'll make a trip to Etienne's place after we get the Honeymoon Suite levelled and you can judge for yourself."

Jacks, blocks, concrete pads and beams were all employed to bring balance back to the smaller cabin. Equipment, and more than a modicum of sweat, blood and grunts were also of assistance (though the blood wasn't of a voluntary nature). No broken bones made the list so we celebrated with lattes after lunch.

"Hey Ben, you look like you're moving easily," Colin remarked as we walked the trail single file.

"It's rather miraculous. A twist and a shove and, voila, it's like nothing was wrong." Holding his hands up he turned to look back at Colin. "Remarkable, really. But then I guess the talent is knowing where to twist and shove."

"Ach aye, laddie," replied Colin in a surprisingly good Scots brogue, "there's really nothing tae it. If ye dae it wrong, the patient will nae be able tae donder again, but that rarely happens, so dinna fash yersel."

There was a noticeable stutter in Ben's stride then a shake of his head.

For the most part the mosquito population could be virtually non-existent during the day out on the deck or the dock, but the concentrations in the trail kept us walking at a brisk pace.

Ben's truck was parked behind our vehicles. He unlocked it with the remote and doing frantic swatting and batting gyrations, we quickly climbed in.

"Should we call Etienne before we drop in on him?" Pearl held up her phone. "You know, I haven't missed this at all." Phone reception is usually okay at The Camp, but for whatever reason we hadn't been able to get a line during our stay. No phone, no internet… it was rather liberating.

"We should be able to call just down the road." Ben tapped his pocket ensuring his phone was there. "Etienne has always been open with his invitations to me and I really enjoy his company. Over the years Sadie, Uncle Carl and I spent many an evening at his place. He's quite the host."

From the back seat of the crew cab, Pearl leaned forward. "As good as Marcel?"

Ben smiled. "You can be the judge of that."

As we drove over the bridge near Ben's cabin, he tapped a button on his steering wheel. "Call Etienne." A few seconds later we could hear a phone ringing.

A modulated baritone came through the speaker. "Good afternoon."

"Hello, Etienne. It's Ben."

"Benjamin! What an absolute delight to hear from you. Are you up north?"

"Yup. Trying to settle some estate issues."

"Ah, my dear boy," Etienne's tone deepened. "I hope that I can be of assistance in whatever manner possible."

"Actually, I was hoping I could come and run a few things past you."

"Perfectly brilliant. I was just wondering what I should do with my afternoon and would be delighted with your company."

"Etienne, you're always so accommodating." Ben was smiling. "I have three friends with me. Would you mind the extra company?"

Without hesitation he replied, "I would enjoy that immensely. When shall I expect you?"

"Is half an hour too soon?"

"Not at all, dear boy, the sooner the better."

"Can we pick anything up before we get there?"

"You're always the perfect guest, Benjamin, but no, thank you. I'm sure I have everything we'll need."

Ben was chuckling. "See you shortly then." His face wore a conspiratorial grin.

"What's with the British accent?" Colin enquired.

"Etienne lives there for a few months each year. His mother moved back after his father passed away."

Twenty minutes later we were on the outskirts of Timmins. Ben turned left up a road that led past the Kamiskotia ski hill and on towards a lake. The entrance to Etienne's driveway was flanked by huge rosebushes in full deep-pink bloom. For the next kilometre, a small forest of poplars allowed sunlight to dapple the underbrush of ferns. It felt both wild and manicured and I wouldn't have been surprised to see a storybook character walking through the setting.

With the exception of Ben, none of us was prepared for the home that greeted us. Pearl was the first to find her voice. "Is it an English cottage or a small mansion?"

Colin whistled.

The two-storey stone structure was barely visible through the limbs of the rose and morning glory blossoms intertwined with English ivy. Mullioned windows peeked through the tangle of colour. I was sure I could hear the hounds baying, the thundering of horses' hooves and the clear notes of the hunting horn off in the distance of my imagination. The scraggly pines that bordered the far reaches of the property were an incongruous note in the otherwise idyllic English country scene.

Twin carved wooden doors opened in unison as we walked up the wide brick path. Emerging into the bright afternoon sunlight was none other than a slightly taller and not quite as weathered Marcel Dubois. This version, however, sported a royal blue golf shirt, well-creased dress pants and dark grey leather deck shoes. The only thing missing was an ascot.

115

I'm afraid we were caught with our mouths open as we stared.

"Benjamin, how wonderfully delightful to see you." Our host clasped Ben's hand in both of his. With a most welcoming smile, he turned towards his gob-struck guests and offered a well-manicured hand to me as I tried to bring my surprise back into the not-so-rude category.

"Mr. Bisette, how very gracious of you to invite us into your most beautiful home with such short notice." I was trying to recover as fast as I could.

"Please, my dear, I prefer to be called Etienne." His smile emanated from a well shaven face and I realized his eyes weren't quite as black as Marcel's but leaned towards a dark blue. Just before he turned to greet Colin and Pearl, I noticed small gold flecks stippling the edges of his pupils.

Ben completed the introductions and we were led into the cool interior of his home. A slate entrance way transitioned into thick, forest green carpeting that flowed into each room.

"I thought we might sit on the patio."

As our host led the way I elbowed Ben in the side and pointed to Etienne, lifting my shoulders and shaking my head. His eyebrows were hoisted in mock surprise while his mouth spoke of laughter. He leaned in and quietly whispered, "It was so worth seeing the look on your faces," and gave my shoulders a one-armed squeeze.

*****

Etienne, with only a short time to prepare, had arranged a tray of vegetables, crackers, smoked cheese and fruits on a large tiled outdoor table under a pergola festooned with more roses and ivy. The man obviously had a gift for creating idyllic settings. Pearl and I could use his talent in our renovation business.

"Coffee? Tea? Or would you prefer something more refreshing?" Opening the lid of a large cedar box Etienne directed our attention to its contents. Nestled in a lining of insulation was a layer of ice cubes hosting a selection of beer, two bottles of wine and an assortment of soft drinks. Colin and I chose wine, while Pearl twisted the cap off a bottle of craft beer.

"I'll take the non-alcoholic beer if you don't mind, Etienne. I'm driving."

Passing a bottle to Ben, Etienne poured himself a glass of wine and joined us at the table.

"It's such a pleasure to have you all visit. Brightens up my whole week." Etienne lifted his wineglass. "May you live to be one hundred years, with one extra year to repent."

The wine was a lovely mellow Pinot Grigio that slipped softly over the tongue. "This is delicious. I'll have to look for it."

"It's actually a B. C. wine – from the Okanagan. I like to have it on hand as it seems to please a variety of palates."

We spent a delightful hour with our enchanting host who wanted to know all about us and was skilled in drawing out the finer details of our lives and interests. He regaled us with colourful tales of his travels until finally we arrived at the purpose of our visit.

"Benjamin, you mentioned settling up the estate. Are there many concerns?"

While Ben filled him in on the real estate issue, Etienne looked puzzled. "You're right, that doesn't make much sense. Sadie never mentioned to me that she wanted to sell or move." He thrummed the fingers of his left hand on his chest in a contemplative gesture. "Would you like me to extend a few feelers? Make some discreet enquiries about this Sterling Harper chap?" His head bobbing reminded me of Marcel's gesture. "I've heard of him, of course I've seen his real estate signs around town, but I don't know much else about him."

"You know, that could be of help - might turn up something I could use." Ben's fingers were see-sawing on his chin so I knew he was in deep thought. Abruptly, they stopped and his eyes lasered in on Etienne's. He hesitated, then slowly drawing in a deep breath, seemed to come to a decision. "You're good friends with Judge Jenkins, aren't you?"

"Ah, the judicious Judge Jenkins…" Pausing, Etienne pursed his lips and produced a few more head bobs. "Yes, we have been friends for a number of years, however, given recent events at a poker night, the

Judge and I are not, oh, how shall I say this… seeing eye to eye." He shrugged as if the matter were inconsequential or possibly out of his control. "Pity."

We gave our host a moment of raised eyebrows and silence, hoping he would fill in the details of the ill-fated event however, he just smiled and left the story to our imaginations. With a nod to our empty glasses, he got up and opened the cooler. "How about another drink?"

Ben stood and thanked our host and insisted that we couldn't impose on his wonderful hospitality any further.

"Impose? You're not imposing in the least. Your company has been simply delightful and I'm afraid I'm going to be quite lonely once you've gone."

I caught Ben's eye and the merest shake of his head. "Etienne, we've so enjoyed ourselves but we still have to drive into town before the stores close, to pick up some supplies."

With promises of another get-together, we made our way back to Ben's truck.

Etienne, with courtly manners, kissed my hand then Pearl's, shook Colin's and then hugged Ben. "So good to see you, Ben. I've missed Sadie – but I would imagine that you miss her a great deal more. I'll start doing a little investigating on that Harper fellow – I do love a good hunt."

*****

The ride into town was as much a fact-finding trip as it was a journey of suppositions.

"So what do you think the story about the judge is?" was Pearl's first question, followed by my, "What does Etienne do for a living?"

Colin cut in. "My burning question is, how are he and Marcel related?"

Ben's smile was broad. "So you noticed!"

Pearl reached from the back seat and gave his arm a soft punch.

Ben turned from the driveway onto the Kamiskotia road. "They had the same father – and I'm pretty sure you have a good idea of what *he* looked like seeing as the two of them look almost identical." Warming to his story, Ben continued. "Their dad was from France and married Etienne's mother who was a rather wealthy lady from England. Some say she even had a title - I've heard both Lady and Baroness, though Etienne has never talked about it and when asked, he skirts the issue. Bit of a mystery there. The father got hooked on the thrill and romance of gold and wanted to try his hand at prospecting. His wife had no desire to change her way of life by moving to the wilds of Canada as she was purported to have had quite the active social life in London. So, you can guess the rest. The father lived a double life and Marcel was the son of a local waitress whom the father lived with when he was here."

This story was getting good. "So how did Etienne end up here?"

"His mother died when he was about ten so his father brought him over. Needless to say, the boy was not impressed to be dragged from his home and friends, plunked down in a small mining town where he had no social status and even less impressed to find out he had a brother. An illegitimate brother. And a stepmom who was a waitress. The stepmom, Gloria, was a decent sort, and she tried hard. But you can imagine the hostility of the young lad, and, to make matters worse, Etienne treated Marcel like a servant, and therein started the lifelong resentment – on both sides."

The lightbulb went on. "Ah, so the fight over the woman that you mentioned was actually about Marcel's mother, Gloria?"

"Well, she was one of the women. There was a lot of antagonism that went on in high school and afterwards between the two. Sadie talked about a number of girls that these two fought over. They were always trying to steal each other's girl."

I noticed Ben keeping an eye on the rear view mirror.

Colin must have noticed as well as he turned to look through the back window. "Is there something going on back there, Ben?"

"I'm not sure. It's probably just my imagination, but that looks like the same SUV that was behind us when we drove in." He looked over at me. "I'm probably just being paranoid, or overcautious."

Colin was still looking back. "When did you notice it?"

"Actually, it was just after we passed the turn-off to my cabin. I'm sure there wasn't anyone on the road behind us after we left The Camp and then, this white SUV shows up, kind of out of nowhere, not going any faster than we were."

Pearl shrugged. "Maybe that one just came out of some side road after picking berries and this one happens to look like it. I mean, there are lots of white SUVs around."

"Yeah, you're probably right." But Ben didn't really sound convinced.

I still had a few questions about Etienne. "So what do you think happened between the Judge and him? That sounded pretty serious if they've been friends for so long."

"Ah, don't read too much into that – Etienne likes a bit of drama."

"You looked like you were getting ready to ask him something serious."

Once again Ben glanced in the mirror as if he had to make sure whoever was behind us couldn't hear. He took a breath then paused, apparently giving his comments a full review before saying them out loud. Another breath. "I know it would have been asking a lot of him, but I figured he would do it for Sadie."

"Do what?" My mind was starting to categorize different possibilities.

"I was hoping he would offer first, but since he didn't I was going to ask if the Judge might be of help. You know, with the will and helping to stop the sale of the properties from going through." Before anyone could comment, Ben rushed ahead. "I know that's not the right way to do things, but I'm stumped. I'll keep fighting the sale but I feel like I'm using a cardboard sword to battle a dragon. And, I know Sadie is gone and she is probably in a place where it really doesn't matter to her anymore, but it matters to me. It matters that someone got away with killing her and is profiting from her death."

Pearl, sitting behind Ben, leaned forward. "Do you think that this Harper fellow is the one who killed her because she wouldn't sell? What about the gold?"

Ben scratched the back of his head. "That's just it, I'm tilting at windmills. Anyway, I thought it was worth asking – I figured the worst he could do was turn me down. And, possibly think less of me."

I reached over and squeezed his shoulder. "I think it would take a whole lot more for him to think less of you. Etienne obviously cares a great deal for you."

We came to the T-junction and turned east on Highway 101 towards town. Merging into a stream of traffic, we lost sight of the SUV.

*****

Since the invention of pizza, there have been many iterations of this gastronomic delight, and I've yet to find one that doesn't have merit. There are favourites, but I'd be hard pressed to pick one, or even five. I pretty much like them all. Okay, I pretty much love them all. Unfortunately, I have no turn-off switch when it comes to this delectable dish and I was in good company. After boxing up the few remaining slices, and before we all slipped into a food coma, we hustled to the stores to get our supplies, cranked the music and headed back home.

With the windows wide open, spilling our music onto the roadway and into the forest, we covered the miles to the Whitefish River in less than seven songs. The road was empty except for the occasional semi.

Passing a bag of penny-candy to Colin and Pearl in the back seat of the crew cab, I noticed a vehicle pulling out of a side road. Twilight hadn't fully invested itself in the evening, but headlights, always an excellent idea while driving in the bush, hadn't been turned on.

Ben's eyes were once again focused on the rear view mirror. "Kate, did you happen to see what kind of vehicle that was?" He turned off the music.

"Sorry, I only caught it as it was mostly turned onto the highway."

"I don't know why I didn't think of this sooner, but there's a pair of binoculars in the glove compartment. Maybe we could get a look at the license plate or occupants."

The road was fairly smooth, but the occasional bumps knocked the binoculars against my face. "Sorry – there's not enough light to see the plate and the windows are tinted. But, it is an SUV and it looks white."

"Okay, let's play this a different way. I don't want to try and slip into your hidden trail off the highway because if we disappear, they'll have an idea of where we are, if, in fact it's the same vehicle and they are following us."

Pearl held out her hand for me to pass her the binoculars. "At this point, I don't think there is any question about that."

"I'm going to keep going for another ten or fifteen minutes. We'll see if they stay with us. Then, when I can, I'll speed up, duck into a side road and wait for them to pass."

With the truck windows opened, the sounds of the roadside frogs became our background music. Colin leaned his right ear towards the window. "I recently read an amazing fact about frogs. They can change the pitch of their call to accommodate traffic noise so they can be better heard by a receptive female."

There didn't seem to be anything to add to that statement so we let it stand alone while we drove past the turnoff to The Camp.

After each bend in the road we all looked back to see if the SUV was still with us. Finding a side road in the distance while travelling at highway speed, and giving us enough time to slow down to make the turn was proving difficult.

Pearl tapped Ben's shoulder. "How about we let them see us make the turn off, then sit and wait to see if they follow us."

"That's an idea however it would tip our hand by letting them know that we're onto them. I'd rather try to see what they're up to before we do that."

"That makes sense."

At this point the highway was bordered by rock cuts that looked seriously sinister as the light abandoned the sky. After negotiating a long curve Ben sped up for a minute then had to slow down to safely make another curve.

"There, on the left! Can you see the reflective marker beside the road?" I pointed into the distance where our headlights had created a brief flash.

Ben sped up then braked hard as he cut onto the side road. We felt the back end of the truck swing out, threatening to flip us over. There was a collective intake of breath from all three passengers. With considerable skill, and the good fortune that the road was wide enough to allow him to bring it back without sending us flying into the trees, Ben had us once again pointing forward. "Sorry about that!"

When we were far enough into the trees he cut the lights and we waited. Within minutes, speeding past the entrance was a white SUV. Ben waited another minute so it would be far enough down the highway to not see us return. Cautiously he backed up without putting the lights on. I grabbed the flashlight that I had found in the glove compartment and shone it out the window to give Ben a bit of light to navigate by. Once around the bend on the highway, he turned the truck lights back on as we headed home.

Pearl whistled. "Wow. That was a bit intense."

Colin pulled his phone out, scrolled through and looked up smiling as the theme song from James Bond filled the cab.

Chapter 32

T he call was picked up on the second ring.
"Well?"

"I think they're on to us." the voice, terse with frustration. "I lost them about fifteen or twenty miles past the turnoff on 144."

"I told you to be careful."

"Hey, it's open road with not much traffic - kind of hard to blend in." The voice challenged. "So what did you find out?"

"Enough to make enquiries."

Chapter 33 – We'll See

"**I** don't think I'll be able to sleep after that little game of hide and seek." Pearl had finished putting away our purchases and was perusing the game cupboard. "Nope, I don't think games are going to do it." She closed the door. "Anyone up for a swim?"

The night still held the warmth of the day and the thought of a swim sounded wonderful. "I'm in."

The guys weren't going to be left out so it was a full contingent that stood on the dock scanning the water.

Colin was the first to voice the concern that we all had. "So, do you think he's out there?"

Pearl said, "We'll see," and gave Colin a quick shove sending him flailing into the pitch-black water. His yell was short-lived as his head dipped briefly below the surface. "Sacrifices must be made to appease the Piscean gods!" Raising her arms above her head she yelled. "Don't worry, my little copper-top quack. I shall not leave you to fend off the evil Lucius on your own!" And with the proclamation still echoing off the opposite shore, Pearl cannonballed her partner.

Ben gave me a quick look. I expected him to jump but instead, grinning broadly, he picked me up and leapt into the lake. Once submerged, I was released, and Ben re-emerged a few metres away.

The water, warmer than the night air, felt deliciously soft and embracing.

With so many questions still plaguing us and the intensity of our car ride home, the pent-up energy of the group needed to be expended. The decision was made to swim together to The Point as we believed, just as fish form bait-balls, we would also find safety in numbers. Upon reaching our destination, we could feel the cooler water of the embedded creek making its way through the warmer water of the bay much like my thoughts percolated through the events of the last six days.

The moon, one night shy of being full, cast an enchanted light making the water and cabin appear to glow. It's moments like this that render words redundant and floating silently, we were caught in the spell. Delicate crackling noises from the shore brought us back and Pearl's voice broke into our thoughts. "I'm ready to go back."

We still found words cumbersome and the return journey was made listening to the various rhythms of our strokes and breaths.

The water had cooled us sufficiently and once I stepped onto the dock, I snuggled into the warmth and comfort of the towel pulling it tight around my shoulders.

After drying off we put on our various night attire and met on the deck but no one seemed to have anything revelatory to add, so uncharacteristically we sat in silence, listening to our own thoughts.

Ben had been standing with his hands on the railing and his back to us. He took a deep breath and turned. With the moon behind him his face was mostly in shadow and I was surprised to hear the sadness in his voice. "I'm so sorry I've brought you three into this. I had no right to expose you to this danger." Ignoring our protestations, he continued. "You've been absolutely amazing and all I've been is selfish and have now put everyone at risk. I can't apologize enough nor thank you enough. If it's okay I'll stay the night and leave first thing in the morning."

We were stunned but managed to present arguments. "Are you crazy? You're not going anywhere." And, "Not a chance! You're not leaving us out of this. No way. We're here until we either find out what happened to Sadie or at least make sure that you get to keep what's rightfully yours."

I stood up, moved directly in front of Ben and took his hands in mine. "No, you can't leave. We're not quitters and we're not going to let anything happen to you – or us! We're all in this together."

126

"Ah, Kate. You've already saved my sorry-butt once. I think that's more than enough. I would never forgive myself if anything were to happen to you." He looked over my head at Pearl and Colin. "...to any of you."

Colin laughed. "Are you kidding, man? This is the best vacation ever and tonight was just a bit of fun. Do you really think someone is going to be crazy enough to take out four of us and think they can get away with it? Come on, this is just getting good. You're not taking this away from us!"

Ben's snort was soft as he shook his head.

"We'll see."

I wrapped an arm around Ben's waist and looked at my two best friends. "No, we'll see." I turned and looked up at him. "We'll see what happened to Sadie. And we'll see that things are made right." Quite the bravado from someone who didn't have a clue as to how this was going to happen, but the sentiment came from deep within, and I've learned to trust that instinct.

Pearl stood up and told us to not move. She went into the cabin and I could hear the clinking of glasses. While we continued to confirm that Ben was an integral part of our group and our holiday, Pearl backed out through the door carrying a tray with a bottle of Irish whiskey and glasses.

With everyone ready, Colin made a toast. "To friends, old and new, and how rich our lives are because of them."

Ben still didn't look entirely convinced but he smiled, closed his eyes and added, "May everyone be as fortunate as I am." He opened his eyes, connected with each of us in turn and added the Irish blessing of health, "Sláinte!"

After a few more rounds of toasts, Ben sauntered off to the outhouse. Pearl's smile was smug as she informed us that Ben would most definitely be staying.

"I don't know – he sounded pretty concerned and convinced that the best thing for us would be for him to leave."

Pearl smile stayed true as she reached into her pocket and produced a set of truck keys. "Maybe, but I don't think he'll get far without these."

Chapter 34 – Double Recap

There was the tiniest space between the bedroom curtains that allowed the morning sun to enter, striking my eyes with the intensity of an interrogation light. A whole horizon exists upon which the sun could rise – but no, it chooses to pick the exact spot that culminates in the rude invasion of my perfectly sound sleep. Then again, the question begs asking, why didn't I close the curtains tightly?

I tilted my head slightly to avoid searing my retinas and my mind cast about for the current that picks you up, softens your thoughts and carries you back into Morpheus' realm. Apparently, that particular Greek god had decided I was no longer allowed to take pleasure in his company. There was neither a current nor a softening of thoughts. Instead, a large white surface came to mind, then faces, vehicles, land deeds and chunks of gold created a perimeter frame. Snatches of conversations wove themselves into a soundtrack. I tried to turn it all into something meaningful but logic and answers were elusive. A dot appeared in the centre and as I watched, a distant image began to form. Slowly, a woman with long black hair began to glide forward into the middle of the setting. She was sitting quietly, bathed in a silvery glow, looking down at her hands. As she progressed to the foreground, the nuggets of gold and land deeds migrated to either side of her then came to rest in her lap. She watched as they settled between her hands then, with startling clarity, she looked up, directly into my eyes. The impact of her gaze was as strong as the sun's had been and my head snapped back on the pillow.

I tried to make sense of my thoughts as they zipped around, dancing, falling, colliding and fading in and out. Being an extrovert creates a bit of an internal maelstrom when I try to think. Often, in order for me to work through my thoughts, I need to verbally express them which helps me to sort and make sense of them. I needed to talk them out. I needed to think outside my head.

Throwing back the covers I slid my feet into my slippers. Even though I was going to wake Ben up, I slowly opened the door then tiptoed over to the bunkbed where he was stretched out with his arms thrown casually above his head.

Like most people, I prefer to be gently awoken and chose to proffer the same courtesy to our guest. I leaned in close. "Ben," whispered gently didn't get a response so I leaned in further with my lips close to his ear and whispered his name again.

A soft rumble rolled around in his chest as his arms pulled me into a tender embrace. He turned his head and nuzzled my neck.

Oh my, but that was lovely! Unexpected, but surprisingly, welcome. I was quite willing to indulge in this particular pleasure as my thoughts stopped scrambling around in my head and receded into the shadows.

His kisses journeyed up my neck then across my cheek, leaving a delicious trail of tender caresses. As his lips discovered mine I found my perspective of the world collapsing into those few square centimetres. His kiss was soft and inquisitive. And enchanting. I could become addicted to this.

One of us moaned.

Ben's lips stopped moving and I heard a sharp intake of breath. This time I was pretty sure it was him. Our eyes popped open, but given our proximity we weren't in a position to look into the other's.

"Ummm."

Pulling myself back a bit I started to laugh after seeing the look on Ben's face. Surprise and guilt vied for the majority of space, while delight danced around his mouth. Searching my face, he settled on my eyes, started apologizing and then stopped as he placed his hand on the side of my cheek. "No, I take that back. I'm not sorry that happened. I've wanted to do that since I met you." He turned his hand over and gently ran the back of his fingers along my jaw. "I'm just sorry that I was sleeping through the first part of it."

I hadn't quite decided where I wanted to go with this, but as I looked into his mahogany eyes then down at his lips there was no doubt in my mind that for now, I wanted to further enjoy at least some of the delights they had to offer. "No problem. Here's a recap."

Chapter 35 – Please Leave A Message

Pearl's eyes were opened wide while her forehead puckered in disbelief. She had walked into the cabin as Ben and I sat finishing our breakfasts, took one look at my face and her mouth formed a perfect 'O' as the sound of the letter slipped into the room. I thought I had set my expression to neutral, but Pearl obviously saw right through that. She pointed to Ben and tilted her head. Ben's back was to her so his eyes were also scanning my face to get advanced warning as to what might be coming his way. I smiled and tried to pull an innocent face by batting my eyelashes. His response was to laugh and add, "Boy, you two certainly know each other well." He half turned and looked up at my friend, his expression one of surrender.

Pearl sighed. "Actually, I think it's probably a bit of that, but also a people-thing. If you were to ask me how I knew, I couldn't give you specifics - I think it's just about paying attention."

"And what are we paying attention to?" Colin had his face pressed up to the screen door, flattening his nose.

Pearl turned, smiled and said, "Well, you're not paying attention to the fact that you look rather funny with your nose mushed up." She turned back to us and whispered, "We'll see if he notices."

"Scrunched up or not, my nose smells breakfast and I'm famished." He opened the door and with a courtly bow he said, "Ladies and kind sir, may I join you for a scrumptious repast?" Not waiting for an answer, he started to walk towards the stove but stopped midway as he looked around the table. He made a, "Hmmm" sound, nodded, then resumed his quest for food.

Pearl popped some bread into the toaster. "So what's on the agenda for today?"

We looked around waiting for inspiration. Ben finally took a deep breath. "I've decided that I have to either talk to a different lawyer – one who's more aggressive or maybe hire an investigator to look into this Harper character. I don't know if he's the developer or just the face of it. "Kate, do you think your father or one of his brothers might know of a good lawyer?"

"I don't have to ask – my aunt is a lawyer." I gave my forehead a smack. "I don't know why it didn't occur to me before. I'm sure she would love to be in on this."

Pearl whistled. "You mean Aunt Maggie? Magical Maggie?"

The guys' surprised look invited an explanation. Pearl shrugged. "Well, Kate, how would you describe her?"

"Um, well, to start with, she has a PhD in law. She seems to thrive on cases that no one else will take. When she first graduated she was practicing at a firm in Toronto. She got into a legal tussle with some questionable characters, received threats against her life and somehow ended up with them offering her protection." I looked at the guys' faces and shrugged at the surprised expressions. "She's rather hard to define, but if I had to sum her up it would be that she's amazing and you want her in your corner."

Colin was intrigued. "And the magical moniker?"

A visual of Maggie was in the forefront of my brain. "Well, she's about five foot seven, with a slender but solid build – you know the kind that can move quickly and also hold her own if push came to shove. She actually looks a bit like a shorter Sigourney Weaver." A memory from long ago popped up. "I was visiting her in Toronto and she had taken me to my first restricted movie when I was twelve. Afterwards we went to an Italian restaurant for dinner. I thought this was the best time, ever! I felt so grown up. When the bill came, they had charged too much so she brought it to the waiter's attention. He wouldn't change it so she spoke to the manager. Maggie pointed to the price on the menu and said that was what should be charged. I guess the manager figured he could bully us and wouldn't back down. He said it was a printing mistake and the price charged was what she had to pay. Maggie just smiled, took out her wallet and put down exactly the amount that should have been charged."

Pearl was laughing. "Oh, I can so see her doing that."

"Needless to say, the manager was furious at having this woman defy him and started yelling and trying to get in her face. She just turned to me and said we were going. I thought this pompous jerk was going to hit her. I mean, his eyes were bulging. He followed us to the parking lot and took down her license plate number." I looked around at the table. "Honestly, I was scared for her but part of me was cheering her on. He tried to block us from leaving but instead of running him over – which I was hoping for, she got out of the car and very calmly walked over to him. He started yelling again and waving his arms around, shoving his finger into her face and all the while she slowly moved so that she had him with his back to the car. You should have seen her – her face was serene the whole time. Then slowly, she put her finger to her lips in a 'Shhh' gesture and leaned in. He couldn't back up without falling over the hood of the car and, I'll never forget this – I can see it so clearly, his arm came back as if getting ready to swing and Maggie just shook her head, said something, and his arm fell to his side like he had lost all of the muscles in it."

Ben was shaking his head. "What did she say to him?"

I shrugged. "I asked her and she merely said that she had pointed out the error of his ways and suggested there were consequences for his behaviour. Then she stressed, '*all* of his behaviours'. I've never been able to get specifics from her but, as you can imagine, it left an impression with me." The movie reel playing in my head stopped and I brought myself back to my friends. "She seems to have a talent for making problems disappear – hence the 'Magical'."

"She sounds like just the lawyer I need. Can we make an appointment with her?"

"Dad mentioned something about her being somewhere in the Middle East – I have no idea what she's doing there or when she's coming back, but we can call. She might even know something about Harper."

The look on Ben's face fed my heart. I saw hope overlaid with admiration. At least that's what I thought he was expressing. Hey, it's what I saw, and truth be told, it felt wonderful to revel in it.

*****

After breakfast, we decided to not run the risk of using the vehicles and instead, chose to take the boat up the main lake where we could get cell reception. The day was overcast and cool so we left the bathing suits behind and loaded up the fishing gear. Colin's hat du jour was a simple baseball cap that said, "Cute enough to stop your heart. Skilled enough to restart it." Ben laughed as he read it. "A gift from Pearl?"

"Actually, no, it's from my grandmother." Colin tapped the bill. "I don't know where she comes up with these things but her gifts are always fun."

Pearl nudged him. "Just like her grandson."

I offered Ben the chance to drive and his grin was wide underneath his aviator sunglasses. I assumed it was memories of other times spent in this boat with Sadie and Uncle Carl that gave him such pleasure.

Pearl and Colin had sat in their usual spot in the middle, so I untied the line and climbed down into the small front seat. There wasn't enough space under the little triangle at the bow for adult legs, so I faced backwards, leaning on a lifejacket, which allowed me to reflect on this different perspective.

In my mind I saw layers. Layers of life, of love – present and past, In the immediate foreground were Pearl and Colin whose relationship had fleshed out in the last year giving it a sense of completeness. On their own they each were solid, fun and amazing friends, so easy to be with. Together, they complemented and flowed into each other and it seemed that any gaps were filled in to create a solid relationship. The next layer was driving the boat. And what a complicated layer he was. Physically striking, smart, funny, compassionate, passionate... oh. Oh yes, passionate... sensitive, strong, capable, tender... hmmm, I was sensing a theme here...

The tap on my foot jolted me out of my daydream. Smiles come in many forms but there was no mistaking Pearl's. Busted.

Ben's head swivelled in my direction and Pearl immediately disappeared from my view. Though his sunglasses hid his eyes, there was no mistaking his smile either. And that smile brought a little happy dance to my nethers, and my nethers had been dancing up a storm today. Our little getting-to-know-you intro session this morning had apparently set my internal stereo to full blast and I found the music compulsive. Ah, but I digress.

Colin leaned in to whisper something to Pearl and I allowed my perspective to shift to the wake of the boat that was sending rolling waves across the bay. It made me think of how each of us goes through life, all of our actions impacting everyone and everything in our wake. This brought me back to the present and our current situation. So many events had transpired to bring us all together. Was there such a force as destiny or were these choices and events just that – truly random choices, and like the waves emanating from our stern, they rolled along until they met up with another wave or obstacle, where alterations in the course would be made.

By that point in my ruminations, we had rounded the corner and were almost on Kenogamisi. Ben opened the throttle and the little Elgin's bow tilted up as we headed north.

I watched my phone and as soon as I saw that we had service I signaled to Ben. He scoped out the terrain and headed for a dot of an island on the west side of the lake. An old pine tree had lost its tenuous hold on the earth and was listing out over the water. Ben throttled down and as we glided beneath it, Colin reached up and snagged the trunk. I tossed the bowline to Pearl who lashed us to it.

When we had first arrived at The Camp, it had only taken me a day to break my technology ties. The freedom from constantly checking social media, texts and emails was liberating. It's quite surprising how quickly these shackles are left behind when you have such great friends and are in a place to which the connection goes soul deep. My phone, which I'm normally never without, felt and looked foreign even as I quickly tapped my way to Aunt Maggie's phone number. I looked up as it rang and three faces were staring expectantly at me.

After three rings it went into voice mail. I put the phone on speaker so everyone could hear the message that said to contact her office as she would be unavailable for another three days. The expectant faces turned to frowns. Bugger!

"I'll send a text so she gets it as soon as she's available."

We stared at each other for a few breaths. Having pinned so much hope onto my aunt, there seemed to be a stutter as to what our next move should be.

Colin was the first to recover. "Well, while we have service – I might as well check my texts and emails. We all shrugged and started to scroll through our various devices and apps. That lasted a minute or two.

Pearl looked up and shook her head. "I just don't want to connect or deal with any of that right now." Colin and Ben had already put their phones away.

I checked three texts that might be important, realized that they could all wait and shut it down. "Well, while we're here, shall we do a little exploring?"

The island took no more than twenty minutes to circumnavigate, and that included climbing over the fallen trees and digging in a spot that Colin insisted was a perfect place to bury treasure. The only items that our explorations turned up were three old nests, a long-extinguished campfire and a bunch of empty beer bottles that we collected to take to the recycling depot.

As we were climbing back into the boat I thought I could hear the whispers of a song. I looked at my friends and no one else seemed to notice. "Does anyone else hear music?"

Colin's forehead became creased, his eyes closed and his head dropped a bit as he slowly swiveled it back and forth. "Sad, no, tragic - and she's so young." He looked up at Pearl. "You do know that's the first sign of going mad – when people start to hear music." His voice lifted to a higher timber with a Viennese accent. "Now tell me, meine liebste, ven did you start to hear voices?"

"Years ago – about the time I met you!" I turned and leaned over the boat as if those few extra inches would afford me better acoustics. "There – there it is."

Everyone became quiet for a few seconds. Ben was the first to recognize the tune. "I'm pretty sure that's Perry Como singing *Catch A Falling Star*, and you know what that means…"

The disappointment of not being able to reach Aunt Maggie was lost in the excitement of meeting up with the inimitable Marcel. As we came around the island we could see the stately Florence serenely sailing down the lake. Ben looked around at us. "Shall we?"

"Of course, my good man. Make haste." Colin's arm was outstretched as if directing our course then he reached down and opened the tackle box. Carefully rummaging around the bottom he pulled out a number of lures and other fishing bits and placed them on the seat. "And, we even come bearing gifts." His smile was vast.

Pearl leaned in and kissed his cheek. "Good call."

As soon as we started heading towards the houseboat we noticed that it was no longer moving forward, its gentle wake subsiding.

Chapter 36 – Sterling Is Not Gold

Marcel's cheeks were crinkled with a smile as he helped us aboard The Florence. From behind the Dutch door came the sharp whistle of a kettle's invitation to tea.

"Heh, heh, perfect timing, this." Marcel motioned for us to go up to the top deck. Within a few minutes he had hoisted up the fixings for tea along with a plate of oatmeal cookies.

Colin had placed the fishing gear on the table beside Marcel's chair. "We were in town the other day and they had a fantastic deal on tackle. I got carried away. Seeing as I only have carry-on for the plane can you make use of it?"

Marcel eyed Colin then nodded. "For sure, lad, that'll come in right handy." A dark cloud began to form in the weathered face. "I've something that you might be interested in." He looked directly at Ben. "Real early yesterday morning, I was checking Sadie's raspberry bushes out back of her place when I heard what sounded like an argument. There were two guys standing over on the shoreline a ways down so I got as close to them as I could. Turns out, it was that smarmy real estate fellow, Harper, with Sadie's brother Raymond. It seems I caught them close to the end of a squabble and couldn't make out exactly what they were yelling about but Raymond had a face on him like a smacked arse."

Despite the possibly disconcerting news, I had to work to suppress a laugh at Marcel's description.

We all looked at Ben, whose own face had hardened. "I knew something was up with those two. Where, exactly, was this?"

"Two properties up from Sadie's place. You know that point of land the young couple from Toronto bought a couple of years ago? The one with the big fancy dock."

Ben was nodding. "You didn't catch any of what they were arguing about?"

"No, sorry lad, a generator started up close by and I couldn't hear anything after that. All I could see was Harper making chopping motions with his arms and Raymond throwing his hands up." We waited for the conclusion. "About a minute later they both got in their vehicles and left."

I reached over and put my hand on Ben's arm. "Do you think Raymond supplied Sadie's signature to Harper?"

Ben's look was piercing. "That's exactly what I think."

Colin was tapping his lips with his index finger. "What are the odds of connecting those two? You know, maybe with a payment or something?"

Pearl shook her head. "Nice thought, Honey, but they could just say that Raymond did some work for him - pretty hard to prove otherwise. Plus, he could have just paid him cash."

Marcel started handing out mugs of tea. Ben passed a bowl of powdered milk and after adding a spoonful I noticed that the colour had changed from deep black to charcoal grey. You could have used this stuff to fix potholes. Marcel was watching our faces. "That there tea has been good and stewed. I start fresh every Monday and just keep adding a new teabag each day. The tenants build up, you see and it kills any parasites you might have in you."

I assumed that 'tenants' meant 'tannins' and I hesitantly took a sip. Tremendous control was exercised in an effort stop my eyes from bugging out of my head. I think it would be an effective killer of a lot of things. Wow, his stomach must be cast iron to drink this stuff.

The pinging of my text messenger sounded so foreign it took us by surprise. I fumbled in my pocket and pulled out the phone. "It's from Maggie!"

Ben leaned in looking expectantly at me.

"She will be home in a couple of days, but in the meanwhile, she'll contact her assistant, Sylvia, and ask her to review all of the property purchases in this area in the past year and get a list of any being bought by the same company or people."

Ben's eyebrows lifted. "That seems like quite a huge task."

Colin was nodding. "And I'm sure Sylvia will enjoy the bottles of wine we'll pick up for her."

Pearl clapped her hands. "Yeah, another trip into town. I wonder if we'll have another James Bond adventure?"

Pearl's comment connected a few dots for me. "Marcel, did you see what kind of vehicles they were driving?"

Our host looked up, scanning the clouds, as if trying to gain a clearer picture of his memory. He was quiet as he scratched the back of his head and appeared distracted as he watched a bird riding the currents above him. We waited patiently.

"You know, the bush is pretty thick there so I couldn't get a good look, but, and I'm not sure about this, I think Raymond was in a white pickup. Harper's vehicle was parked on the other side of it so I never even got a glimpse."

Thoughts had been gliding and colliding around in my head and on impulse I threw out a question. "Marcel, do you know anything about poker games that go on in town?"

His head cocked to the side - the movement much like a rooster that's just spied a tasty bug. Squinty coal black eyes bored into me. "Well, lass, you might be the kind who likes a bit of cards, but I don't think that's why you're asking."

Marcel's gaze was steady as he searched my face.

Oh, I wish I had thought this through before saying anything. A feeling of being stalked left me with a shiver slinking up my spine. I was afraid we would lose this man's trust forever if he found out that we had been socializing with his half-brother.

I did a quick mental tap dance and hoped I could carry off the lie under the apparently all-seeing scrutiny. "Dad mentioned that there were some serious poker games that go on in town and I thought there might be some interesting stories about what happens." I leaned forward hoping to create the illusion of a conspiracy. "In fact, he hinted that some very well-connected players might indulge in some serious gambling."

Ben caught on. "Rumour is that some of the stakes are pretty high with cars, land and even businesses ending up in the pot."

Marcel's face slipped from hawkish to a scowl. "Well now, I do know that there are a few serious games that go on."

He waited for his quid pro quo, which Ben supplied. "Do you think that Harper is involved in any of these games? Could that be what they were arguing about?"

Marcel tapped his forehead. "Nah, Harper is sneaky, but he's not bright enough to play with the serious guys. And, I don't think he has the coin to keep up with them." His eyes were slits. "And that there Raymond, well, he's no better than a tick. I wouldn't trust him with the collection box in a church. And, he's as useless as tits on a bull." He nodded to Pearl then me. "Pardon the expression, ladies."

I might as well play my hand.

"So, Marcel, what do you know about Judge Jenkins?"

He waited me out.

"The thing is, he's the judge assigned to Ben's court case – the one where he's fighting the sale of Sadie's two properties." Marcel's eyes moved from mine to Ben's. Again, he waited until Ben filled him in on the details.

Our host nodded as if ending an internal debate. "Well now, lad, seeing as it's you, I'll tell you what I think." There was still some hesitation. "From what I hear, the judge is pretty fair when it comes to his courtroom." Again, he hesitated. "His shortcomings seem to lie with the ladies." We waited while his rheumy cough took over his story. He stood, leaned over the railing, and donated whatever his lungs had produced to the lake.

Sitting back in his chair he simply nodded and repeated, "Yep, with the ladies." His mouth twitched back and forth. "Well, more to the point, one certain lady - his wife."

Ben couldn't take it anymore. "Is there something we need to know about Judge Jenkin's wife? Or, is it that he likes to…" Ben paused, looking for the right term. "…step out on his wife."

"No, lad, nothing like that. She wears the trousers in that house. She'd flay him alive if he ever cheated on her." Marcel rumbled a chuckle. "No, she's the adventurous sort when it comes to investing.

141

Seems like he's had to clean up after her on a few occasions. You know, deals gone bad, that sort of thing."

Either the old duffer didn't know specifics or he was still being cagey and just shook his head. It dawned on me that he might think we were trying to get something on the judge to use against him and Marcel was making sure his name wouldn't come up. Innuendos can be serious game-changers, but you can't shackle someone on a bit of gossip with no details.

"Yup, that's all I know." Our host decided it was time to move the conversation onto other avenues. "I believe I met up with your Lucius just yesterday." He pointed to the tackle and nodded at Colin. "I had a good-sized pickerel on the line, a right big lad. He had put up quite a fight and I almost had him in the net when this gaping mouth comes from underneath the boat and grabs it. Just grabbed it in one bite, snapped the line and was gone. I was left holding an empty net and my line just a swingin'. Yup, it was your Lucius all right. Teeth a-gleamin', let me tell you, a right monster. That Jasper Lebeau fellow saw the whole thing. Don't think he'll be going for a dip any time soon."

There was a pause as we all scrambled to connect the name.

"You know, Sadie's trapline fellow." Marcel's upper lip was scrunched up near his nose. "I'm not sure about him. Carries on like he knows something no one else does." He gestured to the teapot. "Anyone for more tea?"

I wasn't sure about the rest of the group but my head was buzzing. Interesting bits of gossip but not really clear on where it fit into Ben's situation.

Pearl was subtly inclining her head towards our boat and her eyes were opened wide. She wiggled in her seat and nodded towards the boat again. Ben caught her look and rubbed his hands together.

"Well, Marcel, it looks like it's time for us to go – we have some work to get finished today and we'll probably have to make a run into town."

Colin held out his hand. "Is there something we can pick up for you, sir?"

Marcel's eyes moved around the circle, connecting with each of us. "That's right kind of you, lad, but I'll be going in myself in the next few days."

After we settled ourselves in the Elgin, Marcel pointed a gnarled finger at Ben. "You watch out, son. There are some nasty characters out there that you don't want to come up against if you don't have to." He was shaking his head as he untied our rope and tossed it to me. "Stay together and you should be fine."

Marcel pushed us off and nodded. "Yup, just stay together."

Chapter 37 – Lumbering Along

Returning to The Camp from our trip up the lake, we quickly threw together a picnic-style lunch and loaded up the canoe. While Ben and I paddled up the creek to the landing spot near the spring, Pearl and Colin walked the Trail. The portage to the truck was short and after lashing the canoe onto the roof racks, the four of us set off for Whitefish River.

We had hesitated before driving out of the bush and onto the highway making sure there were no vehicles in sight. Because the highway is lower than the forest and the shoulders are mostly rock and gravel, the track leading into the bush and up to the Trail is well hidden. Over the decades, we've managed to keep the entrance difficult to see which has kept most uninvited guests unaware of our little slice of heaven.

The highway was empty except for two motorcycles and the trip to Ben's cabin was quick. We parked his truck around the back of the building so it would be out of sight from the road. While Colin and Pearl carried the canoe down to the river, Ben and I tried looking for any signs that someone had been here. Nothing new appeared to be disturbed so we unchained Ben's canoe from underneath the lean-to and collected his paddles from the cabin.

My paddle dislodged a few stones as we pushed off the bank and the two canoes slipped into the river and caught the slow-moving current. A cool breeze had slipped in, and as Ben steered us into the middle of the creek, I took a moment to do up a couple of buttons on my red plaid jacket. Though the sun was shining somewhere above the clouds, it was unable to penetrate the overcast skies to supply any warmth.

With our paddles resting on the gunwales we let the world drift by, enjoying the ride. A dragonfly danced above the surface, going about its business. Mesmerized by its movements, I felt myself sliding into a peaceful existence where nothing outside of this space and time existed. A red-winged black bird added its song to the scene, deepening my connection. Making our way around a large bend, we startled a cow and a calf moose who had been feasting on the aquatic vegetation. The little fellow's head came up from his underwater foraging with a long piece of weed hanging from his ear. His mother stepped in front of him and with a graceful execution, herded her little one up the bank and into the woods. Words were redundant.

About half a kilometre down the river, creeping ever so slowly into our idyllic setting, came the sound of a chainsaw. As soon as I acknowledged it I was sucked out of my reverie. I looked behind at Ben who smiled, shrugged and dipped his paddle into the water.

The cooler day provided a comfortable temperature for our workout. As we rode the gentle current, our efforts at paddling were slow and easy. In the distance I was surprised to see the river almost doubling in width, then noticed The Whitefish was joined by another river of almost the same size.

Ben stopped paddling and motioned for Colin and Pearl to come closer. "That's the spot Marcel was talking about." He pointed towards a gleaming white bowrider parked beside a long, T-shaped dock. A boathouse, under construction, had the roof and two-thirds of the walls finished. Just up the hill from that was a beautiful stone home sporting enormous windows and a wrap-around deck. I wouldn't want to see the propane bill when the winter set in. Then again, if they could afford this, I'm sure their heating bill would not be an issue.

Colin whistled then added, "Nice digs. Who did Marcel say owned it?"

"It's a youngish couple from Toronto. I met them last year. They seemed pretty nice – if somewhat intense. Brokers or investors - money-people of some sort. Successful, by the look of it."

The sun found a little patch of cloudless sky and rays streaked into the gray day. Pearl shielded her eyes with her hand. "Do they live here year-round?"

"No, they fly up. That's why the dock is so big. They park their plane there as well."

Slow and easy paddling carried us serenely past the property. A tall cedar hedge defined the lot and just past that was a large pile of felled trees stacked like a cord of wood. The smell of freshly cut lumber was pervasive. Boulders had been moved and the land roughly levelled. The naked lot looked sad and out of place. A large orange backhoe stood as a sentinel to the carnage. Ben used his paddle as a rudder to take us closer to the shore. His forehead was crimped and he shook his head from side to side. "What the hell is this?"

Nobody had an answer.

He dug his paddle into the water and with a few swift strokes we passed the pile of trees and headed towards what I assumed was the next lot. The small cabin sat high above the water. Large slabs of stone were fashioned into a stairway leading down to a modest sized dock. I wasn't sure where we were going and Ben wasn't speaking so I let my paddle rest. A small log boathouse with a red garage door greeted us as Ben turned the canoe towards the dock.

"That dirty son of a bitch!" Ben pointed to the pile of trees. "Those are from Sadie's land."

Beaching the canoes, we climbed out. It wasn't until I was standing up that I noticed the stumps bristling the land. "Who do you think did this?"

"I'll lay odds it was Harper or whoever is behind the numbered company."

He did seem the most likely suspect considering he had signed documents for the purchase of the land.

"Because I'm contesting the sale, he has no right to touch anything." Ben strode over to a wooden box lying in the middle of the stumps. Squatting down I could see him shaking his head as he reached to pick up the box. As I moved in closer he held up a weathered bird house that looked to be in need of a few repairs. When he stood and turned, his mouth was set in a grim line. "I made this for Sadie when I was twelve.

We had nailed it to a tree..." He looked around then pointed to a large stump partway up the hill. "That tree." His snort was soft as his head dropped forward. "We watched a lot of sparrows fledge from this."

My instinct was to comfort him, but before I could move he stood up straight, tucked the birdhouse under his arm and carried it to the canoe where he stowed it in the bow. Reaching into the back pocket of his jeans he pulled out his phone. "I don't know if this will do any good but I'll call my lawyer." The phone was picked up quickly, and with a minimum of words he identified himself, explained the situation and what he wanted done, immediately. There was a pause as he listened then put the phone on speaker. As we moved towards Ben, we could hear cheesy elevator music that was apparently supposed to amuse or entertain the listener while on hold. It usually just annoyed.

"Mr. Brodan?" came the disembodied woman's voice. "I was able to contact Mr. Pachinski who advised me to put the paperwork together for you. I will have it done by noon tomorrow, but he said it would be a good idea to put a notice on the felled trees. Would you like me to help with the wording?"

Half of Ben's mouth turned up in a smile as he shook his head. "No, thank you. That won't be necessary. I'll be in tomorrow at 11:30. Will that give you enough time?"

There was a slight pause then the voice confirmed the appointment.

Ben returned the phone to his pocket. "I think what galls me the most is that I feel like someone keeps knocking my feet out from under me before I get a chance to take the next step. It's like I'm fighting a wraith or something invisible."

Pearl wandered over to the pile of trees about thirty metres away. We watched her looking around as she walked back. "I don't get it. Didn't Marcel say the couple was two lots over?"

Ben pointed to a surveyor's stake near the shoreline. "Sadie's lot ends there and the other lot ends at the cedar hedge."

"So some of the trees were from the middle lot." Pearl waved her hand in the direction of Sadie's denuded hill. Do you think whoever came to take the trees down got the instructions wrong and took out Sadie's trees by mistake."

Ben picked up a small limb and smacked it against his palm. "That's very generous of you, Pearl, but these were cut professionally and anyone who does this for a living doesn't make mistakes like that. They would lose their license and end up with huge legal battles." He looked at me and his lips formed a small circle. "Huh." Pointing to the pile of trees he continued, "I'll bet when we hear back from your aunt's assistant, we'll find that this property has been recently acquired. At least within the last year or two." He turned and stared up at Sadie's cabin on the hill.

"Kate, would you mind going back with Pearl and Colin? I'd like to spend the night here to make sure that if someone comes to collect the trees I'll find out who they are."

Colin raised his hand. "Hey, how about I stay with you. That way, when you find out who did this and have a chat with him, I can patch him up afterwards."

Before Ben could reply, a long, rolling rumble of thunder caught our attention. "Thanks, Colin, but I would prefer you stay with Kate and Pearl. I wouldn't be comfortable with them being on their own."

Normally, I would have been all over that with a lecture, complete with a good finger wagging, but I realized that Ben was just trying to look out for us and it wasn't a commentary on us being helpless females. One death was more than enough. So, I went easy on him.

We hadn't gotten to the terms-of-endearment stage in a relationship, but I felt something along those lines might help to ease the situation. "My dearest Ben, Pearl and I have been taking care of ourselves for a long time and we're pretty good at it. I think it would be a very good idea for Colin to stay – I know I would feel a whole lot better if there were two of you confronting whomever, rather than just one."

Ben was shaking his head so I continued. "It looks like a storm is moving in and there really isn't any time to debate this. Pearl and I will paddle back, take your truck, and if you give me directions, we'll drive back here tomorrow morning, bright and early with breakfast for you both." Before he could refuse I continued, "And, either we can all go into town or one or two of us can stay here if you think that would help. Your call."

Colin moved in and clasped Ben's shoulder. "Trust me, buddy, I know these two. They are quite capable of taking care of themselves. And, it'll give them some time to do whatever they do when we're not around." He pointed towards Sadie's cabin. "Is there somewhere for us to sleep in there."

"Yeah. I've stored most of her personal stuff but left the furniture because I wasn't sure what was happening with it. Sadie always kept a key hidden behind some chinking."

"Great, then let's get these girls off and we'll get ourselves settled in."

Pearl held up a hand. "Hey, you guys can have the picnic that we packed, complete with beer." She jogged back to the canoe and pulled out the repast. Handing it over to Colin, she completed the transaction with a torrid kiss. "Until the morning, mon amour."

Ben looked a little dazed. "It's not often I get filibustered. You guys are good!" His eyebrows arched as he looked at Pearl and Colin. Turning to me, he hesitated, shrugged, then walked over, put an arm behind my back and pulled me in close. "Are you sure you're okay with this? I have to say I have an uncomfortable feeling but what you all say makes sense and I don't want to offend you and your capabilities." His smile was sincere and his eyes questioning.

"Three against one – majority rules."

A second boom of thunder rolled across the sky, and with that, he bent and gave me a very good reason to come back tomorrow morning. Early.

Chapter 38 – Sting Ray

As gentle as the current was, paddling against it proved to be a good workout. Earning a living in renovations can be great for building and sustaining muscles, however, paddling a canoe is an entirely different beast. By the time we pulled the canoe out of the water at Ben's dock, mine were yelling, quite distinctly, at me. It felt like I had bowling balls hanging off my arms.

"Come on, Kate, don't tell me that little bit of exercise did you in."

"Hey, I don't see you moving any faster."

Pearl, always up for a challenge, looked wide-eyed at me, flipped the canoe and hoisted it over her head in one smooth move. "Do you think you can carry the back end?"

Herein lies the paradox. Even though we do the same work and she's built like a pixie, she constantly bests me in the strength department. Frustrating? Why, yes. However, working with someone who is so strong is of great benefit. I've learned to live with the shame.

We raised the canoe up over the cab of the truck lashing it to the padded rails and tailgate.

My arms returned to hanging uselessly at my side.

"Do you want me to drive?" Pearl held out her hand for the keys.

"Thank you, but I'm perfectly fine. Well, all except my arms." I moved closer to my partner. "Now if you would just be so kind as to liberate the keys from my pocket we can get going."

Pearl fished them out, grinned and opened the passenger's door for me. "Do you need help getting in?"

By this point my arms had recovered just enough strength for me not to humiliate myself completely. I chose to answer Pearl's question by climbing into the cab with as dignified an expression as I could muster. "Home, James."

Pulling onto the highway we hadn't travelled more than half a kilometre when we noticed a white truck parked on the shoulder with its hood up. Pearl slowed down as I lowered my window. A man was adding windshield washer fluid to the reservoir.

"Is everything okay?"

He tilted the container back as he looked up. His head slanted a bit to the side as his eyebrows pulled together. He looked at the truck then back and forth at the two of us. "Yeah, thanks." He put the cap back on the reservoir, reached up and pulled the hood down. "Ran out of juice and needed to clean the bugs off the windshield." Picking up the container cap he screwed it down as he moved around the front of his truck. He stopped beside my window and leaned in. I turned towards him hoping the movement would hide the fact that I was reaching down into the door pocket. I let my hand rest on the heavy Maglight.

He was younger than I first thought – maybe in his early forties, with wispy strands of hair hanging out from under his ball cap. His eyes, the shade of a faded sky-blue, kept moving between Pearl and me. He wasn't quite as tall as the cab of the truck and looked like he enjoyed his meals and beer. A good-sized belly poked at his shirt. My father would have politely called it 'Molson Muscle,' while most would label it a beer gut. "So where are you girls headed?"

I tightened the grip on the flashlight. "Down the highway."

Noticing my tone, he held up his hands in a surrender gesture. "Hey, no need to snap...just being friendly." He lowered his hand on the side mirror. "I thought I recognized the truck – belongs to a friend of mine." As he leaned in closer I could smell the beer he had recently consumed.

"Really." Seeing as about half of the vehicles in Timmins are trucks this was sounding more and more like a fishing expedition. Okay, I'll play along – for now. "So who's your friend?"

"An old school mate." His left hand had migrated to the door frame.

"And his name would be...?"

"Hey, not important, if this is your truck." He paused looking up and down the highway. Pearl moved her hand to rest on the gear shift.

Noticing the movement, he tried laying on some charm. "My apologies, ladies. My name is Ray. And you are…?"

Pearl slipped the truck into gear. "Well Ray, as long as everything is okay, we'll be going."

"Hey, don't be like that. I know of a party not far from here. I have lots of beer and a few pharmaceuticals – we could have a good time."

I heard Pearl stifle a gag.

I put on my thoughtful face. "Well, Ray, as tempting as that offer is, we'll pass."

He was not to be deterred. "You girls aren't from around here, are you? 'Cause if you were, you'd know I'm a good time. How about giving me your names or phone number so I can call you. You know, in case you get lonely." Feeling his hand sliding down the back of my arm I quickly reached around, grabbed his thumb and yanked it back until his curses filled the cab.

I lifted the Maglight and waved it in front of his face. "Now Ray, that wasn't a respectful thing to do, was it?" I maintained my grip and pressed his thumb back just a little further.

"Son of a bitch that hurts! Stop! I was just being friendly! Fuckin' stop!"

"Are you sorry?"

"Yes, fuck yes, I'm sorry."

"And you promise to never, ever do that again?" I may have been enjoying this just a bit too much.

His voice had risen half an octave. "No, never again."

"Good man."

Pearl started pulling away before I released his thumb. I found it difficult to believe his promise to me as he hurled obscenities at us with further promises to make me regret having done that.

"Ray?" Pearl scratched the side of her nose. "You don't think that's Sadie's brother, Raymond, do you?"

I thought about the coincidence. "Do you think he was the one following us in the SUV?"

"Could be, though I'm not sure why." Pearl looked over at me before flooring the truck. "It doesn't look like he's following us, but let's just put a bit of distance between us. I don't want to have to deal with an uninvited visitor in the middle of the night."

*****

The thump was muffled, but loud enough to pull me out of my dream. I stayed as still as I could, waiting for the next sound. A minute passed before a scraping noise made me sit up. Someone was on the deck. Had I locked the door?

I swung my legs out of bed and slipped my feet into my sandals. I wanted to peek through the curtains to see if it was Pearl but a mental flash of someone staring back at me from the other side of the window stopped me. If whoever was out there saw me, then the element of me surprising him would be lost. I couldn't call Pearl because our phones didn't work, and even if they had, we both put ours on silent during the night.

I hadn't heard the latch on the door and the well-oiled hinges were not going to reveal any movement. I slipped over and pressed my ear to the bedroom door. Nothing.

I thought of the .22 rifle in the wardrobe but couldn't remember where Dad said he had put the bullets and could I really point a gun at someone? Instead, the Maglight felt substantial and comforting in my hand. I waited for further sounds before opening the bedroom door.

A faint rustling was coming from the other side of the window. Do I go out or wait? The not knowing and inactivity were gnawing at my nerves. We all have our strengths and weaknesses – for me, when the sun goes down, I grow feathers and cluck. It's not the dark I'm afraid of, it's my rampant imagination. It takes me into a labyrinth of possibilities - some realistic, some - not so much. My creativity was feasting on fear – and a fine buffet it was serving.

The sound of scratching liberated my inactivity. The corner of the bedroom door sticks, and I knew I wouldn't be able to open it without making a sound, so I decided to fling it open and jump into the main cabin swinging. If I was going out - I wasn't doing it quietly.

My scream was a cross between a Highland clansman charging into battle and a maniacal, little girl squeal. A detached region in my brain made a mental note to work on my sound effects.

The room was quiet and I immediately saw the hook latch on the door was in place.

Pearl! What if he grabbed her?

Bounding out onto the deck I yelled for my friend. "Pearl! Pearl! Watch out!"

I didn't see anyone on the lake-side so I jumped off the other side of the deck to make sure whomever it was didn't just slip away down the Trail. I was now pumped and primed for action. Screw being scared – I was going to deal with this guy. I rounded the corner at the back just as Pearl burst onto her deck wielding a crow bar. "What? Who? What is it?"

"Someone was on the deck."

We both scanned the area and I finally turned the flashlight on, sweeping it back and forth until the beam caught a movement. I processed Pearl's laughter at about the same time that I identified the culprit. Or, in this case, culprits. The black and white warning flag of mama skunk's tail led the family of four's procession back into the dense undergrowth.

Pearl came over and wrapped her arm around my shoulders. "Come on, Kate, my dear, let's get you a nice big drink."

Chapter 39 – To Judge or Not to Judge

Colin lifted Pearl up off the deck of Sadie's cabin. "Woman, I'm grateful to see that thermos, which I'm assuming holds the most delicious coffee ever made; but nowhere near as grateful as seeing you!" He demonstrated his appreciation by pulling her in tightly and kissing her forehead.

There was an awkward pause as Ben and I each tried to figure out what an appropriate greeting for us would be. He broke the tension as he leaned over, took my hand then pulled me into a hug. Leaning back, he held my shoulders as his eyes searched mine. "I have to be honest, I was not happy to see you two go. Despite Colin's assurances, I was still worried." He exhaled his angst as he pulled me in again. "I never would have forgiven mys…"

The rest of his words were silenced as I pulled his head down and blocked their exit with my lips. His arms slipped back into an embrace.

Colin whispered in our ears, "When you two come up for air, how about you tell us about last night's escapades. Where you and Pearl are involved, there's always the opportunity to make an adventure out of the mundane."

Pearl and I had discussed how best to fill the boys in and not have them go all Rambo on Raymond's butt. We decided to put a positive spin on it. Pearl started. "Well, we now have a little more information."

The guys waited.

"We're pretty sure Raymond and Harper are in this together and Raymond is acting as reconnaissance."

I jumped in. "And, he's not very good at it. In fact, he was pathetic."

Eyebrows were raised and waiting.

As we recapped the events on the highway, I watched their faces. Colin maintained what most would call a poker face however I noticed his breath getting deeper, involving his entire chest. Ben leaned forward and his eyes narrowed. Without a pause I swung directly from our truck adventure into the night's action, not allowing them to dwell on Raymond. By the end, they were both shaking their heads though Ben's eyes searched my face. He was processing. I pressed on. "Look, we don't have anything that anyone would want – no one gains from our demise. We don't have information, land, gold… we're just visiting."

Ben shook his head. "That's not true. Whoever murdered Sadie is obviously either desperate or insane – most likely both. I've brought you all into this, and he or they have no idea what your role is. You could be collateral damage." Ben held his hand up as I started to protest. "There's gold, land, development, lumber… take your pick. Sadie's death was not random. It was premeditated. That, to me, says psychopath."

Pearl came over and put her hand on Ben's shoulder. "Yes, you may be right, or it may be someone who got caught up and went too far. Maybe they were pushed. But, more importantly, right now, is finding out as much information as possible so that we're armed and ready." Out of her backpack, she pulled a sleeve of bagels that we had generously slathered with cream cheese and bacon jelly. "Neither of you look like you got much sleep last night so eat up, have some coffee and let's go into town."

I poured two cups from the thermos. "We thought we would hit the laundromat first."

*****

There was no white SUV nor was there a white truck skulking at the side of the highway and our drive into town was completed in quiet conversation. Our description of Ray left little doubt in Ben's mind that he was, in fact, Sadie's younger brother.

Linens, towels, clothes all got sorted into washing machines. Colin and Ben stayed behind to oversee the laundry, while Pearl and I dropped in on one of my cousins for a quick hello. A visit with Rachel is always a good time and today's was no exception. The unfortunate part was that it was so short. As we were getting ready to leave, Rachel's sister Brenda stopped by. I texted Ben and Colin to let them know that we would be a little late picking them up. Ben had already left for his appointment with the lawyer and Colin had discovered a used bookstore in the neighbourhood so he was quite content to hang there for a while.

I vaguely remembered Dad saying something about Brenda working in the court system so thought I would try to garner any information I could. "So, Brenda, how's work?"

"Work itself is pretty mundane. The people, however, are much more interesting."

"How's that"

"Well, it's not just the crazy things that people think are okay to do, but some of the cases that come up are wild." She tipped the coffee pot on our direction and we offered up our cups for refills.

She regaled us with stories of court cases until I asked her about the people she worked with. There was a hesitation. Rachel tapped her finger on the table. "Now there's a good story." She looked at her sister and continued. "Tell them what you heard."

Brenda's face scrunched in denial but her body was wiggling as if the story was fighting her to gain entrance to our group. She looked back and forth between Pearl and me. Story finally broke free. "Since you two don't know anybody involved, I guess it's okay to tell you." Her eyes got big as she took a breath then expelled it. "So, I'm walking past the judge's chambers when I heard a tinkling of something and a really low moan. Then there was some more moaning but this was high pitched and … almost frantic like. Because it was the judge's chambers, we never just go in, but I thought everyone had left for the day and the sounds were so… I don't know, … insistent? that I just went in."

My cousin stopped to take a sip of her coffee then paused as she made a face, added more creamer then tried another sip. I realized that all my muscles had tightened, including my butt cheeks, which were clenched and caused me to rise up and forward on my seat. My hands were stretched out, ready to rip the rest of the story out of her.

Rachel read the room and jumped in, her beautifully huge eyes were impossibly larger than ever. "Apparently, there's something that couples do with ice cubes, brandy, cocaine and a lighter, that blows all orgasms out of the water; and these two were trying it out." She shrugged and waved a dismissive hand. "Sounds too complicated for me – I prefer the old-fashioned way." Her sister nodded.

Pearl's face had assumed a confused or maybe thoughtful expression as she tried to put the pieces together. "Nope, sorry, just can't put those together and have it come out as anything I'd want to try." She looked hopefully at Brenda. "So what happened and who were they?"

"None other than the Judge's wife and one of the female guards from the jail."

"Wow." Pearl's hand covered her mouth then she pointed a finger towards the ceiling. "That wouldn't happen to be Judge Jenkins' wife, would it?"

My cousins looked at each other with surprised expressions.

I quickly added, "Hey, don't worry, we won't tell anybody. In fact, it just adds to the story we already heard about him."

Expressions changed from concern to inquisitive and the bottle of Irish Cream whiskey came out and was poured liberally into our cups.

Hoping to have Marcel's gossip about the Judge and his wife's shady business deals at least confirmed and at best, added to, I told them what we had heard.

Rachel jumped in like a rabbit into a garden. "It's true. I have a friend, Dave, who lost a hell of a lot of money on one of the Judge's wife's schemes. He was threatening to go public with it but then just backed right down."

Her sister took up the story. "Yeah. Dave was really pissed but then, he got real quiet. It wasn't until his wife and I were out for lunch that I heard he had won a court case against another company that made me put two and two together. I mean, the other guy had Dave dead-to-rights in a traffic incident then, poof, all of a sudden the judgement went in Dave's favour." Brenda pointed at her sister. "We've discussed it a lot and asked around. It seems that the Judge has used his position to bail his wife out on a few occasions."

As we said our goodbyes, my mind was trying to pull all the information together but there were still a few empty ports.

Chapter 40 – Fries, Phones and Friends

The shoestring fries with gravy did not disappoint. Every time my family came on holiday it was a mandatory and much-anticipated experience to have at least one visit to the Shanghai Dragon Restaurant. I don't think the menu had changed in all that time, nor had the dishes. For a paltry sum, thin french fries came loaded on an oblong plate with dragons guarding the edges. I preferred my gastronomic experience to have only half of the fries covered in gravy with the other half naked and ready for vinegar and a little extra salt. I'm a woman of simple tastes.

Ben stabbed a forkful of his fries, savoured the first bite then gave us a brief overview of his conversation with the lawyer. "I need to file a complaint with the police. Apparently, there have been a few instances of trees being logged on lots that are either empty or the owners don't maintain a permanent residence. The police are being more vigilant about checking the logging trucks but so far they haven't found any discrepancies."

Colin added a dollop of ketchup to the corner of his plate. "How about mills? Have they checked them?"

"It's too dicey for one of the legit mills to take stolen trees. There's probably a way to do it but it's not worth the risk. There are portable mills around and they can set up just about anywhere."

I pulled out my phone, searched for portable lumber mills and we all watched a demonstration on how they worked. "Well, that's cool… but it makes finding the stolen lumber a tad more difficult."

"Pretty much." Ben ran the straw around the inside edge of his glass. "And, maybe they're using it to build a log house or whatever. They may not be turning it into two by fours. If they have someplace to pile it – they can sit on it for a long time."

Pearl ran her napkin around her mouth catching a stray bit of gravy. "Did you go to the police?"

"Because there's a dispute on who owns the property, I let them know what happened but it's kind of just sitting in limbo. They said they would go out and ask around to see if anyone saw anything."

Colin scratched his newly stubbled jaw. "So, it may not have been Sterling or Ray if there've been other thefts."

Ben shook his head. "Maybe not. Or maybe they know about these other thefts and are using that to hide their own illegal logging operations. Ray does seem to have an unexplained source of income."

My phone pinged and I looked at it like it was a foreign object. Flipping it over I saw my aunt's office had sent a text. I read it to the group. "Numbered company bought land between Sadie's and the Miletelo's." I looked up at Ben. "Do you think they are the couple from Toronto with the big place?"

"Most likely. I don't recall for sure, but that sounds like the name Sadie mentioned. The Bensons, then the Turcots are on the other side so it's got to be them."

I read on. "The Bensons sold to the same company last January. Will look further into who owns company."

Ben leaned back and stared up at the ceiling. "So someone's buying up the land. Can you ask Sylvia if those properties came with mineral rights?"

I tapped in my thanks to my aunt's assistant then asked if she could find out who owned the mineral rights. Within minutes her answer came back. 'All of the deeds come with them.'

Colin looked around the table. "Well, doesn't that thicken the plot? And, it makes Sadie's land even more valuable."

Ben pinched the bridge of his nose. "We're still no closer to discovering who's behind this and what it's about. We've now added another layer. I was thinking it could have been about the gold that people thought Sadie had stashed but it's looking like the mineral rights are a possibility, as well as land development, logging... who knows. It sure would be helpful if I knew who I was fighting, and why."

Ben's pocket started ringing. He pulled out his phone, looked at the display and smiled. "Well, this could be good - it's Etienne."

We were riveted watching Ben's face for any indication of what was being said. For the first minute, "Umms," "uh hus," and "hmms" were all we had to go on then Ben held the phone to his chest as he addressed us. "So, Etienne is inviting us out to his place. When can he expect us?"

We settled on as soon as we could drive there. We're flexible like that. And excited.

*****

Etienne's greeting was warm and welcoming. We were sitting once again on his patio enjoying iced tea and an assortment of cookies. Resting his elbows on the arms of his chair, he steepled his fingers and tapped his chin with the tips. "I managed to engage a few people in the matter of this real estate fellow, Sterling Harper. He doesn't have the most 'sterling' reputation, however, no one actually said what he has done, they just more or less alluded to pressure tactics and not necessarily having the client's best interests in mind."

Ben leaned forward. "So other people are questioning his ethics?"

"Ethics, tactics, the company he keeps... it appears that some consider him to be a bit of a pariah, though it hasn't stopped some people from dealing with him."

We looked at Ben, who waited for Etienne to get to the good part.

Colin couldn't wait. "Does this mean that there's a connection to Judge Jenkins?"

Etienne smiled. "Once removed."

Ben cocked his head slightly. "Through his wife?"

"Yes, through his wife, Paula. But there's more." Etienne sounded like a hawker on an infomercial. "It turns out that Paula and Harper's girlfriend, Ginny, are best friends."

Ben drummed his fingers on his leg. "So we've got the Judge who, it appears, can be bribed or coerced, his wife who has not only bad business sense but has no problem with questionable business activities, and an unscrupulous real estate salesman who's girlfriend probably has a part in all of this." Ben shook his head. "Wow, that's some wall to come up against."

Colin shook his head. "Ah, now, I wonder if we could look at it another way." He smiled at Ben. "They may be in cahoots and appear to have some power, but that just means that all we have to do is get the goods on one of them and the rest will fall."

Etienne shrugged. "True, but from what I've heard, the women are close - I mean, really close." He had emphasized 'really.'

Remembering the story about the judge's wife and the female jail guard I caught the inference and, by the looks on the rest of the faces, they did as well.

Pearl gave a little chuckle. "I just love small town intrigue. We have this idealized version of how clean and unblemished life is out of the big, bad city, but people are people – no matter what their numbers."

Colin leaned over and gave Pearl a kiss on her forehead. "Ah, my darling pragmatist." He turned back to the rest of us. "And, being people, we love a juicy bit of intrigue."

Pearl drained her iced tea then ran a finger in the condensation on the glass. "It's all good information – I'm just not sure what we can do with it. Even if we could prove they were doing something illegal – are they really tied into Sadie's death?"

I reached over and laid my hand on Ben's arm. "If nothing else, maybe we could stop the sale of her property." The action was not lost on Etienne and he looked back and forth between Ben and me. A slight smile softened his eyes.

Chapter 41 – Trust

Ben sat on the dock, his legs dangling over the edge. He swished his feet rhythmically but his attention was somewhere off in the distance. His arms were stretched out, slightly forward from his broad shoulders. The late afternoon sun cast red highlights as it caught in his dark curls. Had it only been slightly more than a week since we'd met? I imagined the intensity of all that had taken place made it feel more like months. There was still so much I didn't know about this man, but that didn't seem to matter. I had seen him in circumstances that would have crumpled most people, yet he'd held his own and tried to make sure that we were okay as well. I felt a slight pressure somewhere in the region of my heart.

I walked the length of the dock and stood behind him. He looked up and smiled then shifted over to make room for me. Joining him, I looked out to where I thought he had been staring. "Were you thoughtful-gazing or is there something out there I'm not seeing."

He reached over and took my hand. His face looked solemn but his eyes had a depth to them that drew me in.

"Kate, I have a rather large favour to ask of you." He shifted his hips and turned further towards me. "Should something happen to me," his free hand gently pressed my lips as I started to protest. He smiled and continued. "Please, this is important and I need to make sure everything will be okay."

He waited until I nodded then he removed his fingers from my lips. "Should something happen to me, do you think you would be able to sell the gold and make sure that Marcel and Etienne get the money?

And, if you can't, then I think it would be best to just divide up the gold, as best you can, and give it to them. They'll have to figure out what to do with it." He took a deep breath and held it for a few seconds as he scanned my face.

My first instinct was to assure him that he would be around for a long time to come but his eyes were intense and I knew he wasn't willing to accept banal proclamations.

"Of course." I looked over to the far shore then back into his dark chocolate brown eyes. "If the three of us put our heads together, I'm sure we'll figure out something."

His eyes narrowed a bit more. "You are absolutely not to put yourself in jeopardy or take unnecessary chances. It's just that you seem to be well connected in this town, and if you can't dispose of it here, then maybe you could in B. C."

I squeezed his hand and nodded. "Don't worry, whatever needs to be done, will be done."

Chapter 42 – A Reprieve

Ben's back arched when the water-logged sponge ball splatted him squarely between his shoulder blades. The splash-zone extended to cover me as well.

Making the transition from a deep, serious discussion to a water-bomb attack took just a few seconds and we both scrambled to our feet as the next volley assailed us. In one smooth move, Ben snatched one of the balls from just in front of us and lobbed it back towards Colin. The good doctor had outfitted himself with a khaki-coloured pith helmet and he carried a large pot lid like a shield. There wasn't much water left in the sponge ball, but you could still hear the smack of it hitting the metal lid.

Three more balls appeared in quick succession from behind the birch tree. They had us pinned on the dock. Ben hid his mouth behind his hand and whispered. "Do we make a run for it through the shallows or beg for mercy."

My response was a yelled, "You will never take us alive. We will inflict untold damage onto your troops and your town." We leapt onto the shore and made for the tool shed as we dodged more balls. I had seen a couple of giant water guns underneath the bench and thought if we could fill them we'd have a fighting chance.

I pointed to the tool shed and Ben held up three balls that he had collected and he pointed to the outhouse. He was going to re-load them with the water from the bucket. I slipped into the tool shed and grabbed the super-soakers. Peering out the window I couldn't find any sign of the opposing army. They had us pinned down so they must be waiting for us to stick our heads out.

I was surprised to hear Ben whispering through the cracks between the logs at the back of the shed. "They're crouched down beside the birch tree on the far side of the deck. If we go either way they have us, so how about I take the water bucket, climb up the ladder to the roof? We can either wait for them to come and find us, or you can act as a decoy to draw them out."

"Devious. I like that. I'll cut across the blueberry patch and head down the trail. That should give you enough time to get on the roof. If I can, I'll slip down to the water and fill up the guns."

Ben lobbed a chunk of wood to the left to distract them while I slipped out of the shed and moved in the opposite direction. My screams filled the air as I headed for the trail but they were short lived as a water-logged ball made a direct hit to the back of my head. I stumbled but managed to get my feet under me again. I stopped long enough to retrieve the ball then made for the cover of the trees.

All was quiet. After slipping down to the water and filling the guns, I crouched on the side of the hill and waited for any further sounds. Suddenly, the howl of a bugle filled the air and I realized that Colin must have hooked up his phone with its sound effects to the Bluetooth speaker. He and Pearl yelled, "Charge." and I could hear them running around to the back of the cabin.

Their "charge" turned into a howl as I heard Ben yell, "Take that you vile beasts."

Scrambling up the bank I ran the twenty feet down the trail and broke out into the open. Ben had scored a direct hit from the roof and Colin and Pearl were drenched. I aimed the water gun and yelled, "Surrender, or die."

"Never!"

They took off around the corner of the cabin. I didn't have to guess where they were as I just looked up at Ben and he pointed to them hunkered down beside the boat. I left the second gun for Ben then took off to the right, while he shimmied down the ladder, grabbed the gun and made for the left. We had them cornered. We slipped as quietly as we could towards the boat. When we were in range, we opened fire.

With one final act of bravado, Colin yelled, "You'll never take us alive." And with that, he and Pearl turned, jumped onto the little dock then into the water.

Ben and I nodded our congratulations to each other, high-fived then dropped our guns and joined our friends in the lake for a game of Shoulder Soldier or, as Ben called it, Chicken Fight.

The shrieks and laughter were the perfect antidote to the situation in which Ben was mired.

Chapter 43 – Bearly Done

The alfresco supper was a simple affair of salad and cold cuts, topped off with ice cream sandwiches. Grey clouds had rolled in and the early evening's light was unable to penetrate them with any great effect. Colin was licking his fingers when he stopped and looked at his arm. He smacked the mosquito that had chosen to feast on him then swatted at the back of his neck. "Hey, where did these come from?"

Pearl slapped the side of my leg and dispatched another of the little blighters. "We've been really lucky so far on this trip but there seems to be a late crop of the little blood suckers this evening." We grabbed the dishes off the picnic table and moved indoors.

The boys offered to wash up while Pearl and I looked through the games cupboard for our evening's entertainment. A sharp snap and a yelled, "Scored" pulled me away from the piles of games. Colin had the tea towel stretched taut between his hands, while his head swivelled as he followed the buzzing of another mosquito. We watched as he flicked the towel in midair. "Don't know if I got her – but if not, she'll have a hell of a headache."

I turned back to the cupboard and pulled out the box of mosquito repellent coils. Slipping one out of its sleeve, I speared the slit in the centre with the metal holder, placed it on a tin foil pie plate and grabbed a match from the holder behind the stove. The end of the coil lit easily and all kitchen production stopped as we stood and watched the smoke swirl upwards. There was a tiny little tick sound as the first casualty fell onto the table. It was a few more moments before she was

169

joined by others of her ilk and a small, scattered graveyard began to appear on top of the red-checkered vinyl tablecloth. It was quite a thirsty little crowd that had followed us into the cabin. They may have flown in but they were going out in a puff of smoke. Pearl used a paper towel to clear the corpses and tossed them into the wood stove. Satisfied that the coil was doing its job, we returned to our tasks with the long-remembered odour of the pyrethrum wafting throughout the room.

Deliberations over which game we would play ensued. Pearl was confirming that all the marbles to the Aggravation board were in the bag while I pulled out the Risk game.

Ben's finger-snapping got our attention. "Hey, I have a great game back at my cabin. Have any of you played Hotels?"

Colin's eyes were mischievous as he wiggled his dark red eyebrows. "No, but I've definitely played *in* hotels."

Pearl's punch to his arm was gentle. "Perv."

"It's still early and I need to go and grab some clothes and stuff – I'll just make a quick run over there now." Ben's eyes were intense as he looked over at me. "Does anyone want to come along for the ride?"

Pearl quickly wrapped her arm around Colin's waist and kissed him, muffling his "Sure, …" into a half-spoken response. He looked up and smiled. "On second thought, Pearl and I will stay here and finish cleaning up."

*****

Because of its latitude, evening in the north remains surprisingly bright, however the increased cloud cover dampened the sun's enthusiasm. I grabbed two flashlights for the return trip through the more dense areas of the trail. We pulled hoodies on then sprayed each other down with insect repellent.

Ben stepped up to the large window beside the sink and looked in the direction of his cabin. "Those clouds look rather ominous. I'm pretty sure everything's shut up tight but I'm glad we're headed over there. I want to make sure that the trough into the rain barrel isn't plugged with debris. It's been such a dry summer – I want to catch all of the rainwater that I can."

Pearl's voice was half an octave higher than normal. "So, will you two be gone long?"

Ben did a fairly good job of looking innocent. "I might have to do a bit of searching, and... there may be a few other things to take care of…" His hand cupped my shoulder and he rubbed his thumb ever so gently on my neck causing a shiver of delight to tango down my spine.

I looked up into Ben's delicious mocha-coloured eyes. "Yeah, it may take a while."

*****

Halfway to Ben's cabin, the heavens did their best to cleanse the earth's stratosphere with a spectacular downpour. Not being able to see past the truck's front bumper, we ended up pulling off onto the shoulder of the highway and sitting until the worst of it passed. The defroster in Ben's truck struggled to banish the condensation but was losing the battle. Accompanying the moisture-burdened air was a distinct sexual tension. There was no doubt that Ben and I were incredibly attracted to each other – we'd just never had the discussion. You know, the one about what was important to us or what our boundaries were, but it was difficult to keep focused on that when my thoughts kept zeroing in on his lips and their talents. Okay, not just his lips… let's be honest, it was the whole deal. You can have the most amazing body, looks, sensuality, but if you don't have the personality and honesty to go with it, well then, my friend, you're just eye candy that ain't getting' ya nowhere.

I was halfway through turning to look at him when a wickedly intense bolt of lightning struck a tall pine just off to our right. My intended conversation was replaced with a surprised yell as I jumped in response to the shocking thunderous crack. When I turned back to Ben, his eyes were open wide like an owl's and, "Wow, awesome!" was his only comment.

We watched as one side of the pine tree appeared to fall away in slow motion, the branches quivered as the partial trunk bounced on the ground.

I wiped the window with my sleeve to get a better view. "Now that's something you don't see every day!"

"Nope."

We looked at each other and started to laugh. Ben reached over and took my hand, gently squeezing it. "This is quite the summer for excitement!"

He turned back to the windshield and leaned forward to get a better view of the sky. "That strike seems to have signaled the ending of the storm." The rain had downgraded to a soft drizzle and the atmosphere in the cab had also lightened. Ben put the truck back into gear and we resumed our drive.

By the time we reached his cabin the rain had stopped and we navigated around the puddles, and parked beside the small deck. Stepping out of the truck, we both paused to enjoy the ozone-fresh smell. Mother Nature knows how to do a deep cleanse.

Ben opened the cabin and flicked on the lights. The room appeared undisturbed from our last visit. Moving towards the bedroom, he stopped in his tracks and looked down. I stepped around the table so I could see what had caught his attention. A small puddle had formed on the vinyl flooring. Ben had moved to the side and was looking around the floor then up at the ceiling. Pinpoints of soft evening light shone through the pine boards.

"What's going on up there?" Turning he strode out of the cabin and I followed. We rounded the back of the cabin and Ben unchained a ladder. I held it steady while he climbed onto the roof. "Wow. Now that's determined!"

Looking over the edge of the roof he was shaking his head. "A bear tried to get in through the roof! You can see the claw marks in the tarpaper around the hole."

"How the hell did he get up on the roof?"

Ben pointed to a spruce tree whose limbs overhung the cabin. "Probably that way."

As I waited for him to collect the necessary supplies to temporarily patch the hole, I scanned the log walls of the cabin and noticed the distinctive claw marks under two of the windows. "Looks like it tried the windows first. Good thing they're metal."

We grabbed the bucket of tar and tarpaper out of the shed and dropped them by the ladder. Ben returned to get the rest and I started up the ladder with the bucket.

"Hey, I'll get that."

I looked down, smiled and winked as Ben reached out to take the handle of the bucket. "It's okay. I've done this a few times."

His laugh was warm as he shook his head. "Sorry, I forgot."

"If you'll notice, I left the tarpaper for you to wrangle up."

By the time we had patched the roof the light was fading and the temperature had dropped significantly. Clouds were rolling in from the east and the smaller trees were dancing as the wind picked up speed.

After everything was put away in the toolshed, Ben's arm snuggled me into his side as we stood back to admire our handy work. "You were amazing. I'd still be struggling with that if you hadn't been here."

His eyes closed for a moment then he turned to face me. My heart gave a little stammer as he cupped my cheek. "Wow. You know, ever since I met you… I can't imagine where I'd be if it wasn't for you. I'm… I'm not used to being so indebted." Once again he put his finger over my lips when I started to disagree. "No, Kate, you have to understand how much you've affected my life. I'm a pretty independent fellow, but, hmm, you keep being there for me. And, there's another aspect. You, well, you make everything so comfortable." He shook his head. "Comfortable isn't the right word but I don't know how else to say it. Being around you… I don't want to think about what it will be like when you leave."

What could I say? I didn't want to dwell on that either. I felt my mouth turn up at the corners. "But right now, I'm here."

His lips tasted of sweet promises, while his sighs spoke of adventures.

The muffled thump of something landing on the deck pulled us back into the here and now. The snuffling noises left us with no doubt that the bear had returned. Ben grabbed my hand and we carefully moved the short distance to the passenger side of the truck. The startled bear raised his snout, found us and huffed. He hesitated for an instant then stood on his hind legs. Ben shoved me into the cab and scrambled in after me. I slid behind the wheel as he pulled the keys from his pocket. He reached over and leaned on the horn. The bear dropped back down and snapped his jaws, slowly turned and ambled away.

My mouth hung open. Not pretty but honest. "Did you see the size of that beast? He was enormous!"

"The top of that window is six feet high and he was taller than it!"

"Wow! They grow them big in these parts. Big and freakin' terrifying!" I turned and looked at Ben. "And, the next time we go into town I'm picking you up a case of bear spray. You need to have cans everywhere!"

I held out my hand for the keys. "I don't feel like getting out of the truck right now. How about I drive back."

Ben dropped the keys in my hand and laughed. "Walking through the trail should be interesting tonight."

"I plan on singing and making noise the whole way. I think surprising one bear is quite enough for one night!"

Chapter 44 – Well, Son of a B

A chime came from the vicinity of Ben's hip. "Oh!" Ben laughed and reached around to his back pocket, pulling out his phone. Reading the text, he made a small exasperated sound.

The rain had returned with a vengeance and I drove slowly as I tried to identify the difference between lane and shoulder. I waited for him to fill me in on the text message.

I couldn't remember ever hearing Ben swear but there was a distinct muttering that sounded like "… son of a bitch."

Again, I waited. This being patient thing is annoying.

Ben flipped his phone over and slapped it down onto his thigh. He took a deep breath as if he were about to take an extended dive then flipped his phone back to reread the text.

The windshield wipers were whacking furiously trying to keep up with the assault.

I didn't want to enquire in case it was personal, or more specifically, not my business.

"Well, this shouldn't have surprised me."

I waited. Again, with the patience thing.

He sighed and lifted his phone in the air. He jiggled it lightly as if to either shake the text out or perhaps give the sender a physical message.

"Harper."

Well, that explained the wanting-to-throttle mime.

"He's saying that if I don't contest the sale of Sadie's property, he says the buyer is willing to cancel the contract for the sale of my place.

And, I've got twenty-four hours to decide. He's offering to meet me tomorrow night."

"Wow. That's a big decision to make in such a short time." I turned down the wipers in response to the softening of the rain. Ben's breathing seemed to slow as well.

There was a small buzzing from my pocket. I pulled out my phone, pressed my finger to the scanner for fingerprint recognition and passed it to Ben to read.

"Well now, isn't this interesting." His hand touched my shoulder. "It's from your aunt's assistant. She says that they tracked down the principals in the numbered company that bought the properties on either side of Sadie's. It took a bit of digging because the names were buried in a web of multiple developers, which ultimately are all connected to a business called Fantasy Vacations of the North. She said they were trying very hard to remain anonymous – but that just made it more fun to flush them out."

I snuck a quick look at Ben's face. A smile touched his lips so quickly that I almost missed it before his forehead became furrowed.

This time I distinctly heard the "son of a bitch."

I wanted to pull the truck over so I could read the message myself but we were in the area where the road was flanked by steep rocks and very little shoulder.

"What?"

"The Miletelos, you remember the ones with the huge place just before Sadie's? Well, they are part of the group." He stopped, sighed and I waited.

Boy, getting the information from Ben was like pulling a moose out of quicksand. "And?"

"Sorry! I'm just trying to put it all together. It turns out that a Paula Jenkins, Ginny Folkman and the Miletelos all have stakes in the various development groups. And, no surprise here, Sterling Harper was the real estate agent on those purchases." He kept scrolling through the text. "There are two other people mentioned but I don't recognize their names."

I made the turnoff onto the road leading to the Trail and as I navigated the short, narrow dirt road into the woods, I was glad we were in a truck as the huge puddle in the middle of the road would have sunk a lower vehicle.

The rain had finally subsided but the clouds still looked weighted down and ready to burst once more. We walked as quickly as we could down the Trail hoping to not get caught in another deluge. The beam of the flashlight caught the ridges of mud and reflected off the wet, slippery leaves giving us advanced warning of where not to step.

*****

Pearl and Colin had lit a fire in the woodstove and the warmth was welcoming after the cool, damp evening air. We sat around the table with mugs of hot mint tea and oatmeal cookies, rereading the texts.

"Paula Jenkins? You mean Judge Jenkins wife?" I shook my head as if to clear out the fog that was tugging at my thoughts. "And, Ginny? Where have I heard that name?"

Ben was quicker on the uptake. "Didn't Etienne say that Harper's girlfriend was named Ginny? And that she's friends with Paula?"

Now it was my turn. "Well, son of a bitch."

Pearl stabbed her finger on the piece of paper where we had listed all the players in our drama. A spider web of lines indicated the connections between them. Some, like Etienne and Marcel were off to the side with the fewest lines, while Harper, Ginny, the judge and his wife, along with the Miletelos and Sadie's brother Raymond had multiple connections. Then there was the list of whys. Gold/mineral rights, lumber, land development… and who knows what else? "Fantasy Vacations could be about anything. Maybe they're a bunch of hedonistic fanatics; or they plan on starting a grow-op to go along with a theme park." Pearl shrugged. "Or all of the above."

There are moments of clarity that unfortunately, in my case, can be fleeting. However this particular thought lit up my brain like the strip in Vegas. I grabbed Ben's arm. "That's it! That's your answer!" I looked around the table. "The judge!"

Ben smacked his forehead. "Of course. I was so caught up in the why that I wasn't thinking about the who." He looked back and forth between Pearl and Colin. "He's the judge assigned to my case and now

I can petition, or whatever it's called, so he can't take it because of the conflict of interest with his wife being involved in the purchase of Sadie's properties!"

"Well, doesn't this put a whole new spin on things?" Colin raised his mug of tea. "Here's to foiling the evil-doers!"

There were smiles all around the table as we clinked our mugs.

Ben pursed his lips and shook his head. "But that doesn't mean that the next judge won't rule in favour of the sale."

I felt like someone had stuck a pin in me as the air seeped out over my lips.

The ever optimistic Pearl jumped in. "True, however, Ben, at least now you've got a fighting chance. And, I think another judge will be very careful on how he rules because he won't want it to look like there were any backroom deals."

This was turning into a bit of a rollercoaster ride. "Okay, so what's the next move?"

"I'll meet with Harper tomorrow night and tell him that I'll see him in court."

Colin was shaking his head. "You aren't planning on going to the meeting alone, I hope. I don't think we're dealing with a stable fellow."

"It'll be fine. I won't tell him that we know who the players are – in fact I'll just say that I'm not willing to let Sadie's place go without a fight."

I passed around the box of cookies. "Maybe it might be better if you don't mention anything about fighting. Maybe… how about saying that you need more time to think about it. That will give you time to go to your lawyer and tell him what you know and what you want done."

"You know, I'm not trusting my lawyer very much anymore. When does your aunt get back?"

"Didn't she say in a couple of days? But, if she's not back, I'm sure one of the other lawyers in her practice would help. Sounds like anyone would be better than the fellow that you have. He doesn't seem to want to fight too hard about this."

Colin pointed at my phone. "Didn't you say there were others involved in this?"

"Yeah, there were two other names."

I picked up my phone and opened the text again. "You said you didn't recognize the names of the other two but maybe they're related or know your attorney."

Pearl chuckled softly. "This is turning into a total soap opera. Your lawyer may not be corrupt; it could be he's just lazy - or incompetent. How did you pick him?"

"He was Sadie's lawyer. He had her will so I just starting using him to contest the purchase. I'm not really sure how these things work - I guess I should have asked Etienne if he knew a good one."

The crackle of the fire filled in the momentary quiet of the cabin before Ben continued. "If you think it's okay, Kate, I'll try to get an appointment with your aunt's firm tomorrow and tell Harper that I need a few more days. Hopefully that will buy me enough time to figure out what's going on and how to handle it.

Chapter 45

A wall of purple flowered clematis growing along the side of the patio shelters it from the light breeze. Sitting on the glass-topped table under the umbrella is a marble mortar and pestle. The pills have been crushed and are ready to be mixed. There's a prismatic flash as the sun's rays glance off his large diamond ring and temporarily distract him. Taking a moment he admires the bling before picking up the disposable gloves. He pulls them on and makes sure the ring's setting doesn't snag the latex. The respirator is clumsy and hot, but necessary.

Using the mortar and pestle, he easily crushes more of the sleeping pills. After all, he doesn't want any suffering - just a brief transition. Picking up a tin he pours a small amount of the colourless liquid cyanide onto a tin pie plate then sprinkles the contents of the mortar on top. The powder and the cyanide blend easily with his small kitchen whisk to make a watery paste.

This creation needs to be slightly different. The third ingredient is the game changer this time around. Very slowly, sliding the zipper tab on the plastic bag, he opens it just enough to dip in a small metal scoop. Filling it half way with the brown powder he slides it out of the bag and pours it onto the paste in the pie plate. As he blends the ingredients, the powdered heroin turns the white paste into a creamy taupe. After adding a little more cyanide and some green food colouring he studies the effect.

This is his favourite part – the combining of ingredients. He has dubbed himself the Humane Chemical Genius. His creations are simple, clever and never traceable. He's particularly proud of this one.

Little beads of sweat form around the rubber seal of the respirator. Underneath, he smiles at the irony. He will be paid quite handsomely for his creation then paid again to do the analysis of what killed the victims. His lab reports are always meticulous.

He pulls the mosquito repellent coil out from its paper sleeve and compares the colour of the paste to the coil. Satisfied, he dips it into the slurry and ensures the bottom is well coated, then places the coil upside down to allow the mixture to dry.

The timing of the delivery is not his problem. His client is the one who needs to make sure that the container of mosquitos will be released into the cabin.

Placing the items from the morning's work back into the metal box he pulls off the respirator and feels the tingling of cooler air as it hits the droplets of sweat on his face. He takes a moment to delight in the sensation then pulls a handkerchief from his shirt pocket under his lab coat and wipes away the moisture. He'll make sure everything gets washed thoroughly, including the rag he uses to wipe down the patio table.

Chapter 46 – Owls and Omens

Sleep had decided to park somewhere else for the night.

Tap, tap, tap and a whispered "Kate," had me flipping the sheet off my legs as I swung them over the side of the bed.

I ran my fingers through my hair trying to reduce the tangles. "Yah, I'm up. Come on in."

Ben's substantial form filled the doorway. "I heard you tossing around and figured you couldn't sleep either. Thought I'd warm some milk and Irish Cream. Would you like a cup?"

"Sounds delicious." I slipped my feet onto the plush sheep skin rug and stretched the kinks out of my back from the evening's roofing job. I could hear Ben pulling mugs out of the cupboard and pouring in the milk. The keys on the microwave dinged as he chose the settings.

The skies had cleared and there was enough moonlight coming in the windows to allow us to navigate the cabin and not stub our toes.

I sat on the couch, tucked my legs underneath me and worked at the knot that had settled in my shoulder.

Ben handed me a mug and placed his on the window sill. "May I?" he asked as he laid his hand on my shoulder.

"That would be lovely." I took a sip of the warm drink and let the flavours delight my taste buds. I looked out the window as he sat behind me with his fingers searching out the kink that had manifested.

"Mmmm. I don't know what is better; the drink or your massage." His fingers pressed along the length of the muscle and I found myself sighing. As the tension slowly slipped away, his touch lightened and his hand smoothed the last vestiges of tightness as he slid it along my shoulder and down my arm.

I leaned back into the comfort of his chest as he idly stroked the back of my hand. My eyes closed to better absorb the sensations. Ben's other arm wrapped around me and he gently pulled me closer. "Hey look."

A huge shadow was soaring across the water then righted itself as it perched on a stump at the edge of the Point. Folding its wings in, the owl became part of the motionless silhouettes. Mesmerized, we watched as the minutes ticked by. Its head cocked once, then, with a quick flourish, the owl launched itself and we lost sight of it in the long reeds at the edge of the water. Within seconds it reappeared and ascended into the late night sky, the outline of a snake writhing in its talons. Wordlessly, we followed its progress as it glided over the far shore and out of sight.

*****

I cracked my eyes open wondering what was going on. My breath caught in my throat as I looked at the faces of my friends staring at me from the other side of the window. "Huh?" Such sparkling wit.

Expelled air passed my ear as I scrambled to remember the night. An arm released me and stretched before it returned, softly pulling me back in. A sigh, then a soft, "Hmmm."

Colin, grinning like a mad fool, nudged Pearl and mimed like he had a microphone in his hand. "And here we have the reclusive Snuggle Bugs, caught after a night of snugglebugging out here in the wilds of Northern Ontario. We are truly grateful to bear witness to this behaviour as it is rarely seen in the wild. If you look closely, you'll see the contented but gormless expressions on their faces."

I felt Ben's arm stiffen as he pulled back slightly. A deep rumble preceded a laugh. "Wow, I was out cold. Are you okay?" A soft kiss fluttered on the top of my head.

Ignoring my friends, I placed a hand on top of Ben's. "Couldn't be better."

We yawned, stretched and repositioned ourselves on the couch, both staring up at the ceiling, trying to bring the morning into focus.

The door swung open as the dynamic duo entered. Pearl made for the fridge, while Colin cleared his throat and enquired about our night's entertainment.

Ben rubbed his hands over his face then turned to me. "The last thing I remember is the discussion about owls and their mythology."

I let my mind wander for a moment. "Yeah, about how they are the omens of change, but then we got into stories of animals in general."

"Right. You were telling me of the time your cousin from Montreal said he had never seen a moose and within minutes a momma and a set of twins ambled past the Honeymoon Suite."

We were quiet for a moment before I looked up at Colin. "I don't remember anything much after that."

He picked up Ben's empty cup that was still on the window sill and took a sniff. "A little late night libations?"

"Neither of us could sleep. It's Uncle Carl's foolproof remedy."

I poked Ben's ribs gently. "I like Uncle Carl's therapy. Worked like a charm."

*****

Colin had stabbed his last piece of syrup-soaked French toast and was swirling it in the air. "So, what's the deal with the owls and omens?"

Ben finished off his coffee and placed the mug on the table. "There are some First Nations people who believe when you see an owl it foreshadows death. Some see it as ominous, as in the death of someone they love, but it is also believed by others that it can mean the death of a situation – which may or may not be good or bad, just something that needs adjusting to."

Ben's eyes closed and he shook his head. "Wow! I can't believe I never thought of this before." An almost imperceptible snort preceded a smile. "I guess I was a little distracted."

We waited.

"The night I was lost in the woods, there was an owl." He looked at Pearl then Colin, finally settling on me. There was the slightest movement as if he was going to reach out to take my hand, but he simply raised both of his and held them out wide, in an all-encompassing gesture. "I believe that owl foreshadowed the death of a very sad and angry time in my life." He paused as he bobbed his head, "I hadn't put words to it before this... I don't think I even realized it, but since Kate rescued me and you all brought me into your lives, my life has been... well... changed. Like the black hole inside me has imploded and ... is gone. I'm still sad about losing Sadie, and, yes, angry at whomever murdered her, but," his smile slipped across his face until it settled in his eyes as he shrugged, "because you've allowed me to share it with you, it's released a lot of pent up pressure and, well, it's like I'm feeling hopeful. I'm not sure about what, but the horizon isn't as dark anymore."

Pearl reached out and laid her hand on his arm. "It's a two-way street, Ben. Think of all you've brought into our lives." Her eyes cut over to mine then back to Ben's. "You've turned a simple vacation into a great adventure – in more ways than one."

Colin tapped the table. "So, my question still stands, what's with the owl and omen?"

I nodded in the direction of the Point. "We saw an owl catch a snake out there."

A little shiver slipped up my spine as a breeze rustled the birch leaves just outside the window.

Chapter 47 – Lawyering Up

We decided to take my car into town in case someone was watching for Ben's truck. Ben had put on a podcast featuring a variety of comedians. Though the show is usually quite funny, we were both too lost in thought to take in the humour. Pearl and Colin had wanted to go back out to the sandbar and do a bit more treasure hunting so we left them just after breakfast. Shortly before we came to the Whitefish River and Ben's cabin, his phone dinged.

"Of course…it's from Harper." I turned off the radio to better hear him. "Wondering if you got my text from last night. Still waiting to hear if you're interested in keeping your place." Ben closed the app. "I'm not sure if that sounds more like an optimistic sales technique or a threat."

"I think I'd go with poorly veiled threat."

"Yeah. The guy is just so slimy I don't even want to text him." Ben blew out a short sigh. "Better to get it over with. I'll ask for a couple more days." From the corner of my eye I could see him hit the send button with a deliberate jab.

"I'm going to give Etienne a call." Ben put the phone on speaker and the call was picked up after only two rings. Etienne's cultured "Good morning, my dear lad," came through. "Can I hope that you and your friends will be joining me for coffee or lunch today?"

This put a smile on Ben's face. "Hello, Etienne. That's kind of you but Kate and I are going into town to see about getting me a new lawyer."

"Ah, may I enquire as to whom you have been dealing with up until now?"

"Gerald Pachinski. Do you know him or of him?"

"My dear boy, actually, I do. Gerald Pachinski is as thick as a cast iron frying pan and about as deep." There was a slight pause before he continued. "As a matter of fact, he's on the fringe of the poker group that I mentioned."

"Fringe?"

"Yes, he's a wannabe. Not a regular but someone they can call to fill in as a last minute replacement. And, he's not a good player so we can always expect his money to get divvied up around the table."

The phone and the inside of the car were silent.

"And yes, Ben, I do see how having him as your lawyer might impact your situation."

I looked over at Ben. His eyes were closed and his mouth was pursed in a tight line. His thoughts were hanging in the air as if he had spoken them. And just as the sun breaks through the clouds to brighten the day, Ben's smile came full on.

"Etienne, thank you! It always felt like I was coming up against brick walls and now I know why. This is brilliant."

"You're more than welcome. I'm delighted I could be of help. I just wish we had talked sooner."

"Etienne? Kate here. I just want to tell you that the smile on Ben's face is lighting up the car!"

"Ah, dear Kate. How delightful of you to say."

Ben's finger hovered over the "end" button. "Etienne, I'm going to call Kate's aunt's office to make an appointment with one of the lawyers there."

"And might I enquire as to whom Kate's aunt is?

"My Dad's sister, Maggie O'Malley."

"Ah, yes, the marvelous Maggie. I should have guessed. You'll be in good hands, lad. Do let me know how it goes."

"Thanks, Etienne, I will."

Slipping my phone out of my pocket and turning it on I passed it to Ben. "Here, dial her office from my phone. The number's under 'M'." Ben once again put the phone on speaker. When Maggie's assistant

Sylvia answered, I identified myself and we had a brief catch up moment before she asked if the information she had sent was useful.

"Sylvia, you have no idea. Thank you! And, to that end, we're driving into town now and Ben was hoping that if Maggie's not back yet, one of the other lawyers could take his case. Does anyone have some time free?"

"If you can wait two days Maggie said she'd like to handle this personally." Sylvia lowered her voice. "She said something about being delighted to, and I quote, 'knock the legs out from under some people who give the legal profession a bad name.'"

I looked over at Ben.

"Sylvia, Ben here. That would be excellent. I've heard some amazing things about Maggie and would love to meet her."

My aunt's assistant laughed. "I'm sure you have and, they're probably all true. How about we put you in for four o'clock, two days from now. That will give her time to sort out a few of her other clients first. Kate, I'm assuming you'll be coming in as well?"

"Wouldn't miss it."

I slowed the car down and pulled onto the shoulder. "Is there something else we need in town today or shall we turn back?"

Ben was still smiling as he shook his head. "I can't think of anything. Do you mind if we stop off at my cabin to check on our repair job?"

"Sounds like a plan." I put the car back into drive and pulled a U-turn.

*****

Light poured into the cabin as Ben pulled back the curtains. We had a good look around and couldn't find water anywhere on the floor so we celebrated the repair job with a high-five.

"Nicely done, Ms O'Malley."

"It's always a pleasure working with a professional, Mr. Brodan."

"I was thinking of pumping some water on the roof to test it but I'm pretty sure the rain last night would have been a better indicator of the reliability of the job. How about we…" Ben's phone pinged and he stopped, mid-sentence to read the text. "Can't extend offer. Tonight only."

I leaned against the counter watching his face. "What do you think?"

"I wonder why they're pushing this. They seem intent on moving this forward quickly. I'm trying to figure out what the rush is."

A text from Sylvia came in on my phone. "Contacted realtor about paperwork and he's stalling. Says he'll get it to us in two days. Will try sending courier over this afternoon to see if we can expedite this."

"Okay, now I'm really curious to see what he has to say. I'm going to meet him here tonight and tell him, 'no deal'. Then we can see what their next move is."

Ben tapped his reply to Harper and pocketed his phone. "I told him to meet me here at six thirty."

"You mean, us."

"No, I mean, me. This is something I want to do on my own." He smiled as he tried to read the look on my face.

And I tried to read the look on his. Lowered eyebrows and lips pressed tightly together said 'Determination,' loud and clear, so I acquiesced. For now.

"Let's not waste the day – how about we go back to The Camp, take the canoe and go out to do a bit of exploring?"

"Sounds like a great idea." Ben turned and slid the curtains closed returning the darkness to the corners.

Chapter 48 – We Otter Have Known Better

We loaded the canoe with lifejackets, a small minnow dip net in a bucket and some snacks. The rhythmical movements as we paddled enhanced the tranquility of being on the water. We slipped past the Point and instead of turning towards the main lake, we both dipped our paddles on the right side of the canoe and headed north. It wasn't long before cattails, fallen trees and debris reduced the waterway to a narrow passage. We explored the shallows with the dip net, dropping our treasures into the water-filled bucket. Bugs, larvae, and unidentifiable swimmy-things were scrutinized and released.

A soft slipping sound caught my attention, but when I looked behind, only an undulating set of concentric circles were to be seen. It wasn't the sharper snap of a fish jumping, but more like an undemanding, silky sound. After the second time, I carefully twisted so as not to upset the canoe and waited. This time, the sound was a chirp and it came from off to the side, somewhere in the reeds. An echoing chirp on the opposite side had our heads snapping in that direction. And, not too smoothly, I might add. The canoe rocked and we both grabbed the rails to steady ourselves.

And, quick as a flash, an otter popped up in front of us. It checked us out then made a half chirping-gurgling sound and slipped with the utmost of grace back underneath the surface. And then it was gone.

The afternoon passed like a summer cloud, quietly gliding along, filled with easy conversation and comfortable silences.

Pearl and Colin were waiting for us on the dock with a pitcher of iced tea and snacks. We filled them in on the events of the morning and Ben's plan to meet Harper in a few hours. There was a bit of discussion about him going on his own, but in the end he insisted that this was something he wanted to take care of by himself, so we backed down.

When six o'clock rolled around we watched as Ben slipped his wallet into his back pocket, pulled his ball cap over his head of thick, dark brown hair and grabbed his keys from the bowl on the table. "I'm rather looking forward to this. I might play it out a bit – just so I can enjoy the look on this face when I tell him I've switched lawyers."

I wanted to remind him that Sadie was murdered and not to get too cocky, but in the end said nothing, and he set out down the Trail.

We watched as the forest swallowed all traces of him.

Chapter 49

He hands the packet of cash over and notices the ring as the chemist quickly flicks through the bills. Business must be good, he thought.

Few words and a small unmarked brown box are exchanged along with a taped paper bag that buzzes.

The chemist watches as the man in the dark blue suit turns and walks back to the white SUV.

Chapter 50 – Chasing The Dragon

Colin looked at his watch. "So how much time are we going to give him before we follow?"

"I thought about ten or fifteen minutes. I don't want to be too far behind, but not too close in case Harper is late." I started clearing up the dishes.

Pearl poured the hot water into the large metal washing dish on the wood stove. "Have you thought about what we might have to bring?"

We all stopped and looked at each other. I shrugged. "I was just thinking of bringing us. You know, a show of force. Four against one."

Pearl was not convinced. "What happens if Harper has something awful planned and we need to stop him?" She looked back and forth between Colin and me. "Do you think it might be an idea to bring the .22? You know, it might come to a little more than us just showing up."

Colin and I thought for a moment then we both shook our heads. Neither of us was comfortable with that idea.

As we cleaned up, I kept imagining disturbing scenes playing out between Ben and Harper and felt my anxiety level ramping up. "I'd like to leave now. I was thinking that we could get there before six thirty and park down the road and hide in the bushes so neither of them sees us."

Colin and Pearl agreed so we grabbed our jackets, phones and the binoculars and were walking down the trail within minutes. Pearl's voice sounded far behind me. "Hey, slow down and wait up."

I realized that my breathing was shallow and I was walking with a decided forward lean. Taking a deep breath, I slowed my pace. "Sorry."

*****

We had to park a little further away than we wanted but felt it was important to keep the car hidden. I'm sure we looked quite silly trying to sneak up on the cabin but as long as we weren't seen we were okay with that.

It was six-forty and only Ben's vehicle was parked beside his cabin. After five more minutes we decided to see if everything was okay and approached the door. We couldn't hear anything inside so I finally knocked and called out for Ben.

Nothing.

I pushed the door open and the smell of burnt almonds hit me. Colin was right behind. "Why does it smell like licorice or burnt brown sugar?"

We heard someone coughing in the bedroom. Moving forward, Colin told us to immediately open the door and all of the windows.

He had disappeared around the bedroom door. "Kate, Pearl, get in here."

Entering the room, we saw Ben lying face down on the bed with Colin checking his vitals. "We need to get him out of here NOW."

My heart was hammering in my ears as we pulled him onto his feet with Colin under one arm and me under the other. Pearl held the door and moved chairs so we had a clear exit. Ben had the idea of moving his feet but his execution was slow and unsure.

Once outside, we propped him up on the steps. "Take deep breaths, Ben. Deep breaths."

Ben's head was rolling around then flopping forward, like his neck muscles weren't engaging.

Colin held Ben's chin and lifted it up, checked his eyes, pulse then smelled his breath. He looked up at us. "Did you smell the licorice?"

I was holding Ben's limp hand and noticed that his eyes moved in slow motion under half opened lids and couldn't seem to focus on anything. "I'm not sure. What struck me first was the smell of burnt almonds."

Pearl was standing by the door and took a tentative sniff. "I'm smelling the almonds but not the licorice, more like scorched barbecue sauce."

Colin looked past Ben at Pearl. "Honey, please move away from that door." His tone was firm and Pearl responded immediately, moving back towards us.

"I'm not exactly sure what's going on but it looks like Ben was drugged and/or poisoned."

I looked from Colin to Ben and back again.

"Drugged? How?"

"I'm just taking a wild stab but the burnt almond that you smelled could have been cyanide. He's having trouble with his equilibrium and his heart rate is elevated – all signs of cyanide poisoning. To add to that - the licorice or barbecue odour… that's what burning heroin smells like." Leaning Ben back he patted his front pockets, reached in and pulled out Ben's keys. "We need to get him into the hospital. I've got a naloxone kit at The Camp, which is closer, but I'm out of my league when it comes to cyanide. And, I'm just guessing. We need to move fast."

Pearl opened the passenger door on the truck and jumped inside so she could haul on Ben while Colin and I pushed. They got him strapped in while I held my breath, closed and locked the cabin door.

Pearl drove while Colin monitored his patient. He instructed me to call ahead to the hospital with the situation. Ben's breathing deepened slightly but his head continued to loll, so I rolled up my jacket and put it between his head and the window. It was the longest ride of my life.

*****

The ambulance met us on the highway and once Ben was safely transferred I felt the conflicting emotions of relief and worry. He was now in the care of a medical system that could help him, but the question of what had happened to him had us reeling.

A simple finger prick for a blood sample confirmed the presence of cyanide so the police were called in. Initially, it appeared that the officer believed it to have been self-inflicted, however after we filled him in on a bit of the history, his attitude shifted and he took a lot of notes. He called the Inspector in charge of field operations who then contacted the Ontario Provincial Police as the incident had occurred in their jurisdiction. Detective Tuffanski and the Forensic Identification Unit were assigned to further investigate.

By eleven o'clock we'd each repeated our story multiple times, after which Detective Tuffanski closed his notebook. "We'll need to talk to Mr. Brodan in the morning. I'll have the nurse give me a call when he's awake."

Ben had been given inhalation therapy of amyl nitrite followed by an I.V. of other antidotes, but was still groggy so he had been put into a room for monitoring.

We decided to grab a hotel room so we could be close by.

Sleep wasn't much of an option so we stretched out on the two queen beds and spent the next couple of hours trying to come up with ideas of how it had happened. Around one o'clock Colin rang the hospital and was told that Ben was doing much better and would be released in the morning.

Pearl grabbed Colin's wallet and told us she'd be back in a couple of minutes. True to her word she reappeared with a bottle of rye, a litre of ginger ale, some ice and two bags of chips. Colin's wallet was lighter and the night desk clerk was richer. We managed a few hours of sleep after reducing the contents of the bottles.

Chapter 51 – How Brilliantly Evil

In the history of hugs, I'm sure there have been many as heartfelt as ours; however, given the here and now, for me, this one was the sweetest. I'm not sure who let go first, Ben or I, but before we could totally separate, Colin and Pearl joined in pinning us back together.

When we finally pulled apart, I looked up into those amazing deep chocolate eyes and felt a thump in my chest.

His hand cupped my face. "I'm fine. But," he looked at each of us, "once again, I owe it all to you! You can't imagine how thankful …"

I leaned in and smothered the rest of the sentence. This was becoming a habit.

Pearl pulled us apart. "Later, you two. Ben, what the hell happened?"

Ben ran his hand through his hair and sat back down in the hospital bed. "I went into the cabin to wait for Harper and found I was getting eaten alive by mosquitoes. There were hordes of them, so I lit a mosquito coil." The skin between his brows furrowed as he stared off above our heads – like he was trying to find the answer somewhere up on the wall. "It had a really weird smell – not at all like it usually smells."

I leaned forward. "Like burnt almonds or sugar?"

"Yeah, sort of. Maybe not the burnt almonds, but definitely burnt sugar or maybe licorice. Then, the next thing I know is you three hauling me out of there – but that part is really kind of hazy. It's almost like everything was in slow motion, or blurry, and like… like something was wrapped really tightly around my chest."

Ben pointed to the nursing station outside his room. "The doctor said I was treated for cyanide and heroin! What the hell…?"

Colin was shaking his head. "Wow. That's some evil genius. That must be how they killed Sadie."

Pearl looked at me and shrugged. "Sorry, I'm a little slow on the uptake. Just how did they do it?"

Colin was smiling. "It's brilliant." He touched Ben's shoulder. "Sorry, dude, sick, but brilliant." He held his hands slightly apart forming a circle. "The mosquito coil… they/he/someone must have somehow manufactured or doctored one of the coils with heroin and cyanide." He paused for a moment. "And, most likely something else… maybe something to make you sleep so you were sure to get a lethal dose."

Pearl is a quick study. "And, they must have let a bunch of mosquitoes loose to ensure that Ben was going to light the coil while waiting for Harper. So, putting it all together, it has to be Harper who did this. I mean, who else knew Ben was going to be there?"

Thoughts were skittering around my head like a newbie on roller skates. "Actually, it could have been any one of the stakeholders in Fantasy Vacations. I mean, they would have known that Harper was going to talk to Ben last night about changing the deal. In fact, they may have been behind it. Harper could just be the fall guy."

Ben pressed his hands over his mouth, dragged them back across his cheekbones then dropped them to his lap. He shook his head and made a few strange noises, like he couldn't decide which sounds went together to form words. Finally, "Un-fucking believable." came out. And was repeated – this time with emphasis on each word.

"Now that's a new one on me."

We turned to see who had said that. The OPP detective from last night was standing in the doorway shaking his head. He was wearing the same brown plaid sports jacket and tan pants but this time his face was sporting a smile.

He strode in and offered Ben his hand while flashing his badge with the other. "Hello Mr. Brodan. I'm Detective Tuffanski." He nodded to the rest of us. "Good morning." Turning back to Ben he continued. "I talked to your friends last night and now I need to find out exactly what happened to you." The officer pulled out a notebook, tapped it with a pen, then sighed. "So, Mr. Brodan…"

"Please call me Ben."

"Right, Ben. Shall we start with what happened when you arrived at your cabin last night?"

Tuffanski was a good listener. He let Ben go over the details without interrupting, then spent a minute reviewing his notes. "Okay, that fits with what the doctor said, now, let's get to the why. Your three friends gave me a lot of information last night, but I'd like to hear the history from you." He consulted his notes. "So you were supposed to meet a real estate fellow by the name of Sterling Harper. He didn't show? What do you think happened?"

Ben leaned forward and stared at the officer. "I think he got there before me and set this up."

"So he didn't contact you?"

"No." He looked around. "Where's my phone?"

Pearl looked in the locker in the corner of the room and found a large white plastic bag with Ben Brodan marked on it. She brought it over to him and he dumped the contents on his lap. Sorting through the clothes he came up with his jeans and pulled his phone out of the pocket. "Hah! There's a text from Harper." He opened it scowled and passed the phone to the officer .

"So Harper sent you a text fifteen minutes after you were supposed to meet him saying he was held up signing papers with some other clients. That would be an easy one to check out."

Ben's eyes drooped and he released his breath in a sigh. All the fight seemed to have gone out of him. I wondered how much of the exhaustion was due to the drugs and how much was from emotions. But Ben is a strong, determined man and as he took a deep breath, you could see the strength revitalize his face and body. "I was so sure it was him. It's tough fighting an invisible opponent."

I felt that we had faded into the background until the officer asked Ben how he had met us.

Ben smiled, reached for my hand and retold the story. He summarized the ensuing days with the rest of the information we had gleaned.

"This is quite the list of suspects you've given me." One of Tuffanski's bushy eyebrows lifted. Again, he tapped his pen on the pad. "A judge, his wife, the couple from Toronto, a real estate agent and a brother; it's going to be both interesting and a bit tricky questioning them." He broke into a smile. "I do love a challenge."

Chapter 52 – Regroup

Detective Tuffanski arranged for his forensic team to accompany him and Ben to the cabin to collect evidence. While still in cell range, I sent my aunt's assistant, Sylvia, a text outlining what had happened and let her know that we would be in for the meeting tomorrow afternoon. She responded immediately, insisting that we move into town and offered the key to my aunt's house.

A very brief discussion resulted with our declining the offer and reassuring her that no one knew where we were – we would be fine. Besides, the police were involved and we were sure someone would be arrested soon.

The doctor suggested that Ben not drive for a few more hours, so I took the wheel and the three officers from the forensic identification unit followed in their two vehicles. After parking at Ben's cabin, a petite, blonde officer suggested that we stay by the truck and give her a quick reconstruction of events, while Detective Tuffanski and the two other officers put on Hazmat suits and prepared to process the scene. We opened the tailgate and sat on the edge letting the sun rejuvenate our tired minds while we once again repeated our story. I found my thoughts wandering and let my gaze take in the scenery. Pearl was at the point in the story where we had just arrived at the cabin when, through the trees, I noticed a flash that brought my attention to what appeared to be a white vehicle.

I pointed and yelled, "Hey, look."

Everyone turned and peered through the foliage trying to get a glimpse of whatever was on the other side of the trees. There was another flash of light and then the slamming of a door. I jumped off the tailgate as the sound of gravel rocketing off trees, then the squealing of tires on the pavement shattered the silence.

The officer, whose name I couldn't remember, turned to me with eyebrows raised, silently asking for an explanation.

"I think that's the SUV that's been following us. We've got to see who's driving it! Pearl, come on."

I was stopped by a hand coming down on my shoulder. The officer shook her head. "No, that's not wise. We can't allow you to go tearing off after someone. We'll handle it."

I was about to argue that they were getting away when she smiled and shook her head. Turning, she walked over to her unmarked car, slid into the driver's seat and grabbed the microphone of her radio sending out instructions to investigate the white SUV on Highway 144 headed towards town, just north of the Whitefish River.

It's nice to have the police around.

Pearl finished recounting the events of the previous evening and Colin filled in some of the medical details. A tall, slender officer came out of the cabin and removed the headgear from his Hazmat suit. "Mr. Brodan, where did you say you put the mosquito coil?"

"It's right there on the table, in a tin pie plate."

The officer looked at us. "Did any of you see it?"

Colin stepped forward. "Yes, I did. Absolutely. It was right there on the table." I shrugged and Pearl commented that she was too busy opening windows.

The officer looked back at the door. "Do you remember if you locked up?"

I did a quick mental video review of my actions. "I'm pretty sure I did." I rewound the video and played it again. "Yes, I definitely locked it." I reached into my pocket and pulled out Ben's key ring. "I remember thinking I didn't want anyone else to go into the cabin."

The officers exchanged glances. Tall and lanky shook his head. "The door wasn't locked when we got here and there's no mosquito coil or tin plate." He turned and stuck his head back into the cabin. "And, since the windows are open, all the smells are gone." He picked up a case from the steps and nodded to his partner. "I'll check for smoke residue if you want to do the fingerprints."

We were told that they would need to get our prints before we left. They weren't holding out much hope of finding any other ones in the cabin because the job looked to be well planned.

It took only a few minutes to collect our fingerprints on the electronic scanner. I gave Detective Tuffanski a detailed map of how to get to The Camp should they need to reach us, along with my aunt's contact information.

Pearl and I walked through the bush to my car. Fortunately, it was still there and hadn't been molested. Colin was not about to miss any of the action so he stayed behind with Ben, insisting that he needed to keep an eye on his patient.

Paranoia had crept into our thoughts and even though the white SUV had been travelling north, we scanned all of the side roads and kept an eye on the rear view mirror as we headed south towards The Camp.

"Hey!" Pearl slapped her hand on the console between us. "Do you know for sure if that was an SUV that you saw back at Ben's or did you just assume."

"Hmm." I briefly cut my eyes over to Pearl. "Now that you mention it, I'm not sure. It was white so I assumed it was the SUV."

"Yeah, it could have been, but it also might have been Raymond's truck."

"Well, shit."

"So the cops might be looking for the wrong vehicle."

"And," I did a quick scan in the rear-view mirror, "there could be two vehicles trying to track Ben."

"Now do you want to take the .22 out and load it?"

Scanning the highway for another vehicle, I slowed down to make the turn into the bush then looked over at my friend. "Pearl, you're scaring me with your gun enthusiasm," I said with more bravado than I felt. As I navigated the remnants of a once-huge puddle I thought it might be a plan to at least have the gun handy. For Pearl's benefit I added, "Nobody is coming to kill us all. So far, it's been all rather…" I searched for the right words, "…underhanded and sneaky. There haven't been any confrontational attempts, and, quite frankly, now that the police will be checking alibis, I'm pretty sure they will have to back off. It's too obvious. Besides, there are four of us. Do you really think someone is going to take all of us out?" I put the car in park and turned to my friend. "And, I'll bet there will be an arrest within a few days."

*****

Pearl and I had just toweled off after a quick swim to the Point. It had started as a race but even with my longer limbs, Pearl's superior strength and lung capacity had me bested half way there. The exercise had been helpful in getting rid of the accumulated nervous energy. We were sitting on the deck when Colin, then Ben appeared in the clearing followed by our new best friend, Detective Tuffanski.

We all took seats on the deck and Pearl busied herself getting everyone something to drink.

The officer looked around and whistled. "Wow. This is a super sweet spot! I can't believe no one else is allowed to build in the bay." He picked up his glass of ginger ale. "Do you have any idea what people would pay for this?"

"Yeah, actually, my family has turned down some generous offers."

"I'll bet they have. Anyway, to the point." He put his glass down and leaned his elbows on the picnic table. "I wanted to make sure that I knew how to find Ben so I thought I should ride out with him but I also wanted to let you know that I heard back from the forensic team at the station. They said that everyone you mentioned has alibis." Scratching his head with his pen he continued, "But, that's not really relevant as anyone could have put the mosquito coil in the cabin at any time. And, they would have all made sure that they could be accounted for at the time that this Mr. Harper was to present the deal so it doesn't let them off the hook."

Colin tapped his lips with his index finger then held it up. "Did any of them seem nervous when they were questioned? Did they appear uncomfortable?"

"Apparently not. Each and every one looked genuinely surprised, but that doesn't really tell us anything. Some people are very accomplished liars."

A hummingbird chose that moment to visit the feeder hanging from the birch tree. I watched without really seeing as I tried to process the information.

I turned back to the officer as a thought slipped into my head. "Hey, but the evidence was removed. Do they all have an alibi for that time frame?"

"When they were questioned, we broadened our time frame to include the whole day and night – that gives us a better idea of their movements. Still no unaccounted-for time."

Tuffanski pulled out a couple of business cards and passed them around. "We'll keep in touch about anything that we find out, and, of course, you can call me, or the station, at any time should anyth... should you think of something."

My stomach felt like a hand was squeezing it as I wondered if he had been about to say, 'should anything else happen.'

Chapter 53 – A-luring

We lapsed into silence after attempting to put together a picture from all the pieces of information. The fragments remained unconnected.

Colin swirled the last of his tea around his cup. "Ben, don't go getting upset – I'm only trying to cover every possibility."

Ben just nodded.

"I know you really like Etienne, but he keeps coming up in association with the Judge and that group."

We waited for Colin to explain.

"He lives a somewhat extravagant lifestyle – do you know how big a gambler he is? I mean, maybe he has some serious gambling debts. Where does his money come from?"

Ben pursed his lips then let them slide into a big smile, all the while shaking his head. "Etienne isn't a serious gambler at all. He's more a… a collector of information. He likes to know what's going on. The people who play poker are a rather diverse group, which makes the games a good source of material, and Etienne is a very good listener. He's also a bit of a card counter so he does well at the table. His money, however, comes from his mother's estate. She may have chosen poorly when it came to her husband, but she made some very savvy investments and he lives off the dividends of those and others that he made as well." Ben shook his head again. "No, it's good that you're not leaving anybody out, but it's a pretty safe bet with Etienne. And Marcel, for that matter."

At the mention of Marcel's name, a little nagging thought zipped through my head, but too fast to catch it. I tried chasing it but found there was a lot of debris floating around in there and I lost the trail.

Ben stood up and stretched. "I'm feeling lucky. Anyone want to see if we can catch a few pickerel for supper?"

Colin started to say that he was in but Pearl commented that "they" had some laundry to see to. His response was a simple. "Oh, right."

Ben nodded towards me. "Kate?"

"You bet I'm in." I grabbed a hoodie and the tackle box, while Ben collected the rods.

It felt disrespectful to disturb the silence of the late afternoon with the intrusive noise of a motor so we had slipped the oars into the metal oar locks on either side of the Elgin and Ben quietly rowed us past the Point towards the deeper waters.

Letting my lure skim across the surface, I found myself becoming entranced by its rhythmic dancing and the soft ripples of the wake it created. It felt good to let my mind drift and I gave in to the sensation. Music from a party barge out on the main lake slipped around the edges of my consciousness. And, once again, at the periphery of my thoughts, shimmered an apparition that chose to remain transparent, resisting any attempt to solidify or identify it.

Ben had stopped rowing and was watching my face. "Now that must be a deep thought. Your eyebrows are nearly touching."

The apparition dispersed to unchartered galaxies as I took a deep breath. "There's something nagging at me and I can't get hold of it."

Ben brought the dripping oars into the boat. "I usually find when I don't chase them they come back when I'm thinking of something else." He wiggled his eyebrows. "So let's lure in a few fish and see what else comes along."

My belly chose that moment to remind me that I hadn't eaten since breakfast and my focus was now on some fried fillets with buttered new potatoes and a salad. I swallowed, almost tasting the feast as I sent my lure arcing through the air.

*****

207

"It has something to do with Marcel or something he said." I placed my cutlery amid the few crumbs left on my plate. The pickerel had been as hungry as I and it took no more than twenty minutes to catch our limit.

Colin started gathering up the dishes. "And you have no idea what it is.

"Nope. There's something there, but it prefers to be elusive."

Pearl wondered if we should go out and see if we could find him and to jog my memory.

We looked out at the dwindling light and Colin nodded. "First thing in the morning."

I poured tea into the four mugs, topped it off with an Irish Cream liqueur and we moved outside to the deck.

The early evening breeze conveyed the sounds of a forest getting ready for the coming dark, lulling us into a quiet inertness.

Draining her cup, Pearl stood, offered her hand to Colin who rose up to place a kiss on her cheek. After good-nights were said they walked hand in hand back to the Honeymoon Suite.

I turned to see Ben watching me with a softness to his eyes.

Standing, I held out my hand to him. His eyebrows lifted ever so slightly. I smiled and gave a slight nod.

His embrace was all-encompassing and felt like I lived within its depth. His kisses; tantric. The summer night transposed into sublime sensation.

Chapter 54 – It's Still Magic – Even If You Know How It's Done

The sputtering of brewing coffee began the introduction to our morning. As Pearl hollered about getting our butts out of bed, Ben pulled the sheet over our heads and began a journey of kisses down my back. The exquisiteness masked the outside world until Colin's persistent pounding on our door dragged me back. With great hesitation, I might add.

"Come on, you two. We have a nightingale to find. Let's get a move on."

Looking for Marcel wasn't on either of our minds at that point but with a shrug I kissed Ben's shoulder and neck knowing that had I made my way to his lips we wouldn't be going anywhere for a while.

As Ben and I emerged from the bedroom our friends handled the situation with their version of decorum. Colin popped a bottle of bubbly, while Pearl poured orange juice into glasses. Adding the prosecco to the juice, he then passed out the glasses. "To Kate and the smile on her face. May it linger there for a long time to come. And to Ben, the maker of said grin and beamer of his own smile. Well done."

Truth was, I was grinning too hard to say much else other than "Jackass."

*****

Within an hour we were idling at the edge of Kenogamissi Lake deliberating whether to turn left or right. Ben suggested that Marcel might have returned to his blueberry patch so we turned north. Sure enough, the "Florence" was nestled in the bay and we could see the wiry little man hunkered down with a bucket collecting berries for his winter supply. He met us at the shore and beckoned for us to throw him a line.

"Well now, this is a right good surprise. I'll go aboard and put the kettle on."

Ben clasped Marcel's weathered hand. "That's kind of you, but we've just had a huge breakfast. But, you might want to slip this into your fridge – the butcher cut it extra thick."

Marcel eyed the peameal bacon and smiled. "Oh, that'll be a right treat. Thank you, lad."

Pearl eyed the bountiful blueberry shrubs. "These are amazing. I don't think I've ever seen so many berries."

The gnarled outdoorsman placed a finger to the side of his nose. "Heh heh, I helped them along. They were getting a little long in the tooth – kind of like me – so I burned them last year then loaded the soil with compost from fish and seaweed. Makes them grow like they were repopulating the world."

Colin pointed to the bucket. "Can we help you pick them?"

"That's kind of you, lad but let's sit a while."

Marcel scrambled up onto the deck and passed down two chairs. "Here's for the ladies, and us fellows can sit on that there fallen log."

As we settled in, the sounds of the blueberry patch became more obvious with the droning of bees and flies and the gentle lapping of the water on the hull of the boats. We filled our friend in with the events of the last few days. His head shook in disbelief as he peppered our adventures with mild expletives, apologizing to us 'ladies' after each one.

Marcel's coal black eyes were squinted in pain as he looked at Ben. "Lad, I don't know what to say." He swept his gaze around the rest of us and tears glistened between his lids. "I'll bet it was Sadie who sent you three out to make sure Ben was safe."

It felt like the whisper of a breeze blowing across the back of my neck. It wasn't cold and ominous, but more like a warm caress. I could have sworn the trees sighed. And then it hit me. The elusive phantom at the edge of my thoughts turned into a man holding a fox pelt.

"Marcel, you said that you saw the man who was helping Sadie with the trapline. What was his name?"

His nose scrunched like there was a bad smell. "Lebeau. Jasper Lebeau."

"And you said that you didn't really trust him."

"I see where you're headed with this, lass, but a trapline isn't anything to kill over. There's less and less of a living to be made off it – it's more of a lifestyle."

Pearl drew in a deep breath. "But, what if it's not about trapping? Marcel, you mentioned the rumours of Sadie's gold." She was careful not to look at any of us.

Marcel's eyes narrowed slightly and he didn't answer right away. "Well now, there is that." He turned to Ben. "Those of us who live an outdoor life still need money for the big items. So yeah, the rumours were probably true, but we never talked about it." He paused again. "In truth, I don't rightly know how killing Sadie would be the answer. If someone wanted her gold, it would make more sense to," he turned to Ben again, "...sorry lad, try to... uhm, force it out of her. A body can't give up secrets."

Good point.

"But mind you, I'm not letting Lebeau off the hook that quick."

Neither was I.

*****

As we got close to the Point, Colin pointed at The Camp. "Who do you think that is?"

A lone figure was sitting on the deck. As we approached, our mystery guest stood and waved. I turned to look at Ben. "It's Aunt Maggie!"

She came down to the dock and grabbed the line from the boat.

After hugs and introductions were made we settled ourselves around the picnic table on the deck. In the years since I'd last seen her, Maggie's stunning auburn hair had matured into a beautiful blend of silver and brown curls and the soft lines around her eyes paid testament to all that she had witnessed. The years had treated her well.

She took the cover off a deli tray filled with an assortment of cheese, crackers, sliced meats and veggies. "You'll find some lovely chardonnay in the fridge and a charming merlot on the counter for when the mood strikes."

Colin stood. "I would say the mood has struck me. Anyone else?"

We all agreed and he went into the cabin to retrieve the wine and glasses.

"I'm so excited that you're here! We were coming to your office in a little while."

Maggie's face was happy as she looked around. "I love any excuse to come out here and I don't manage it very often. This seemed like a good time." She kept her head turned in my direction but her eyes shifted to Ben's face. She studied him for a moment before smiling. "Besides, I thought you might like to hear the good news sooner rather than later."

It wasn't as though she was speaking quietly, but we all leaned in closer.

"I'll wait until Colin rejoins us."

"I heard my name – I'm assuming it was not being used in any derogatory manner." Colin backed out through the door then placed the tray on the table.

Drinks were poured and Maggie raised her glass.

"Always remember to forget
The things that made you sad.
But never forget to remember
The things that made you glad."

In unison we added, "Cheers." Glasses were clinked, drinks were sipped and we all turned to Maggie.

"All right, enough suspense. Ben, the Offer to Purchase your aunt's property has been withdrawn and after reading her will, her brother doesn't stand a chance at contesting it."

Disbelief was written all over Ben's face. "But how? How come? How did you manage it?"

Maggie studied the ruby liquid in her glass then smiled. "Well, I'd like to say that it was due to brilliant legal negotiations on my part, but in truth, I think it was the police questioning everyone involved that scared them off."

"That's it?" Ben still looked incredulous.

"Well, there were a few, shall we say, inconsistencies in their offer. When I pointed them out to their lawyer, who, by the way, has a reputation for being inconsistent himself, he did a bit of sputtering." She chuckled. "You could almost hear his back-up-beeper as he tried to salvage his pride."

"Wow. This is amazing." Ben looked like a death row inmate who has received a last-minute reprieve.

I sat back and watched my aunt.

Pearl was the first to rise, congratulate Ben and lean over to give him a hug. Colin followed. I could feel their eyes on me, while I continued to regard Maggie who turned and gave me the most innocent smile.

"You're not telling us everything."

"My dear Kate, you always were the observant one." Maggie turned to Ben. "I had a little chat with our friend, Judge Jenkins, and asked how his wife, Paula, was making out in her business venture with Fantasy Vacations. He played innocent and said that the name was familiar but he didn't get involved with his wife's business dealings. I suggested that he might want to review his docket." Maggie raised her hands in a supplicant's gesture. "There might have been a bit of coughing and sputtering from him as well."

My aunt picked a piece of cheese and wrapped some salami around it before biting it in half. I crossed my arms and continued to watch her until she finally swallowed and laughed. "Oh Kate, I do miss you. Should you ever decide you need a change of scenery you could come and work with me." She gave Ben a quick glance then turned back at me.

My god but I adored this woman! "And now the rest of the story…?"

Her laugh was full-bodied. "Well, okay, but let's refill our glasses first."

Once again, Colin did the honours, except for Maggie, who insisted on switching to water as she was driving.

My aunt tucked a strand of her silvered hair behind her ear. "Well, let's just say that I had a peek at the agreement between the principals of the company called Fantasy Vacations of the North." She pointed a finger at me. "And no, you're not allowed to ask for details on how. I have access to some very clever investigators. I asked my assistant to check things out and by the time I returned home last night I had a most interesting file waiting for me. The Miletelos have a fascinating history. This isn't the first company they've formed and it's safe to say that they've always come out on top while their partners haven't."

She sipped her water. "I won't go into details but this Fantasy Vacations venture is very cleverly written so that this couple can walk away with everything. It seems that they sell an idea to locals who are, hmmm, not to be judgemental, but who are more greedy than bright."

Ben waved a hand. "Wouldn't the Judge have read the agreement before his wife signed it?"

"You would think. But apparently, she and her… friend, Ginny, entered into it without consulting him. And, as I'm sure you've heard, whatever Paula wants, Paula gets, so her husband just chalked it up to an indulgence."

Pearl's brow was furrowed. "So he knew Ben's case involved his wife and he didn't recuse himself?"

"I think he was going to play it out to see how it went. It would take quite a bit of investigating to find out who the principals are because of the numbered companies and the way the corporation is structured and he probably figured that no one would make the connection." Maggie shrugged. "As I mentioned, he appears to be under his wife's spell."

Ben brushed some cracker crumbs off the table. "I'm particularly impressed that you were able to stop everyone in their tracks in so short a time. I don't know what to say."

Maggie covered Ben's hand with hers. "You don't have to say anything. I like seeing our Kate happy. Besides, you're only as good as the people you work with and, quite frankly, I've managed to surround myself with some of the best."

Maggie always did shy away from the spotlight.

We spent the next hour catching up on family and recent escapades before my aunt said she had to get back to the office. I hated to see her leave. There was always a feeling when she was around – a sense that everything was going to be okay, or that you're safe. She's magical like that.

Chapter 55 – As The Evening Retires

Ben and I decided to row out to the main lake for cell reception. We had just passed the spot where the pickerel fishing is the best when the chime on Ben's phone sounded loud in the silence of the lake.

After glancing at the screen his brows pinched together and he shrugged. He commented that he didn't recognize the number before he answered the call.

It was mostly a one-sided conversation with Ben giving me very little to go on. "Yes… hmmm… I'd like to think about that before I give you a definitive answer… Okay, sure. Yes, we could meet there. Tomorrow morning, nine a.m. Okay."

It took him a few seconds to collect his thoughts before he pinched his brows together again and said, "That was Jasper Lebeau."

I waited for the rest.

"He wants to get my permission to continue to work Sadie's trapline. He says he'll compensate me, but I'm not really sure I want to. And, I don't know why I'm hesitant. I mean, someone is going to – I guess it might as well be him."

We let the idea hang there for a minute before I asked him if he thought it was because of the way Marcel had talked about Jasper.

"Yeah, you know, that could be it." Ben tapped his phone against his leg before slipping it back into his pocket. "Anyway, as you heard, we're meeting tomorrow morning so I can get a feel for him myself."

We spent the next ten minutes checking texts and email before pocketing our phones.

I pointed to the oars. "How about I row back?"

We switched seats and Ben decided to do a bit of casting as we made our way into the bay.

The whine of a chainsaw echoed off the trees.

As we approached the small dock the abrupt cessation of the high-pitched whine was a welcomed reprieve. The rhythmical creaking of the oars in the locks and dripping water once again accompanied us to our journey's end.

Colin strutted down the hill sporting safety goggles and a huge smile. The thwacking of an ax hitting its mark followed him. He grabbed the rope that Ben tossed and snugged us up to the dock. "Pearl let me buck up that dead tree." I thought his chest looked a tad inflated. "I just might have to get myself a chainsaw. That was fun!"

"Yeah, 'cause you have a lot of use for one of those." I play-punched his arm.

"Well, just in case I ever decide to build myself a log cabin."

Pearl drove the axe into a chunk of wood, neatly splitting it in two. "Hey, Mr. Lumberjack, you still have to pile the wood."

He turned and bounded up the hill. "Coming, my darling little axe-wielder."

*****

We watched the evening retire, enjoying the warmth of the flickering light from the bonfire as it danced into the night. The fire mesmerized, and the only sounds were the snapping of sparks and the crackling of the wood as it was being consumed.

Chapter 56 – Ba-Doom

The windshield wipers slapped the rain away only to have the ejected water replaced by a never-ending deluge of its kin. We were soaked from our sprint through the trail and the defrost fan was on full-bore trying to erase the moisture accumulating on the windshield. That and the incessant rain pounding on the roof made conversation difficult so we rode to Ben's cabin in silence.

Turning onto his road Ben motioned ahead. "Looks like Jasper came early."

A man in a yellow slicker stood on the small porch. Ben pulled the truck under the roofline in front of the stairs and we joined his visitor.

The man extended his hand. "I'm Jasper and you must be Ben." A smile curved his mouth. "By god but Sadie thought the world of you. I'm finally glad to meet you, though I'm awfully sorry that Sadie's not here with us."

Ben nodded, said hello, then introduced me. Jasper's handshake was firm but quick as he turned his attention back to Ben, who was busy unlocking the door.

"Thanks for meeting me. I'm sorry to drag you out in this weather."

My pocket started playing the theme song from The Good, The Bad and the Ugly – my brother's favourite western. I answered the phone with the usual, "Reagan, how the hell are you?"

Pearl and I often got referrals from my brothers' construction business. They only did new builds, while Pearl and I preferred renos. Ben turned to look at me and I motioned that I was going to take the call in the truck.

Through the moisture-laden side window I watched the distorted forms of Ben and Jasper going into the cabin.

Twenty minutes later Reagan and I wrapped up our call. We had discussed some future jobs he had lined up for us and I gave him a quick outline of what was happening out here. His parting words were to stay safe and give Aunt Maggie a huge hug.

The rain had reined itself in to a soft drizzle and I let my mind wander, immersing myself in the most delightful events of the previous night. The slamming of the truck door hauled me back from an outstanding replay.

I took a deep breath as Ben chuckled. "Wow! Where were you just now?"

"Oh, just lost in space." I pointed to Jasper's retreating back. "So, how did it go?"

Ben shrugged as we watched Jasper climb into his truck. "Fine. He seemed nervous or uncomfortable at first but I think he's okay. I'm not sure if there's something up with him or if he's just … I don't know – maybe socially awkward. I figured since Sadie took him on, I had no reason to not let him continue." The engine rumbled to life as Ben turned the key.

"That sounds fair."

A muffled blast rolled over the forest. I looked over at Ben who had leaned closer to the windshield. "What the hell?" He turned the wipers on and through the short-lived cleared arc, a large black cloud, followed by a duller grey plume of smoke could be seen in the distance, billowing up above the treetops. When I turned to look back at Ben, his face had also taken on a greyish hue.

"Son of a bitch!" He threw the truck into gear and floored the gas.

"What is it?"

His eyes barely left the column of smoke long enough to check for oncoming traffic as we pulled onto the highway. "I'll lay odds that's Sadie's cabin."

"Why do you say that?"

Ben didn't answer right away. He seemed to be either concentrating on driving or deliberating what to say. Finally, he took one hand off the steering wheel, made a sharp chop in the air and slapped it back on the wheel. "It's a hunch." I waited. "Jasper let me know that he wants to buy Sadie's place but couldn't afford it right now. He offered to rent it and when I said I would have to think about it, he then offered to keep an eye on it whenever he was in the area." He let out a huge sigh. "I know it sounds crazy, but when Jasper said it, I got a weird sensation up my spine. Like a chill." He paused. "An ominous chill."

I'm okay with stuff like that. In fact, I get them myself. But something wasn't sitting right. "Do you think he'd be that obtuse as to give you a hint that he might do something to her cabin?"

Ben gave me a quick glance. "I don't think it was him. I mean, I don't think he was threatening me. Look, I can't seem to explain it very well right now, but it was more like… like… I don't know… like he knew something. Or, honestly, it was more like I was having a premonition."

The back end of the truck slid as Ben made a quick turn onto Sadie's road. The trees were tall and thick but a huge, dirty column of smoke could be glimpsed rising above them. "If it is Sadie's, how do we put the fire out?"

"We'll have to pump water from the river using the generator." Ben gave a soft snort. "Man, I hope there's gas in it."

It took us another five or six minutes to arrive at the blaze. The back wall of Sadie's cabin had been blown out and the ghostly shapes of her furniture shimmered in the inferno that had engulfed them. The fire was rapidly consuming the contents and structure, turning all into charred memories. We got out of the truck and I followed Ben down the lane as he made his way towards the river.

The roar from the fire dominated all other sounds.

A lone figure skirted around the flames and heat. A colourful sarong was hoisted up allowing the woman to run. She yelled and beckoned us around the building. A man was spraying the front deck and roof with a stream of water from a garden hose in what appeared to be a futile effort to combat the blaze. There wasn't much of anything left to save. The woman had bent down to retrieve a bucket filled with water. She walked over to a wooden patio set that was just out of reach of the flames, poured the water over it, shrugged and returned.

Ben had taken over the hose and was spraying down the bushes and small trees in the vicinity. A feeling of impotence overcame me and I just stood and stared as my vision and mind became consumed by the flames as well.

The rain decided to throw its assistance into the struggle and started pouring down with a vengeance. Ben twisted the nozzle on the hose until it was just a dribble. His stance was wide as if defying the flames but I saw his shoulders slump as he let the hose slip from his grasp. And just as quickly as the deluge had started, it stopped.

The fire had lost its enthusiasm but the smoke and steam continued to swell up into the morning sky.

I moved to stand beside Ben. He spoke softly, as if to himself. "It's like someone is trying to erase all evidence that she was here." I slipped my arm around his waist and he exhaled loudly as if to rid himself of the disquieting thought.

Ben turned to the couple. "Thanks for helping out."

The man was tall – well over six feet, with a full head of blonde hair, square jaw and his cream coloured linen shirt was smudged with bits of debris. The woman was barely five feet tall, sporting a bikini top that matched the sarong. Her hair had the look of an expensive salon blend of highlights.

The man held out his hand. "You're Sadie's nephew, aren't you?"

Ben hesitated a fraction of a second then shook the proffered hand. "Hi. I'm Ben. Sadie was like family but not my aunt. And this is Kate."

"We're Joyce and Jack Miletelo. Our place is just two over." They looked back towards the blaze. "I'm so sorry we couldn't do more. It was pretty much over as soon as it started."

"Do you know what happened?"

Jack put his arm around his wife's shoulders. "We were having coffee on the deck when there was a tremendous explosion and then the fire. It all happened so fast and was so intense…"

Joyce picked up the thread. "We're assuming it was the propane tank. I mean, it was such a violent explosion."

I pointed up the river. "Yeah, we heard it from way up near the bridge on the highway."

Ben removed his arm from my shoulder and slipped his hands into the front pockets of his jeans. He once again widened his stance. "Have you seen anyone around lately that you didn't recognize or, you know, didn't look like they belonged?"

The couple looked at each other and shook their heads. Joyce said, "We're usually here only on weekends. We flew up late yesterday afternoon and didn't see anyone then. And this morning we slept in."

Ben picked up the hose then looked at the river. A small generator sat in a wheelbarrow on the edge of the water. A cord reaching up out of the water was plugged into it. "Is that your generator and pump?"

Jack smiled. "Yeah. It's small but handy."

"It certainly was today." Ben turned the nozzle back on and walked towards the cabin. Most of the roof was gone and the rain had done an admirable job of soaking the structure and contents. The steps leading to the deck didn't show any signs of damage so Ben carefully tested to ensure they would hold his weight.

I knew he was being cautious, but my words came out without hesitation. "Please be careful."

Ben explained that Sadie's deck was built with a product made of PVC and wood fibres which didn't burn as easily as wood. He aimed the spray through the blown-out front windows. A groan followed by ominous creaking came from the side of the cabin and Ben leaped off the deck as one of the side walls collapsed. And, like a book that has been finished, we watched the structure fold in on itself, closing the cover and ending its story.

Our silence consumed all sound.

Chapter 57 – Coming To Terms

We were sitting in the sun porch of the Miletelos' cottage. I wasn't sure if you would call it a cottage or a home as it was beautifully decorated and featured a state-of-the-art kitchen, four bedrooms and a deck that was bigger than my apartment. Joyce had supplied Ben and me with clean, dry clothes while Jack threw ours in the laundry. A carafe of coffee and a bottle of rye sat in the middle of the glass-topped rattan table. Joyce poured the ingredients for Coffee Royal into the hand potted mugs and checked to see who wanted cream or sugar. Ben hadn't joined us at the table but stood at the large side window staring off in the distance at the skeletal remains of Sadie's cabin. As I approached him, he gave no indication that he was aware of my presence. I wondered what consumed him more right now, the past or the future. I let my hand and forearm rest gently on his back and felt the slow rhythm of his breath. His eyes looked at the cup but I wasn't sure he actually saw it. He glanced back to the window, shook his head slowly then turned and took the proffered mug. Tilting it towards our hosts, he nodded his thanks then drank deeply. Tasting the alcohol, he shook his head and handed the mug back to me. "Thank you, but I have to keep a level head right now."

Jack was drumming his fingers on the table; the lines between his brows were deep. "Ben, this is probably the worst time to bring this up but there's no hiding it. Joyce and I and a few others were the ones who had put an offer on Sadie's property."

Ben responded with a simple, "Yes, I know."

"Right." continued Jack. "It came to our attention that there was a concern about Sadie's signature on our original offer and that's why we withdrew it. Unfortunately, because we're here only once or twice a month, we have been relying on our local connections to pull things together." Jack's glanced at his wife before continuing. "We won't be making that mistake again. Our local partners in this venture are enthusiastic to move this project along so last night we asked the real estate agent to draw up a new offer – one that was considerably closer to the value of the property than the last offer. We understand that the will is being contested, which will hold things up for a bit, but we wanted to have an offer on the table as we were hoping to move our project forward sooner rather than later."

Ben began rubbing the back of his fingers on his chin but said nothing.

"The agent was going to present it to you today, but I want you to know that we'll be withdrawing the offer. We're just so upset that this happened this morning and want to ensure that you know we had absolutely nothing to do with it. That's not how we do business."

Joyce stood up and laid her arm on Jack's shoulder. "Ben, we're so very sorry that you lost Sadie and now her home. Truly, if there's anything we can do to help you in any way, we'd appreciate being able to do so."

Ben acknowledged her offer with a slight nod.

We let the silence sit for a few moments.

Curiosity got the better of me. "Can I ask what Fantasy Vacations is about? The name sounds rather intriguing."

Joyce's face lit up as she held out an index finger then asked us to wait a minute while she retrieved some papers. She quickly returned with a large cylinder of what appeared to be architectural drawings and invited us over to the kitchen counter where she was unrolling them.

"We are interested in what makes people tick. What their dreams are; what their unfulfilled fantasies consist of. We've been rather successful investing people's money, but once they amass their idea of wealth, we want to know what plans they have for it. Some people only want to keep making more thinking that once they have the next milestone – maybe a million, maybe ten million, they'll be successful or happy or complete. Of course, that time never comes because they're looking at the wealth to fill their needs and wants, yet they don't even realize what those needs and wants are. So, Jack and I came up with the idea of offering people a peek into their own ideas or fantasies. An opportunity to understand what excites them and why. To connect with what they believe will make them happy."

I glanced over at Jack and got the impression that this was more his wife's idea than his as his eyes were more relaxed than afire like Joyce's and his smile appeared more tolerant than enthusiastic.

When I looked back at our hostess she was watching me. "And, yes, this project is more driven by me than Jack. His passion is providing the physical experience whereas mine is the psychology behind it."

Jack stood and moved to his wife's side. He held down two corners of the papers while Joyce held the other two. The sketches were not professional architectural renderings but pencil sketches of various buildings and activities and a long list of ideas. Jack pointed to the largest sketch. "This is the main building with six guest rooms, a dining area and a lounge. So that participants can fully immerse themselves, there will be no outside communication except, of course, for emergencies."

Ben's attention appeared peripheral. He was staring at the paper but his eyes weren't moving from sketch to sketch. He surprised me by asking, "What kind of fantasies are we talking about?"

Joyce jumped back in. "At first, we're going to offer outdoor type of ideas. Things like giving people a wilderness adventure complete with survival games. Or maybe a hedonistic or sultan type of experience where they are completely pampered and their every whim is granted – so long as it doesn't involve physical pain to anyone else. We will also be offering a virtual experience that could include pirates, safaris, old west – pretty much anything."

"So why here?" asked Ben.

Our hosts looked at each other before Jack answered. "Many reasons. First, the land is a lot less expensive, it's remote yet easily accessed, there are four seasons and a lot of wildlife. Plus, with the unemployment numbers being what they are, we'll have no shortage of people to build and work once it's operational." Looking directly at

Ben, Jack continued. "We've acquired most of the available land around us and the rest is Crown land so we won't be disturbing any neighbours." Jack realized his lapse in judgement as he shook his head. "I'm sorry, that sounded insensitive and points the finger at us as being the culprits in the fire." He leaned on the drawings as he spoke in a lower tone. "Truly, we will walk away if you end up choosing not to sell. We have scouted other locations and are lucky enough to have the resources to simply sit on these property acquisitions." Jack put an arm around his wife and gave her a quick hug. "As I mentioned, I've withdrawn the formal offer and will deal with the others involved. Maybe a year or so down the line we can talk again, but," Jack paused as he looked briefly at his wife, "I'm starting to get a bit uncomfortable with all that has gone on here and think it's a good idea to slow this project down."

Chapter 58 – Strange Bedfellows

Pearl raised her hands towards the sky. "It just never stops. You can't seem to catch a break."

The clouds had sailed off to the west and the warmth of the summer sun was doing its best to dispel the evidence of the recent storm.

Colin joined us on the deck with a pitcher of iced tea that he placed on the picnic table. "Buddy, this has not been your year." As we sat down he poured out four glasses and passed them around. "So what do you make of the Miletelos? Do you believe them?"

Ben looked at me before turning back to Colin. "I'm not sure. They seemed sincere enough, but, I don't know, almost too sincere."

"That was the impression I got, as well." I swirled the ice cubes around in my glass. "Maybe I'm stereotyping, but can you be that successful without being a bit ruthless?" The coarse caw of a crow overlaid the smoother song of a red winged black bird. "You know, it's not just that. I can't say specifically what it was, but it felt as if there are layers to those two and what we saw today was them covering up those layers with frosting."

Ben pursed his lips and slowly nodded. "Yeah, that's a great way to put it."

"What happens now?" inquired Pearl.

"I talked to the fire department in town and because it's outside city limits they'll contact the Ontario Fire Marshal to investigate if it was arson."

At hearing the last word, Pearl shivered. "So what do you make of them removing their offer?"

Ben shrugged. "Could be genuine or it could be more smoke and mirrors." He tapped the table. "Maybe it's time to visit Etienne to see if he's heard anything at the poker table."

*****

Etienne's arms were wide open as he once again welcomed us into his home.

"Now here's a bit of gossip that might interest you," Etienne said after we were seated on his patio. "Guess who was spotted going into a motel on the other side of Nighthawk Lake?"

He raised his eyebrows waiting for us to guess while we all looked at each other and shrugged.

"Harper's girlfriend Ginny."

Ben said, "I'm assuming she was meeting someone?"

"Oh yes. And not someone that you would ever suspect." His pause was pure dramatic effect. "The one and only Raymond Ramier."

There was a collective dropping of jaws. Ben was the first to find his voice. "Sadie's brother? What do those two have to do with each other?"

"Precisely, my dear Benjamin. The chap who saw them said he drove by an hour later and their vehicles were still there."

Ben leaned back and crossed his arms. "Do you have any ideas as to why?"

"An afternoon tryst seems the most obvious answer but as to why those two – well, my first guess would be that there's something Ginny wants Raymond to do and she can be very persuasive. I can't see any other explanation. I'm sure she wouldn't even acknowledge him on the street let alone hook up with him if there wasn't something in it for her. She runs with an entirely different crowd and Raymond's simply not in her league."

Ben's voice was deep yet soft, as he leaned towards our host. "Do you think he's capable of arson?"

Etienne's eyes narrowed as he parroted the last word. "Arson?" He looked for the answer on Ben's face, closed his eyes then shook his head.

As we filled him in on the day's events, he slumped in his chair as if physically burdened by the news. "This is getting to be too much. It's out of control." He rubbed his forehead then his hand slipped down and stopped over his heart.

A late afternoon breeze blew a strand of hair across my face and I saw the man in front of me divided into slices. Pulling the wayward strands back, Etienne became whole again.

"What do the police have to say?"

Ben stood up. "The fire marshal will look into it, but right now, if you'll excuse me for a moment, I want to call Detective Tuffanski."

Our host stood as well and indicated that Ben should move into the house for privacy. Etienne remained standing then walked over to the edge of the patio where he stared out at the woods. We all needed some quiet time to process.

Ben returned within minutes. "It went to voicemail. I briefly recapped and said we'd be at The Camp shortly if he wanted to come out."

"My dear boy, you can't return to the woods. You're far too vulnerable. I insist that you stay here. All of you."

We thanked Etienne for his generosity and explained that no one knew the connection between Ben and us and should anyone figure it out - finding The Camp wasn't easy. Realizing that he couldn't change our minds, he acquiesced and rephrased his offer to a standing one should we change our minds at any point.

"I wasn't going to say anything because I don't have proof, only a vague feeling, but the Judge was pulling up on his betting the other night and I was surprised. He's usually an aggressive player, but either he was distracted or possibly short on cash. I've never known him to play shy."

Colin had been unusually quiet up until now. "But if his wife has spent more money on this business venture with the Miletelos than they could afford, he could be both distracted and feeling the pinch... and lord knows what else is playing out in that household."

Chapter 59 – Reel Or Not

The clank of a horseshoe hitting the stake preceded the exclamation of, "Excellent." then Colin's, "Not to worry – it's only a leaner – easy to knock off." However, his horseshoe flew wide of the target and Pearl's 'leaner' remained.

Ben and Pearl had teamed up against Colin and me for the inaugural game of 'Losers-Have-To-Catch-Cook-And-Clean-Supper Horseshoes'. Ben was careful to throw his shoe to the other side of the stake so as not to knock Pearl's off.

I was feeling antsy and needed to expend some energy. I didn't think sitting quietly in a boat was going to do it for me right now. The incentive of an invigorating swim (and no cooking or cleaning duties) gave me the motivation to not only knock Pearl's shoe off the stake, but also ensure that my throw was closer than Ben's. I mentally drew a line to the stake and felt the heft of the shoe before swinging my arm back. Releasing the arc of metal, along with my breath I watched as it sailed just over the top of the stake, hitting the sand behind with a dull thud. Ben and Pearl's victory dance was not pretty.

Colin and I decided to go out onto the main lake to see if we could land a pickerel or two. Though rowing would have given me a chance to work off some nervous energy it was going to take too long, so we connected the motor to the back of the Elgin and set off. Sitting in the bow I was Colin's lookout for deadheads, but over the course of our stay, my good friend had learned where most of the submerged logs were and was able to easily navigate his way out to Kenogamisi. It was a bit late for the fish to be looking for their supper so we drifted around for a while until we got a nibble. Colin was content to jig with a worm while I was finding the rhythm of casting helping me move back into a more relaxed state. Watching the spinning of the small spoon at the end of my line was therapeutic.

Colin let his rod rest on the edge of the boat as he turned towards me. "We haven't had much of a chance to talk lately." He shifted the brim of his baseball cap to better block the early evening sun. "How are you managing in all of this… insanity."

I leaned back against the horizontal red wooden triangle that constituted the bow and stretched out my legs. "It's quite a ride."

Colin lowered his sunglasses. "You do understand that Pearl's and my first priority is you. Ben has become an integral aspect to our lives, however you come first. If this is getting to be too much, or more specifically too dangerous, we can pull the plug. Anytime."

Knowing my two best friends as I did, there was no question that they would do anything for me and to protect me.

"I'm okay. No, better than okay. I couldn't walk away – not after all we've seen and been through. And, honestly, I couldn't imagine what this trip would have been like without Ben." I watched as a smaller deck boat passed by, slowed down then slipped into neutral. "Are you and Pearl concerned about…?" A flash of light reflecting off something on the other boat made me duck down and put Colin in between.

"Colin, hand me your hat, please, and don't look behind you."

Without waiting for an explanation, he pulled the cap off his head, letting his lengthening red curls spring free. I pulled the visor down low and drew my hair around my face.

Being aware of how sound travels well over water, I whispered, "That boat – it's just stopped and I'm pretty sure someone is looking this way with a pair of binoculars. Is there anything behind me that they could be looking at?"

He stretched up to see over me. "Nope, nothing but water and trees."

"Then I would say we're being checked out."

"Could they be looking to see if we are having any luck fishing?"

"Maybe, but don't you find it odd that they stopped so suddenly? And normally you acknowledge someone in another boat… but I'm probably just being paranoid. I guess all the goings-on lately have my imagination running rampant."

Colin started reeling in his line. "Kate, I've never second-guessed your gut. Let's see what happens." He made a show of shrugging his shoulders and pointing to a couple of small islands. In a moderately loud voice, he suggested that we should try our luck over behind them.

As he turned to start the engine I twisted so only my back would be visible. We slowly made our way over to the islands and slipped between two of them. Making a production of taking out our rods we started casting. I keep my back to the other boat while Colin dropped his line on the opposite side so he could keep a watch on the watcher.

"It looks like there's only one guy on board. He's getting something out… it's a fishing rod. He's casting on this side of his boat."

The wind was gently moving us behind the island where we were obscured by the trees. It stood to follow that our mystery boat was being pushed in the same direction. It didn't take long for us to be back in view of each other once we'd drifted past the island.

"Let's give it another five… oh bugger, I've got one." Colin gave a quick tug to set the hook. "Whoa, it must be huge. It didn't budge." There was a slight zinging of the reel lock.

As my friend tried reeling in, we realized that we were simply moving back over the original spot. "Looks like you caught a log. Either that or it's one enormous sturgeon."

"Sturgeon? Here?"

"Oh yeah. There are parts of this lake that are a good seventy metres deep. 'Here there be monsters.'"

Colin's eyes were opened wide with possibilities. "Really?" In the excitement, the other boat was momentarily forgotten as he tugged his line in all directions trying to get a feel as to what might be down there. Pulling directly up, his line then his face went slack.

"Ah, sorry Bud. That would have been something to snag one of those prehistoric creatures – even if it is catch and release."

We watched as his line was reeled in, waiting to see if the hook was still there. "Looks like the sturgeon are safe today but that log certainly put up a hell of a fight." Colin said as both hook and worm reappeared from the depths.

We finally noticed that the wind had shifted directions and was bringing some dark clouds along with it. Colin zipped up his jacket. "Shall we do a bit of the old deke and seek?"

"Only if you put on your James Bond music."

"Coming right up." He whipped out his phone and within seconds we were enjoying the theme song once again.

His plan was to go down the lake, past the turn-off to The Camp and slip into a bay where we would wait to see if we were followed.

The deck boat didn't immediately follow us so Colin opened the throttle. The little motor did its best but we weren't going to be breaking any speed records. It wouldn't be hard for the watcher to keep us in sight for a while, which was unfortunate as the weather was getting a little more aggressive and home was looking like a good idea.

"Here. Here's a little bay – let's have a look."

Colin directed the boat into the sheltered waters where we dropped anchor to wait and see if we were followed.

Within minutes, the mystery boat could be heard approaching. We took up our rods to give the appearance that we were fishing. I could hear the boat approach but kept my back turned. The engine throttled down as it passed us and Colin confirmed that the driver was looking in our direction. It wasn't more than thirty seconds before it sped up and continued on its way.

I shrugged. "He could have just been checking to see if we knew of a potential fishing spot or maybe he was just being nosy."

"Or, it could have been someone who recognized you and is out to find Ben."

"Let's head home and fill the other two in."

*****

We made it back before the storm broke. Pearl met us on the dock waving her phone. "Hey, some good news – we finally have cell service again! They must have fixed whatever was wrong. It's kind of weird being connected again." We disembarked with our fishing equipment and she hauled the boat up onto the shore and tied it to the spruce tree.

It had been a strange transition to have a connection to the outside world when we were away from The Camp, but it was surprising how quickly we had adapted. And I was sure we would just as quickly and easily move back into the world of technology.

Pearl and Ben had been busy putting together a meal just in case we showed up empty handed. The warmth from the wood stove enveloped me like a favourite sweater. Spaghetti sauce was simmering on top and right beside it the pot of water was maintaining a slow rolling boil, just waiting for the noodles. A loaf of crusty bread had been taken out of the freezer, popped into the oven and the smell of butter and garlic made me realize how hungry I was.

Pearl poured the wine, while Ben submerged the noodles in their culinary bath.

With a deep breath, Colin filled them in on our encounter. "So, what do you think?"

Ben reached over and put his hand over mine. "Like you said, it may be nothing but someone being nosy. Or it could be someone trying to find me." He gave me a gentle squeeze. "Raymond, Jasper and the Miletelos have all seen you, Kate, and let's face it, no one is going to easily forget you,"

I gently shoulder checked him. "Ah, you're just saying that because it's true."

Ben's smile slipped slowly away. "If they find Kate, they find me. And if whoever it was did recognize you, then they have a better idea of where we are."

Pearl got up to stir the noodles but stopped half way to the stove. "We'll be able to see anyone approaching by water and we could always booby trap the Trail.

Colin bounced in his seat. "Oh cool, let's do that. We could set up bells, launch balloons filled with something disgusting… so many possibilities."

"Or we could just set up a trail-cam." interjected Ben.

Colin's smile slipped away. "Well that just takes all the fun out of it."

I turned to Ben. "I think the three of us are out of our league here. What does it involve?"

"There are a lot of different types, but for our needs here, probably an infrared with wireless would work best. That way we could connect it to our phones. I'm not sure but it might be a bit more complicated with multiple phones – but that's something we can check on." He tapped the table. "I could go into town tomorrow to pick one up. It would be useful afterwards, either at my cabin or even back at home down south."

I felt a little ping somewhere in my chest at the mention of his other home. It had been so easy to forget the world outside – it felt more like the ghost of a memory than something tangible.

Looking up I saw Pearl had been watching me. Her eyes were soft with understanding.

Colin and I cleaned up, Pearl brought in more firewood and Ben researched trail cams. The storm blew over and the evening sun brought its gentle light back into the world.

I was kneeling at the end of the little dock filling the water bucket for the outhouse when the whine of a jet ski made me look up. It was getting rather late for anyone to be out playing around on one of those so I waited to see what it would do. Turning into the bay it slowed down then skimmed along the far shore. As it approached I could see a lot of dark hair flowing straight behind a woman wearing a deep purple wetsuit. Her face was obscured by an incredibly large pair of sunglasses. After passing The Camp she did a quick turnaround and gunned the machine, which sent waves lapping along both shores in the narrowing channel as she headed back out of the bay.

Ben joined me on the dock and we watched the woman and machine disappear round the corner. "Are you up for some Rumoli? I've got money just burning a hole in my pocket and Colin is desperate to win it." He grabbed the bucket off the dock. "I'll meet you inside." He leaned in and kissed my cheek. "Make sure you bring your cheque book."

It was past midnight before we wrapped up our game. My wallet was a bit lighter but so was my mood.

Chapter 60 – Tracks

The ringing of my phone was a startling intrusion to my second coffee of the morning. By the time I'd located it the music had stopped and a ping sounded letting me know that I had a voice message. Before I could listen to it, Pearl, who had gone out to pick blueberries, was calling for us to come and check something out.

"Looks like we had a visitor last night."

Expecting to see a moose or bear track, I looked at the spot on the trail Pearl was pointing to, just at the edge of the woods. I wish it had been one of those two. Instead, it was a boot print, clearly defined in a drying muddy patch. The ridges were deep, indicating a new boot that definitely didn't belong to any of us.

Colin and Ben, who had been splitting wood, joined us.

Ben's comment was short and to the point. "What the hell?" He looked at me with eyes that started out as questioning but quickly turned into disbelief. "But I didn't hear a thing!"

Assuring him that none of us had heard anything didn't really assure him, or us, of anything. Quite the opposite. "Son of a bitch, they found us."

Forest sounds slipped slowly back into my awareness as the four of us stood there stewing in our thoughts.

Colin was the first to verbalize what we were all thinking. "Maybe it's time we moved into town."

Ben shook his head. "No, maybe it's time I just gave up and sold the property. I'm pretty sure all of this will go away if I do." He ran his hands through his hair. "This has gone on too long and I can't endanger anyone or anything else."

I turned and stood directly in front of Ben, hands on my hips. "It's your property to do with as you wish but let me ask you one question. What would Sadie do?"

Ben's sigh accompanied his head shake but before he could answer, whistling could be heard coming down the Trail. We stood transfixed.

Within a minute a man's voice broke through the trees just before he did. "Well, that's quite the greeting committee." Detective Tuffanski held one hand up in a self-defence gesture. His other hand was occupied with four take-out cups nestled in a cardboard tray. "Is everything okay?"

The tension that had been mounting was expelled in a collective breath. Pearl, Colin and I all stepped back and left Ben to fill the officer in.

"Wow. I can certainly see how you came to that conclusion, however, you can relax – it's not what you think." Tuffanski pointed to his boots then the track. "That was me. I was attending an out of town wedding and only got your message late last night. I came out first thing this morning to make sure you were okay, but everyone was sleeping and there didn't seem to be any signs of trouble so I went and had a look at the fire scene." He offered the tray to Ben. "Cappuccinos. Sugar on the side."

I didn't know if I wanted to slug or hug him.

We sat around the picnic table on the deck and sipped from the take-out cups while the officer filled us in. It would be another day or so before the Fire Marshall could make it to Sadie's but the detective said it looked like someone had blown up the propane tank on the BBQ that had been stored in the shed on the back deck.

"Propane tanks just don't explode. They have a release valve to prevent that. The temperature would have had to be really extreme." Tuffanski drained his cup. "The blast blew away a lot of the evidence but I found enough remnants of wood underneath where the tank was to be convinced it was arson. Besides, it's just far too coincidental. So, we're still looking at all the same players.

"I've asked for a few more cruisers in the area but I would strongly suggest that you all move back into town. This is far too remote for us to protect you."

We let the thought sit for a moment before Colin stood up, watched a duck fly along the water and splash down. "I understand your concern but if Ben was in town, wouldn't he be an easier target? We don't know how many people are looking for his truck, and what connections they have. At this point, no one knows where he is." He pointed down the Trail. "We were going into town today to buy a trail cam but maybe it's best if only I go. No one has seen me with anyone so I wouldn't have to worry about being followed."

"That sounds like a good idea." I placed my hand on Ben's shoulder. "Besides, there are a few projects around here to finish up. It would be nice to have a day without so much adrenaline."

After Colin and the detective left, I got out the scraper and silicone to reseal some of the small panes in the mullioned windows, while Pearl and Ben cleared the dead underbrush and limbed two fallen trees. Pearl wanted to leave the cutting of them for Colin so he could use the chainsaw again.

It was just after lunch when Ben's phone rang. Colin was asking him to bring the wheelbarrow to the entrance of the Trail. Pearl and I shook our heads. Ben, catching the movement waited for an explanation.

Pearl smiled. "Let's just say that Colin, left alone in an electronics store, is a very expensive beast. His… how shall I put this… curious and childlike personality emerges and dominates. Tell me, Ben, are trail cam boxes big?"

Ben caught on and looked excited. "Not particularly. Well, this ought to be good. Let's see what new toys we have to play with."

Pearl and I put our tools away and gave the cabin and deck a thorough sweeping while waiting for the boys to return.

I picked up my phone and the short vibration reminded me I had missed a call. Checking the message I heard Aunt Maggie's voice tinged with a shade of excitement. "Kate, this is getting quite intriguing. I'll be out to see you shortly."

The kettle had just boiled when I heard voices coming down the trail.

"Ladies," Colin shouted. "Look who we found."

Maggie was out in front with her arms waving off a persistent deer fly. "This fellow has lived a long and evil life of torture. Kate, do you have a zapper?"

I ran back to the deck and returned swinging the electrified tennis-style racquet at the exasperating v-shaped fly. The snap and sizzle was a perverse reward for us, not so much for the fly.

Pearl had set the mugs on the deck while Colin presented his purchases, complete with his version of dramatic flair. "And for our edification, safety and entertainment... three trail cams.

"I thought we should have one set up in the parking area. That way, we get early detection as it uses infrared and can be hooked up to a phone so we hopefully can get a license plate and vehicle image as well." He moved to the second package. "These two are for either side of the cabin. They've got a wide-angle lens so it should cover where the trail comes out and most of the buildings out back, while this one would overlook any approach by water."

Maggie nodded her approval. "Thorough!"

"Ah, but wait, there's more." Colin pointed to the largest box still in the wheelbarrow. "The piece de resistance. Voila." And with a flourish he pulled the box out of the bag.

Ben's voice was incredulous. "A drone? You bought a drone?"

"Mais oui." Tilting the box so we could all admire the picture, Colin explained, "If we get pinged, we can send the drone out."

Pearl raised a hand. "But wouldn't we already have their image from the camera."

"Yes, you're right. But, this way, whoever it is, now knows that we are watching them and are not likely to come any further or try anything because they have been recorded. It's more of a deterrent to any nefarious behaviour."

Maggie was nodding. "That's really thorough. I like the way you think."

Colin gave a courtly bow. "I aim to please." He joined us at the table. "So what scintillating bit of information brings you out on this fine day?"

Maggie leaned her elbows on the table and looked at each of us as she spoke. "Well, this is particularly devious. I've had a few people digging a little deeper on your friends, the Miletelos. As I mentioned before, they are no slouches when it comes to investing, but it turns out they have left a wake of broken lives and emptied bank accounts over the course of the last ten or so years." She pulled a folder out of her satchel. "We interviewed a few of their past partners and it's pretty amazing how these two jokers have gotten away with their schemes and no one is the wiser. They carefully choose their victims and get them to invest in some outlandish real estate scheme, which never gets off the ground for one reason or another, then they turn around and purchase the land from them at a fraction of the original price. They pull this big 'Oh, we're so sorry we got you into this' act, and offer maybe thirty cents on the dollar because that's all they can 'afford'. Their partners usually are happy to be getting back at least some of the money."

I was confused. "But, Maggie, then how do the Miletelos make their money back?"

My aunt's smile was broad. "Because they always have another plan. Seeing as they are investing their professional clients' money – they pre-sell them on a particular land development. They then go in and dupe local people with some amazing scheme and set up a bogus company that then buys the land with these starry-eyed investors. The scheme always falls through and the Miletelos buy the land from the locals for a fraction of the cost. Their original clients then pay the Miletelos the full price."

As disgusted as we all were, there seemed to be an element of appreciation for the complexity yet simplicity of their plan. Ben was the first to comment. "You know, the Fantasy Vacation plan just never made sense to me. I mean, first off, how could you even begin to cover the range of possibilities? They are endless. The staff, buildings, equipment… especially up here where, admittedly, it's beautiful, but realistically, the winters feel endless and the summers are plagued with bugs… it just doesn't make sense!" He paused then nodded. "And that's why they chose the players that they did – because of their, oh how shall I say this… more adventurous proclivities. They would more easily be excited about these fantasies and willing to invest."

Maggie was smiling. "Exactly! In fact, it appears this couple design schemes to match the appetites of the locals, which makes the schemes easy to sell."

Pearl voiced the question that we were all wondering. "So now what? Are they going to offer to buy it from the investors then sell it to developers?" Pearl paused. "No, I guess the real question would be what is so valuable about that land?"

Maggie tapped the papers. "They might have just wanted the land for themselves but more likely there's a commercial gain."

I was getting excited. "Hey, didn't you say the land came with mineral rights?"

"Mineral and timber."

Ben's snort was sharp. "Little late for the timber." Maggie's quizzical look prompted him to fill her in on the logging operations.

Her response was to the point. "Buggers!"

"Unfortunately, we don't know who logged Sadie's lot."

"And I guess no one saw the lumber truck taking it away seeing as Fantasy Vacations has bought up the neighbouring properties."

Ben replied, "Ah, the trees are still on the property. No one has come back to claim them."

Maggie picked up her phone. "I have some friends with a mill. Are you interested in at least getting some money for the cut trees? You could always do a trade-off where they would keep some of them as payment and supply you with lumber to rebuild the cabin, if you wish."

"You really are magic. That would be great if it can be arranged."

Maggie's chuckle softened the afternoon. "Now on to more pressing matters. You know, Ben, if you don't sell, that gives the Miletelos the excuse not to go ahead with the project."

And then it hit me. "Which would really piss off the investors. They have everything to lose, not the Miletelos."

"Well, that narrows the list of suspects!" Colin was getting excited. "That would leave Harper, Raymond, Ginny and Paula."

"You're right, Kate. And in the agreement paperwork that I saw, the Miletelos have the controlling shares so they can pull the plug any time they want, forcing the others to sell the shares at a fraction of what they paid."

Colin was looking dazed. "Who would be foolish enough to invest money and have no real say in the company?"

This time, Maggie's laugh was full throated. "Oh, my dear, Colin, you have no idea how many deals I've seen like this. People want to be part of something big, get in on the ground floor and make a one-time score to set them up for life. They've all heard the golden stories and figure this is their shot at it. Unfortunately, there are hordes of hustlers with unending scams and delusions of wealth who will take advantage of these people." She tapped the table. "And, the funny part is that they're looking for the same big score."

"Ah, the circle of greed." Pearl's comment gave us pause.

I turned to Ben. "That makes perfect sense. The Miletelos told us that they were pulling the offer, which makes me wonder if they just wanted the land for themselves. Maybe they will eventually sell the mineral rights or they don't want neighbours or… who knows."

Ben's response gave us pause. "Then that should mean an end to this all."

I studied his face as I wasn't sure if he believed it or if he hoped that was the situation. Or, if he was just trying to convince us. "Do you really think so?"

His arm reached out and pulled me in. "I'm going with optimism. It's been such a long stretch of intense emotions, I'm not even sure I know how to do normal anymore." He took his free hand and placed it over mine. "But I'd sure like to try."

"Buddy, I can't imagine what your adrenal glands have been through. I think they could use a break." Colin pointed to the box with the drone. "And this might be a perfect antidote."

"But we're still going to install the trail cams, right?" I enquired.

Colin stood and picked up one of the boxes. "Of course. We're optimistic, not idiots. Besides, it would be really interesting to see what kind of critters roam around these parts."

While Colin and Ben set up the trail cams, Maggie, Pearl and I got busy with the drone. I was not about to send it out over the water so we restricted our flying to open areas around the buildings. Fortunately there was little wind and we had to climb trees on only two occasions to rescue it. I loved the completely different perspective it offered and could see how people got hooked on them. Maggie was particularly adept at the controls and managed to fly it half way down the Trail just as the guys were returning.

"Impressive!" Colin said as Maggie handed him the controls. "That was a decent bit of flying."

Maggie wiggled her eyebrows. "I've had a bit of experience."

The afternoon had quietly slipped into early evening when we finally put the toys away and got the barbecue ready for the steaks and veggies. Maggie was easily convinced to stay and kept us enthralled with stories of her adventures. By nine o'clock the sun was straddling the treeline and still giving enough light to navigate the Trail without a flashlight. Ben insisted on walking out with Maggie while Colin tried his hand at accompanying them with the drone. We watched on the computer monitor as the pair stopped beside Maggie's car and had a conversation that ended with Ben reaching out to shake her hand, my aunt tilting her head then encircling Ben with a hug. They shared a laugh then both pointed at the drone and waved. I wished there had been a microphone on board.

By the time Ben returned, Pearl and I had started a bonfire down by the horseshoe pit using the limbs and brush that had been cleared earlier in the day. We slipped into a comfortable silence as we sat and let the flames consume the tension and worry of the last weeks. With night encircling us, the invisible bonds of comradery felt even stronger. Pearl's gasp punctuated the crackling of the fire and brought us sharply back into the present. Her eyes were opened wide and her mouth formed a perfect circle as she pointed behind me. Dancing with sinuous grace across the sky was the most extraordinary display of greenish-blue hues as the Northern Lights shared their magic with us. The ballet was perfectly reflected on the mirror-smooth surface of the water and completely absorbed us in its elegance and beauty.

Mother Nature's whisper enveloped us.

Chapter 61 – Semi Aware

I wasn't sure what gently drew me from a dreamless sleep, momentarily bringing the bedroom into awareness, but the weight of the hand resting on my hip anchored me further into the peace of the night and I succumbed to its call.

My next moment of awareness was Ben's whispered breath as he softly kissed my forehead, eyes and cheeks. His lips hovered over mine and I could feel the want pulling me in to their embrace.

A deep sigh escaped both of us as a sharp rap at the window and Colin's voice yelled at us to get out of bed putting an end to our plans.

Pearl was setting up a pot of coffee by the time we emerged and Colin was pointing to the screen on his laptop. "Oh, I think you two will want to see this."

He had been reviewing the videos from the two cameras outside the cabin. The time stamp on the camera focused out over the water said 2:47 a.m. and not far off the dock we watched as a lone canoeist surveyed The Camp. The green hued screen was surprisingly clear, but the bill of his baseball cap obscured his face. He stayed for only a few moments then slowly turned the bow of his canoe back towards the Point and paddled away.

Ben poured coffee for everyone and returned to the table. "He's not sitting very high up so I'm assuming he's not very tall. It's hard to tell with his jacket but he looks like he doesn't get a lot of exercise."

Pearl nudged him. "That's a nice way of saying he's overweight." She looked around at us. "Did anyone hear anything?"

We all shook our heads.

"Wait, something did wake me up at some point, but I have no idea what it was and I don't remember hearing anything in particular. I think I went right back to sleep."

Colin had zoomed in on the man in the canoe and was studying it. His top lip pushed out his bottom as he concentrated. "I'm the only one who hasn't met Raymond, but given your descriptions of him, it kind of looks like he could he be our night stalker. What do you think?" As we studied the image he continued. "I still don't think he poses a threat to us all. I don't know what his deal is with Ben, but maybe it's time we pay him a little visit – just to let him know that he's on our suspect list."

"No, I don't think any of you should confirm that you know me – we need to keep our…" Ben paused as he looked at me. "…keep our relationship quiet - from that group, for now. I think he's pissed because he didn't inherit anything from his sister." Ben blew a deep sigh that vibrated his lips. "What does he gain if I'm out of the picture? I don't know if he can still contest Sadie's will, Maggie said he doesn't stand a chance. So how does he benefit?"

I had been mulling this over for a while. "Maybe he doesn't know that the Miletelos have pulled the deal. Maybe they haven't let their partners know…"

As I paused while contemplating my final thought, Colin jumped in. "Yeah – I think you're on to something, Kate. Or it could be that they lied to you, Ben, and the offer is still on the table… maybe they've asked Harper to hold off presenting it to you."

Pearl finished his thought. "Then the group still thinks you're a threat to their fortune."

Colin picked it up again. "So if you're out of the picture maybe Sadie's estate will revert to Ray because it hasn't been settled, or if that's not how it works, then maybe whomever you leave it to in your will could be convinced to sell." We all turned to Ben as Colin continued. "You do have a will, don't you?"

Ben scrunched his face as he shook his head. "Nope, no will."

My brain was zipping off in all directions as I tried to hone in on what that might mean. "Okay, so without knowing what would happen to Sadie's place if you weren't…" it was causing a crisp pain in my chest to complete the thought, "…in the picture, we can assume that the Miletelos would still come out on top. As Maggie said, they control the company and can pull out at any time. Maybe these locals haven't thought of this as a possibility. They may be so hopped up on the whole investment idea that they haven't even considered that they could be getting conned. As far as they can see, you are the one standing in their way. And, this works in the Miletelos' favour."

We were so focused on our conversation that it took a few minutes to realize that a jet ski was making its way towards us. Colin was the first to reach the binoculars. "Purple wetsuit and long brown hair - same woman as before." He pointed to the drone and wiggled his eyebrows. "Let's send Intrepid out for a little reconnaissance."

Pearl was shaking her head. "You named the drone?"

"I named her after you, my courageously heroic love." Colin kissed Pearl's forehead and plucked the sombrero from the back of the door and shoved it on his head. "This helps keep my identity a secret plus lets me see the screen in the sunlight." He then grabbed the drone and remote control while Pearl opened the door for him. As he stepped onto the deck she turned to us and shook her head. "He never does things by half."

The whine of the jet ski dropped as the driver caught sight of Colin. There seemed to be a moment of decision before it returned to its former speed. The drone lifted smoothly out over the water. As soon as the driver realized what was happening, she did an abrupt about-face and headed back out. Colin was making encouraging comments to Intrepid who zipped along after its prey.

Pearl had turned on Colin's laptop that had been set it up to stream the video from the drone. We watched as the driver slowed then looked behind. Her mouth pursed into an 'Oh shit!' grimace as she caught sight of the drone coming up on her left. She opened the throttle and sped towards the main lake.

"Woohoo, look at that baby go." We were pretty sure Colin was talking about the drone. "Oh no. Bugger!"

The picture on our screen showed the drone turning around and coming back. We joined Colin on the deck.

"It has a built in GPS that brings it back to its home base before it flies out of range. I guess we know how far it will go."

Ben was looking excited. "Colin, this is great. The drone made it all the way out to the main lake – that's quite a distance. And, the woman now knows that we have her picture so it's like an insurance policy should something happen. She's not going to show up again!

"Pearl, can you send me a screen shot of her. I'll text it to Etienne to see if he knows who she is."

The transfer took less than thirty seconds. Before we could finish laying bets as to whom we thought it was, Ben's phone pinged.

I put my hand over his, blocking the screen. "I say it's Harper's girlfriend, Ginny for five."

Pearl nodded. "I'll take that bet. My money's on the judge's wife. What's her name again?"

Three of us responded with "Paula."

After all bets were placed I released Ben's hand as he turned on his phone. He hid the screen from us then looked surprised. "Hmm."

We waited. "Well?" Pearl tugged on his arm.

"Hmm – as in not what I expected. It's from a neighbour of Sadie's saying he got my number from the Miletelos and that I need to come as quickly as possible. Someone is loading up the trees that were cut down."

We grabbed our phones, keys and wallets, locked up and started running down the Trail.

Pearl yelled ahead to the rest of us that we should take two vehicles in case we had to split up. Ben and I jumped into his truck while Pearl and Colin followed in their car.

Ben was hunched forward as we sped down the highway. "It's going to be so sweet catching this guy!" He noticed that I was hanging on to the grab handle above the door and he sighed and slowed down. "Sorry."

"Don't worry, you don't need to slow…"

I never finished the sentence because just as we were rounding a corner a white truck that had been sitting on the shoulder pulled out in front of us causing Ben to swerve. The front left tire hit the gravel on the opposite side of the highway and as Ben corrected the trajectory I found a scream rocketing out of my mouth. We were in the direct path of a semi that was bearing down on us.

The white truck was running parallel with us, matching our speed. The semi wasn't an option and neither was the solid rock wall on the left side of the road.

My head snapped sideways upon impact when we muscled the white truck off the road. I watched in horror as the tires caught in the gravel, pulling it into the steep grassy ditch where its momentum carried it to the treeline. There was a sickening bang and crack as the truck slammed into a large pine tree.

By the time Ben stopped the truck, Pearl had pulled in behind us and Colin was already exiting the car. As Ben was asking me if I was okay, Colin tried to open my door but the crumpled metal on the right fender blocked it.

"I'm okay! I'm okay!" was all I could manage as the pounding of my heart dominated my chest.

Ben had removed his seatbelt and seemed unaware that blood was dripping down the side of his face. "Can you take off your seatbelt?"

My hand was shaking and weak as I tried to push the release button. It took a couple of tries before it released and I turned to see Ben wiping blood out of his eyes. "Are you sure you're okay?"

"I think I fared better than you." I grabbed some napkins from the centre console and gently dabbed at his cut.

He held my face with a tenderness that one would use with a newborn chick then stared intently into my eyes looking for visual confirmation that I was fine.

"Honestly, I'm okay." I took his hand as I turned to see what was happening with the other truck. "Let's go help Colin."

I had to navigate my way over the console to Ben's door where he held it for me. The driver of the semi had stopped and was making her way over to us. "Are you guys okay? I saw the whole thing. It was completely the other guy's fault. He pulled right out in front of you. You didn't stand a chance. Man-o-man I've seen some shit-bad driving but that was close." As she crossed over to our side of the highway I found her voice became background noise to the loudness of the bling that she sported. Huge gold necklaces swayed over her sizeable chest, while the chiming of a dozen or so bracelets accompanied the jingling of multiple hoop earrings. The chunky jewellery was in stark contrast to the black golf shirt, jeans and work boots. I finally noticed the huge crowbar she was waving around. "Let's get that other fellow out of his truck." she growled as she stomped right past us and lumbered down the ditch.

Ben's eyes were wide and his lips were making little fish gulping movements before he took a breath, shrugged and turned to follow her. I scurried after them. The woman slowed down and held out her hand to me, "Here, hold these," and dropped eight gold rings into my palm.

The driver's door needed a bit of persuasion but they got it open and Colin leaned in to start his examination. He was there for only a few seconds before loud curses backed him out of the cab. "Son of a bitch. Did you see that asshole hit me? He could have killed me. What the fuck did he think he was doing?" The yelling got louder. "He ran me off the road. Look at this truck – it's ruined." A set of legs swung out of the door and the rant continued, ramping up. Colin put a hand out to stop the driver, which just made him increase his volume as he started repeating himself. As he stepped down from the truck it took a second for me to recognize the guy that Pearl and I had encountered stopped by the side of the highway.

Ben spat out the name. "Raymond!"

Raymond's tirade stopped in mid threat as the semi driver created a loud crack as she smacked the dented side of his truck with her crowbar. "Enough, you asshole. Shut the hell up. I saw the whole thing and it was all your fault. You could have killed these good people…" Her tirade caused Raymond to cower, which egged her on. She was now waving the crowbar around and had gotten right into his face. "And I'll be showing the police the footage from my dash cam. Oh, yeah, that's right. It's all been recorded." She stepped back and triumphantly shouted, "You, you miserable asshole, have been busted!" She turned and smiled at us. "I've always wanted to say that."

It wasn't until that moment that I realized her hair was streaked with rainbow colours and cut in a seventies' style shag. Heroes come in all shapes and disguises. She held out her hand towards me and I thought she wanted to shake mine, but her palm was facing up and I realized I still had her rings clutched tightly in mine. A quick dip of her head indicated a thank you, as I relinquished what must have been thousands of dollars' worth of jewellery back to its owner. "Did anyone call the police?"

Pearl stepped up and waved her phone. "Yes, I did. They weren't far away and should be here shortly. The ambulance will take a bit longer."

"Right then. I'll wait for them in my cab 'cause I have to make a few calls myself and let my company know I'll be a bit late with my delivery." And without further comment she stalked off turning only to nod and wave as if getting rid of a pesky fly when Ben tried to thank her.

Colin stared after her. "I'm sorry, Pearl, but I think I'm in love."

Pearl's response was, "Yeah, me too."

The wail of the police siren punctuated the statements.

Chapter 62 – One Ringy-Dingy

While the police and Colin checked Raymond over, Ben pulled out his phone. "I'm going to call this fellow who texted me to see if the loggers are still there."

I had totally forgotten our mission. Ben pulled up the number that came with the text and hit the dial then speakerphone icons. We looked in surprise at each other as we heard the ringing in stereo. The second sound was coming from Raymond who picked up his phone; saw the number displayed then quickly shut if off before stuffing it back in his pocket.

Ben's face hardened. "That miserable son of a bitch!" He walked over to one of the OPP officers and suggested that it might be a good idea to confiscate Raymond's phone explaining that this whole incident had been a set up. Ben let them know that he was calling Detective Tuffanski as this was an on-going investigation. At the mention of the detective's name, the officer tucked his notepad into his pocket and walked over to Raymond. There was a short-lived show of bravado with threats about calling his lawyer and police abusing their power but after the officer had a quiet word with him he handed his phone over. When the cop returned, Ben showed him the text on his phone and said he believed the same one would be found on Raymond's. After checking, he gave Ben a slight smile but didn't say anything.

By the time Detective Tuffanski arrived, Ben had received confirmation from Etienne that the woman on the jet ski was indeed Ginny Folkman; girlfriend, paramour and main squeeze to Sterling Harper, Paula Jenkins and, according to local gossip, Raymond Ramier.

Chapter 63 – Whew

Detective Tuffanski arrived early in the evening after putting together as much as could be garnered from Raymond about the whos, whys and hows of what had happened. It came as no real surprise that Raymond had been a lackey in the whole operation. It was just after Sadie's death that Harper had contacted Raymond with the offer of cash and a job at the Fantasy Vacations Resort if he could get Sadie's signatures on the backdated real estate deal. Raymond claimed he never would have gotten involved had he known what Harper had done or was going to do. Raymond believed Sadie's death was accidental and he realized that Harper's offer was the only way he could get money out of the estate. Once he heard about what had happened to Ben at his cabin he finally grasped that Harper must have killed Sadie using the same method. The confrontation with Harper hadn't gone well for Raymond. The realization that he would look like a prime suspect had made him desperate.

After Tuffanski left with promises to keep us informed we sat in stunned silence for a while before Colin pulled out the tequila to drink a toast to Sadie.

Pearl tugged at her ear lobe in thought. "Remember Marcel said he saw Harper and Raymond arguing over at Sadie's property?" She paused to give us a moment to collect that memory. "Could that have been the confrontation the detective was talking about?"

"Yeah, that could have been." I tried reviewing the timing in my head. "But that was before Harper… set the coil at Ben's." I couldn't bring myself to say that he had tried to kill him. "I wonder if it had anything to do with the logging of the property."

Ben gave a mild snort. "Raymond claims his innocence or that he was a victim to Harper's schemes, but he was the one who sent me the text this morning then tried to kill Kate and me on the highway."

A shiver invaded my spine.

*****

Celebrations are generally loud affairs with music, lots of drinking and rehashing of overcoming adversity. I think we were far too stunned to believe that it was over and that consequences for greed and bad decisions were going to be meted out. Instead, we listened to stories of Sadie and Uncle Carl; we talked about life's choices – forks in the road, attractions, strengths and weaknesses. We shared our gratitude and expressed our sorrows. The bottle of tequila, half consumed, sat quietly off to the side on the counter as the night slipped by.

Chapter 64 – Nuggets Of Insight

Ben dropped the two pouches of gold on the picnic table. I picked one up, feeling its weight. "I had completely forgotten about these." Opening it up I pulled out the magnet. "So, what's the plan?"

"I really don't have the first clue on how to sell this stuff and, quite frankly, with all that has gone on – I just want to settle everything so I gave Etienne a call and straight up asked him if he had any connections. He didn't sound at all surprised and didn't ask any questions about where it came from." Ben scrunched his eyebrows together. "Just in case this ever comes back to me, I told him that you three didn't know anything about it." He stood up and stretched. "I'm going to run this over to him, then meet up with the detective and go over to Maggie's to sign some papers. I'll pick up supper while I'm in town."

Five minutes after he left, our cell phones pinged and we laughed as Ben waved goodbye at the trail cam. Though I knew he couldn't see me, I waved back.

By lunch time we had finished giving the windows a quick cleaning and Colin had contributed greatly to the pile of firewood in the shed. After washing up he folded the hand towel over the metal bar at the side of the sink. "It's different without Ben, kind of like there's a hole in the group or the dynamics have changed." He watched my face for a reaction.

I tried to find words to express my feelings but the thoughts tumbling around in my head were not willing to be restricted to words - at least not yet. I just nodded and sighed.

Feeling restless after lunch, I decided to row out to the sandbars. Colin and Pearl had settled in to read and nap so I guided the oars into the oarlocks, slid the Elgin into the water and set out. I lost myself in the rhythm of rowing and was exhilarated by the power of the stroke as the old boat cut through the water. I slowed as I neared the Point and turned to watch a mink quickly scamper onto a deadhead with a small fish clutched in its jaws. The long reeds promptly swallowed up the little critter as it headed for the shore.

Before I could resume my journey, the memory of my first sighting of Ben caught me off guard. I hadn't realized that I had rowed directly to the spot where he had been standing on a submerged log – what seemed like a life-time ago. It would have been impossible to know just how much that encounter was going to change our lives – mine in particular.

The sun warmed my shoulders as I pulled on the oars and a low buzzing caught my attention. I turned to see the drone zipping up behind me and Colin standing on the dock at the controls. I gave a quick wave as the little flying machine blew past me and turned to the left around the far side of the Point. I lazily headed to the right and lost sight of The Camp.

The problem with rowing is that you're facing backwards, seeing where you've been rather than where you're going. Looking behind me to give a quick scan of the deadheads, I caught sight of a large motorboat moving at quite a clip. And, headed towards me. I dipped my right oar in, moving the Elgin towards a large pine tree that had been partially submerged for decades. If I was going to get swamped, I was aiming for something to hold on to. I watched in fascination as the boat made straight for me, not slowing down until the last minute. Before the swell of its wake could rock my boat, a woman with oversized sunglasses and long brown hair was aiming a flare gun at me. Her face was looking several shades of crazy.

"You miserable bitch. You've ruined our lives and now you'll pay." She levelled her arm out and sighted the gun directly at my chest. "We had such a perfect opportunity and you and that…"

I could barely make out what she was saying as the pounding of blood rendered my ears useless but I did notice her gaze shifting to something behind me. I didn't want to take my eyes off her but a small white shape caught my peripheral gaze and I turned to look. Hovering beside me was the drone. She aimed the flare gun at it and fired. The drone zipped up and over as the flare impotently flew by and sizzled into the water.

As she reloaded the gun, I tried reasoning with her. "Ginny, this isn't going to get you anywhere. Please put the gun down and let's talk."

"No. Talk is bullshit. This is all bullshit. You have to pay for what you've done." She raised her arm again.

"Ginny, you're being recorded. If you stop now, there won't be any further charges but if you pull that trigger, there's not a jury in the world that won't find you guilty of murder. You can make a good decision and just turn and leave." My heart was pounding and was sure you could see it through my t-shirt.

Colin decided to take direct and immediate action and flew the drone straight at Ginny causing her to jerk backwards and lose her balance. Her arms windmilled ineffectually as she stumbled over the edge of the boat. I watched in horror as she fell towards a deadhead. She almost missed it but in her flailing, her left arm caught the log and it bent at an unnatural angle. A primal scream echoed across the lake. Scrambling for the oars I rowed over and grabbed her by her shirt. I snagged the life jacket beside me and tried to slip it over her injured arm but panic had seized Ginny and she fought to drag me into the water with her.

"Stop fighting me. I'm trying to save you."

"You're trying to drown me you fucking bitch." She followed that up with a string of obscenities so I let go of her and leaned back, waiting for her to realize what her options were. Her anger and hatred overcame her pain and I saw the bright orange of the flare gun still in her right hand. Regardless of whether or not it could fire once it had been submerged, I wasn't going to take the chance and wait to find out. I leaned back as far as I could, which caused me to slide backwards off the bench seat. I was below the gunnels so I couldn't see where Ginny was aiming the gun but it was her scream that had me scrambling to my knees. It was not a howl of pain but a higher pitched scream of terror. "What the hell was that? Something just hit my leg! Get me the hell out of here!" She was kicking wildly as she hung on to the back of the Elgin propelling the boat towards open water. Her shrieks of terror and pain continued to overshadow all other sounds as I dragged her into the boat, the flare gun no longer in her grasp. Her rant drained off to a chattering of teeth and I assumed she was probably going into shock as she rocked herself and cradled her arm. She was sitting on the back bench seat enabling me to keep an eye on her as I rowed back to the dock.

The drone hovered for a few moments then zipped back to The Camp. Colin was waiting with the emergency kit and a blanket, while Pearl had collected some bits of wood strapping and a tensor bandage to stabilize the break. Colin fashioned a sling to secure Ginny's arm to her chest all the while speaking to her in a calm and soothing voice.

While Colin ministered to his patient, Pearl beckoned me into the cabin. "As soon as Colin caught sight of her bearing down on you he had me call the police. I'm going to meet them on the highway because they most likely won't be able to find the entrance."

I gently grabbed Pearl's arms and shook my head. "If you don't mind, I'd prefer to go. I need to run this adrenaline out of my system and I think I'll just set Ginny off whenever she looks at me."

I slipped my phone into my back pocket and Pearl gave me a quick spray with the bug repellent before I started my run to the highway. The dappling of the sunshine through the leaves made the uneven ground a little tricky to navigate in a full-out sprint and I quickly slowed to a jog. My phone pinged as I passed the trail cam letting me know I had activated the motion sensor.

The O.P.P. cruiser was parked on the shoulder across the highway and the officer was just getting out. I waved and beckoned him to drive the vehicle over the high spot in the ditch and on through to the dirt road hidden in the trees. Introductions were quickly made and I tried to summarize the situation for the two constables as we hurried through the Trail. Unfortunately, I think my coherence factor was scoring in the basement. Just before we broke through into the blueberry patch I stopped and turned to the officers and tried to pull the story together until one of them stopped me. "Don't worry – I think we have a handle on this. It's all anyone at the detachment is talking about. We actually have been looking for Ms. Folkman to bring her in for questioning." He turned to his partner. "Looks like she's bought herself some serious jail time with today's stunt."

*****

After consulting with Colin about Ginny's injuries, the officers called in an O.P.P. boat to transport her to the boat launch on the main lake where they would meet them with their cruiser. Colin replayed today's drone footage for the officers. Their response was a succinct "Excellent."

By the time Ben returned with enough Chinese food to feed a small village, the three of us had just sat down in the lounge chairs on the deck with Caesars. "Well, you three look like you're ready to wind down for the evening. Did you have a good day?"

Colin got up to mix Ben a drink. "Kate, do you mind if I tell him what happened?"

Ben had been leaning in to give me a kiss but stopped in mid pucker and searched my face. "Please do." My smile reassured him that all was well and I confirmed it by guiding his head down to my lips.

By the time the details of the day were fleshed out and we had watched the drone video, Pearl had topped up our drinks. Time was needed to release the stress of reliving the events before we could even think of eating. We moved indoors and Ben drew me in to his chest with his arms wrapped protectively around me. As I settled in I matched my breathing to his.

Pearl put on some music and we let it fill the gaps between our thoughts.

An idea popped into my head. "Hey, do you think it was Lucius that bumped Ginny's leg? I mean, that's his typical modus operandi. We all smiled at the thought. "Now we have to take back all of the nasty things we've said about him!"

I leaned forward so I could turn and look at Ben. "And, how about your day? We haven't heard how you made out."

He kissed my forehead. "It was a hell of a lot easier than yours. Etienne said he would take care of the gold." He paused and took a long pull of his drink and I noticed that he had taken a deep breath.

"And?"

"And Etienne said that all this was his fault."

Well now, there was a show stopper.

Pearl's one eyebrow raised. "Oh?"

Ben's face looked conflicted then he pursed his lips and took a breath. "He said that it was he who introduced the Miletelos to Harper."

Colin leaned forward. "Say what?"

"I wasn't going to say anything because he really isn't responsible – certainly not on purpose. He was just trying to help out one of his investment people. His guy works in Toronto at the same company as the Miletelos. He said they were looking for some property up here and asked for a contact. Harper had lost a lot of money to Etienne at the poker table and so Etienne gave this guy Harper's name. He says that if he hadn't, Sadie would still be alive and none of this would have happened."

The term 'knocked the wind out of our sails' zipped into my mind. There was a brief pause while we let Ben's news sink in and we each grappled with our personal thoughts.

Colin was the first to cut straight to the point. "And how do you feel about that?"

Ben ran his thumb up and down the cord of muscle at the back of my neck while keeping his other arm around me. He took his time before he answered. "I struggled with it." His thumb slipped down to run along the muscles at the top of my shoulder. The pressure became a little firmer. "I kept running through the what-if scenarios but, of course, that's not how it works. I finally came to the fact that a what-if isn't a what-is. Etienne may have inadvertently set in motion events that ultimately ended up with Sadie dying but I realized that his action was only one event of many and he was in no way responsible for all of the decisions that the others made." He stopped to take another drink and after putting his glass down on the side table he wrapped both arms around me and gently pulled me in even closer. "Though I would give anything to have Sadie back, I think I would also give anything to ensure that I had met you three." He kissed the top of my head. "Anything."

Chapter 65

The lab tech hadn't shown up at work for two days. He hadn't called in nor had they been able to reach him. He was a dependable fellow, reserved but very good at his job. He had a talent for conducting and supporting scientific investigations and experiments, took care when calibrating equipment and his reports were thorough and timely. The department supervisor was more than happy with the man's work, even though he wasn't all that popular with the other staff. By the second afternoon the supervisor took a drive out to the man's house.

He walked around to the side, passing a wall of clematis that marked the edge of a patio. A respirator and a pie plate with a whisk sat on a glass topped table.

The side door was unlocked and when he called out, there was only silence. Knowing the man was more or less a recluse, he wasn't comfortable just walking into the house but he wanted to make sure that his employee was okay.

A white kitchen curtain gently shivered as a warm breeze slipped through the window. Again he called.

His footsteps sounded so loud in the silence that he found himself walking on the balls of his feet as he made his way through the house. He wasn't surprised to find each room exceptionally tidy, even the bathroom sink was free of clutter. Almost sterile.

The distant cawing of crows caught his attention as he headed towards the back door. There was a squabble happening around a small shed set back in the garden. A lone raven was being harangued by a small contingent of crows, his gurgling croak overridden by their raucous calls and his singular status no match for their numbers.

A sliver of light could be seen through a small separation between the curtains. The birds made a few attempts at discouraging the man but he waved his hat at them and they settled on the roof and nearby trees, while they continued their verbal tirade.

Why he hesitated, he wasn't sure. Once again he called out the lab tech's name but the only sound was more grief from the crows.

There was a tremor of foreboding as he reached for the doorknob. Simultaneously registering the legs splayed on the floor and the unquestionable odour of death gave his stomach a heave as he closed the door and reached for his phone.

Chapter 66 – Golden Memories

Pearl's laughter caught my attention as I turned the bacon over. Looking through the large mullioned window towards the Trail, Pearl swung in and then out of sight; back and forth. I was surprised to realize that in all the time we'd been here – no one had been on the swing. It was another of The Camp staples. The red wooden seat and metal chains hanging from the limb of a large jack pine had gifted countless hours of simple enjoyment over the decades; the rhythmical cadence gave contentedness a place in the day. Pearl was completely stretched out with her face open to the sky above - purely in the moment.

Ben came and stood in front of me. He picked up my hand, turned it over, and placed a small royal blue velvet box onto my palm. "I had this made for you when I was in town." Looking up into his eyes I felt my heart stammer slightly at the depth of emotion they expressed.

"Oh." was all I managed as I smiled in response.

The miniature hinge gave the tiniest of squeaks. Sitting proudly atop more deep blue velvet was a heart-shaped nugget of raw gold fastened to a gold chain.

"Oh!" My heavens, could I be any wittier?

I lifted the little blue tab, pulling up the base to release the chain. Dangling the nugget from my fingers, I looked from it to Ben then back again. "It's absolutely stunning. I... I... Wow! I love it!"

"May I?" Ben held out his hand.

"Please! Is it from Sadie's... collection?"

Standing behind me, Ben fiddled with the clasp, while I held my hair out of the way. "It is. I figured she would have loved to give this to you herself." He came back around to face me.

"Etienne picked it out from the bags." I felt a quick prick of guilt that I had taken some of the gold meant for Sadie's two friends. Ben smiled as he guessed my thoughts. "Don't worry. When I told him about what she wanted me to do with the gold he refused to take any money from the sale of it. He insisted on giving me a couple of the nuggets and once he sells the rest, he wants Marcel to have all of the money."

"He's not going to forgive himself, is he?"

"No, I don't think he will, not completely. I went back to see him after I finished my errands and told him that he couldn't be blamed for other people's decisions and behaviours and how I never would have met you if it all hadn't happened."

"How did he take that?"

Ben ran his fingers down my arm to once again take my hand, which he then lightly brushed his lips across. "I think it helped. At least he smiled and then told me what a rare beauty you are – in every way… or maybe it was me who said it…"

*****

Pearl and Colin were both excited to be given their own nuggets, not mounted as jewelry but each nestled in its own small, round box.

"Oh, I know exactly what I'm going to do with mine!" Colin's grin was mischievous as he rubbed his hands together. "Kate, the next time I see your Dad, I'm going tell him I found this down near the horseshoe pit and thank him for letting me 'work his claim'."

Ben looked confused so we filled him in on Dad's practical joke on Colin.

Pearl's laugh was soft as she shook her head. "Wow – that seems like a lifetime ago." She grabbed some of Colin's hair and gently shook his head. "Underneath that kind, brilliant, handsome exterior of yours beats a truly evil heart." She kissed his forehead. "And I love it!"

Epilogue

Ben stared at the For Sale sign and wondered what the point had been. The devastation to so many lives – and for what? What had been the purpose of the Miletelos' existence? To make money? To succeed? To… what? How had greed and wealth done them any good? He wondered what their last thoughts were as they called in a Mayday and struggled to restart the stalled engine just before their plane hit the trees, scattering their remains into the forest.

Making his way from the Miletelos' home over to Sadie's property he pulled on his leather work gloves and ran through his task list for the day.

The smell of a house fire never really goes away. Ben hardly noticed it anymore as he watched the backhoe remove the collapsed wall of Sadie's bedroom from the debris. He was surprised to see that the fire hadn't completely consumed the contents of the room and signalled the backhoe operator to stop. Sunlight glinted off broken pieces of mirror and glass, spearing the surrounding debris with their beams. He removed his safety goggles to wipe the sweat from his face.

The dresser was scorched on one side but he was able to jockey the drawers open. It felt so invasive to be going through Sadie's personal effects, but he had to clear away what was left of her home so he could start construction of the new cabin. Relieved to find no surprises among her clothes, he dumped the contents into garbage bags and threw them onto the lawn. Her jewellery box, beautifully handcrafted by his Uncle Carl, had been nestled in a drawer surrounded by sweaters and had escaped the heat but not the smoke. Ben ran his hand along the rich, red grain of maple. Elegantly simple yet deceptively difficult to construct - the hand-planed curve of the sides - almost perfect. He carefully placed it in the box destined for the ozone chamber. A few days in there would remove the pervasive smell of smoke.

Ben took a deep breath as he surveyed what was left of the room. A sliver of silver peeking out from under the bed caught his attention. He squatted down and carefully slid it out. Picking up the picture frame he turned it over. His chest heaved with a sigh and he was comforted as he stared into the eyes of the man in the picture.

*****

Ben pressed the phone tightly to his ear as he waited for his long-distance call to be answered.

He smiled when he heard her voice. "Hey you! How's the demolition going?"

"Demolition is moving along, and so am I."

There was a pause before she answered. "I'm not sure what that means."

"It's pretty simple. It means I'm moving out to the west coast." He smiled when he heard her squeal. "Does that work for you?"

Kate's reply was a simple, "Absolutely!"

The End

Acknowledgements

I'm not shy about making phone calls to find answers and have left a few people either worried about my mental state or at least scratching their heads. I mean, how many sons get a voice message from their mother asking the best way to blow up a propane tank? And the local O.P.P. detachment – well, I'm sure they've done a thorough investigation of me after I called asking what would happen if someone were poisoned. (I did explain myself but she sounded really concerned and asked for all my contact information.) Heaven forbid my search history ever gets checked! But that's all part of the fun.

Thank you to my brothers; Wayne, for his expertise in the building of The Camp, trapping, all things animal and wilderness and for his castors-on-the-board, (oh yes, it's real), and the 'broncheckles", and Robert, for his knowledge of gold, mining, the smelting process, and for keeping The Camp in the family.

My children, Tyler, Travis and Kaily were so helpful with information on the outdoors, motors, memories, blowing things up (and putting the fires out) and for all of the absolutely amazing holidays we had there (yes, and you, too, Jerry).

Many thanks to my writing group who kept me grammatically legit and motivated with their enthusiasm: Catherine Bianco, Debra Henry, Gillian Bridge, John Paterson, Julie Warren and Alex Greer. Julie gets extra credit for coming up with the one-hour writing challenge, as does Catherine who was kind enough to edit the entire book. And Mary Sedgewick gets a big shout-out for her keen editing skills – please note you're now my official editor!

Michael Phillips, my physio therapist gets a thank you for helping me with Ben's mal positioning of his sacroiliac joint, as well as Berny Stansa, Chief Training Officer for the Timmins Fire Department for his help with explosions and the department's response.

Ellie Horgan, I truly need to right a wrong. I neglected to thank you in my acknowledgements in CLAMMING UP, for helping me correct my porcupine error by coming up with the idea of the 'swan chapter'. My sincere apologies and thanks.

Should anyone know Barbie Zipp and Steve Smith, I'll give you a heads-up. If you encounter them, beware, as they are fervent in promoting my endeavours (and are the most amazing friends and agents - unfortunately, unpaid, except for my eternal gratitude).

To the hundreds of people who have enjoyed The Camp over the decades, contributing to the enchantment of it, I hope you enjoy some of my memories.

And finally, my heartfelt thanks to all of you who have given me the gift of allowing me to share the love of my favourite place on this planet, The Camp.

Author's Note

The Camp is real, as is the magic of it. I have changed some geographical aspects as well as names and ask that you respect my family's privacy should you happen upon it. The characters in the story have been completely fabricated, though I'm sure we all know people just like them. Well, some, anyway.

About the Author

Lee-Anne Stack is the author of CLAMMING UP, the first novel in the Kate O'Malley adventure/mystery series. Her stories have been published in international and local magazines and her photography has appeared in a variety of publications and galleries with her favourite being the Smithsonian Institute. (Honesty prevails... it was a photograph of the winners in the World's Best Camera Club, but it *was* the Smithsonian.)

She now lives in Victoria, B.C. where she can indulge her passions of photography, music, the ocean, having adventures and enjoying family and friends.

Manufactured by Amazon.ca
Bolton, ON

17889981R00153